LOSS AND LOYALTY - MOABITES

LIGHT OF NATIONS

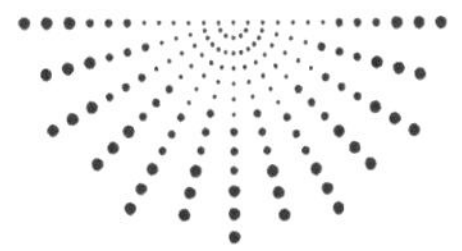

CHRISTINE DILLON

www.storytellerchristine.com

Loss and Loyalty - Moabites (Light of Nations #5)

Copyright © 2025 by Christine Dillon

Cover Design: Lankshear Design

ISBN: 9781923012110

For my workmates in the OMF office in Sydney. If one has to do an office job, then I'm grateful mine is with you.

I will make you as a light for the nations,
that my salvation may reach to the ends of the earth.

Isaiah 49:6b (ESV)

Even if my father and mother abandon me, the LORD will
hold me close.
Psalm 27:10 (NLT)

LIST OF CHARACTER AND PLACE NAMES

Fictional Characters

Arielle — adopted daughter of Naomi.

Many of the minor characters are fictional including **Tozbi** and **Kozbi**, Arielle's Moabite friends.

All of Boaz's friends are fictional.

Biblical Characters (found in the book of Ruth)

I have chosen to use more Hebraic-anglicized versions of the familiar names. This helps us approach the story with different eyes and hopefully makes the biblical parts, feel less familiar.

Naomi — wife of **Elimelech**. They have migrated from Bethlehem to Ar in Moab.

Ruth — wife of Naomi's son, **Mahlon**.

Orpah — wife of Naomi's son, **Kilion**.

Boaz — farmer of Bethlehem.

Rahab and Salmon — Boaz's parents but they've died before this book begins.

There are many mentions of earlier historical characters — A'dam, Yehoshua, Job …

Ar — a major city in Moab. It is likely to have been in the southern part of the Arnon Valley, which is part of present day Jordan.

The Arnon Gorge - a natural boundary in the north of Moab.

Jericho — only ruins and just north of the Dead Sea (thus north-east of Bethlehem).

Heshbon — east of the Jordan River and north of Moab.

Bethlehem — Naomi's home village. Part of the inheritance of the tribe of Judah.

Shiloh — a town 50 kilometres (31 miles) north of Bethlehem. It was the site of the Tabernacle, the central place of worship for all Israelites.

PROLOGUE

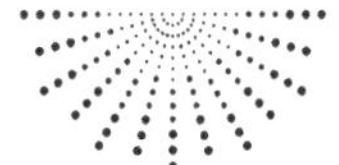

Moab

c. 1130 BC

"Wait for me," Arielle whined as she tried to keep up with her older brothers. Her shorter legs couldn't cover the ground as fast as theirs.

Ahead of her, Kilion nudged Mahlon and they increased their speed.

"Don't," Arielle wailed. "Ima would want you to wait."

At the mention of their mother, her brothers stopped, frustration written all over their faces. They were always trying to sneak off to go fishing, but Arielle had been waiting and watching near the place they kept their fishing gear. She'd started after them the moment they left home.

As Arielle approached, Kilion said, "We like to go on our own. You're too noisy."

When Arielle got bored, she chatted or threw stones. Fishing always sounded exciting when her brothers talked about it, but it never was. Yet there was seldom anyone her own age to play with and she hated to be left alone.

"I'll be quiet this time."

"You've said that before," Mahlon said.

She had. The last few times, at least. It was a mystery to her how such normally boisterous boys managed to sit so still and for so long when they were fishing.

They arrived at the escarpment, and the boys had to help Arielle scramble down. Once at the pool, the boys threw out their lines and they all settled down like three statues.

The heat absorbed by the rocks all day oppressed her and a fly buzzed. Arielle swatted at it and continued to sit. Sweat prickled along her hairline and she licked her dry lips. What a way to spend an afternoon!

Every now and then, the boys checked their lines and replaced the bait before throwing them back into the water with a plop.

It was boring, boring, boring but she never gave up seeking to be included. Never gave up trying to bridge the years between them. Only last night, she'd overheard Ima and Abba talking about the boys' betrothals. Many children were betrothed much earlier, so maybe their parents had hoped to find girls of their own kind. Girls from back home in Israel.

But there weren't many people from Israel around. There was still a famine in Bethlehem, where Abba and Ima had come from many barley harvests before. Ima said her home was many days' walk away. The thought of that long walk made Arielle's legs tired. Or maybe she just felt tired because she was bored. It was amazing how doing nothing was sometimes the most tiring thing of all.

Arielle tapped her foot against a rock. Mahlon glared at her and she stopped. Moments later, she was cracking her knuckles.

"If you can't keep quiet, go away." Kilion glared at her.

"I want to do something else." Arielle cracked her knuckles again.

"We told you not to come," Mahlon said.

"I don't want to play by myself." The boys always had each other, but who did she have? The local children kept away because their parents didn't want them playing with children whose parents worshiped a foreign god.

Kilion huffed. "We want to fish, not play."

"But you're my brothers. You're supposed to play with me."

"You're not our sister," Kilion muttered.

It felt like someone had punched Arielle in her stomach.

"Shut up!" hissed Mahlon as he slapped Kilion's shoulder.

Arielle looked from one boy to the other. "What do you mean, I'm not your sister?" Her voice was hoarse.

The boys looked at each other but said nothing.

"What do you mean, I'm not your sister?" Arielle asked again, an ache in her stomach and her voice rising. She'd learned long ago that persistence usually paid off.

"Ima is going to be so angry at you, Kilion," Mahlon said, his face pale. "She said it was a secret, and now your big mouth has blabbed it out."

"What do you mean—"

"Yeah, yeah, you'll keep asking until we tell you, but we're more scared of Ima and Abba than you. You'll have to ask them," Mahlon said.

Arielle couldn't stay here another moment. She had to get away. To get away and think. She jumped to her feet, hopped across the rocks, and started up the steep path.

"Come back, Arielle," Mahlon yelled. "You shouldn't go off on your own."

Well, if she did, it was their fault. She kept scrambling up the winding path but it wasn't long until she heard them behind her.

Her breaths were loud in her ears and sweat ran down her back.

"Help, help."

Arielle stopped. Had she imagined the faint calls? She checked behind her. The cries had not come from the boys. She cocked her head to one side.

"Help!"

Arielle shaded her eyes with her hand and looked up towards the rim of the ravine. Someone was up there. A girl, waving with both hands above her head. Arielle squinted. It looked like Kozbi. Kozbi and her twin brother, Tozbi, sometimes snuck away from home. They'd played with Arielle a few times over the years, but not a lot because the twins' abba was a wealthy man and he would not have approved. Not only because her parents, Naomi and Elimelech, weren't wealthy but also because their family were foreigners and followers of Yahveh. Arielle sometimes wondered what it must be like to live in a home where she would lack nothing.

Kozbi waved again, her arm jerking as though she was panicked. Arielle licked her already dry lips. Had something happened to Tozbi? She hoped not. He was much more willing to play with her than her own brothers.

Arielle waved back at her friend to let her know she was on her way and pressed on. With a final push Arielle reached the top of the path and looked around for her friend.

"Over here," Kozbi called, waving again.

"What's happened?" Mahlon came up behind Arielle.

"Don't know yet. Let's go and see," Arielle said.

Kozbi saw them coming and turned to lead the way. Mahlon, Arielle, and Kilion followed.

Kozbi led them to a jumble of rocks and stopped, waiting for them to catch up. Her face was streaked with tears. "We were just jumping from rock to rock and he fell."

"How bad?" Mahlon asked.

Kozbi gulped. "I can see the bone."

Arielle's stomach lurched. What use would the four of them be?

"He's over there," Kozbi said. "I can't bear to look."

"I'll go and see what can be done." Mahlon climbed carefully down the rock face.

He came back, looking pale. "Kozbi and I will run for help. You and Kilion need to stay with him. Don't look."

But of course they did. Kilion turned a funny color and went and vomited in the bushes. He obviously wasn't going to be much help.

"Take off your tunic," Arielle said.

Kilion spat and wiped his mouth. "Why do you want my tunic?"

"We need to cover Tozbi up and keep him warm."

Kilion gestured at the sun. "It's a hot day."

"Ima says that injured people get cold and must be kept warm."

Kilion grumbled, but he did what she said. The tunic could also cover the injury. After considering the horribleness of the injury, Arielle drove two sticks into the ground either side of Tozbi so the tunic wouldn't touch his wound. Then she draped the tunic over him and tucked it in around his shoulders.

Tozbi's eyes flickered open and he groaned.

Once when Arielle had fallen out of the tree in their courtyard, Abba had sat beside her and held her hand, so she sat down next to Tozbi and took his hand. He didn't pull away.

He mostly rested with his eyes closed. Every now and then, his mouth twisted with pain. He opened his eyes again. "Story. Tell me a story."

At least that's what she thought he said, for she had to lean down close to hear the words.

"A story?" she asked.

He squeezed her hand.

Arielle had told a few stories to the twins when they had tired of their games. She blew out a breath. Which story was best? Maybe the Noach one, about how he was saved when all the rest of the world was judged and destroyed. She took a shaky breath and tried not to think about the horror of Tozbi's injury.

"Many, many years ago, after the creation of the world, people walked further and further away from Yahveh. Every inclination of people's hearts was evil all of the time, so Yahveh regretted that he had made people."

Tozbi's hand relaxed in hers. She didn't know how much he heard, but by the time the rescue party arrived, his breathing was stronger and more regular.

She didn't want to stay around while they picked Tozbi up and put him on the stretcher they'd brought. Didn't want to hear and see his pain.

She tugged on Mahlon's arm and they set off home. Once well away, they turned and watched as the men took Tozbi home too.

"You're only a child," Kilion said. "How did you know what to do?"

"Im—" Arielle had been about to say "Ima" but now she didn't know if that was true. If Ima wasn't her real mother, who was? Was Arielle still allowed to call her Ima or would she have to call her something else? It was all so confusing and made her head ache.

"Ima," she said boldly, daring the boys to contradict her. "Ima said all girls need to know how to look after injuries. She taught me to keep people warm and calm."

"Well, it helped," Kilion said. "You did a good job."

The rare praise warmed her but didn't ease her confusion. Who was she? Why didn't she live with her parents? Were they even alive?

She'd ask Abba. He'd always had the answers for her in the past.

* * *

*I*t wasn't until sunset that she finally had time to talk with her abba. If he actually was her abba.

"Abba." Arielle sat beside him.

"Yes, my dove." He took her hand.

She loved it when he called her his dove.

"Someone said I wasn't Mahlon and Kilion's sister."

"Hmm," Abba said. "Did they indeed?"

Arielle looked up at him. "But it's not true is it?"

Abba squeezed her hand. "There are different ways of being a sister."

She put her head to one side, not really understanding.

"We always knew we'd have to tell you one day." His voice was warm. "I guess today is the day."

The sadness inside was stifling. "So I'm not your child?"

"You are a child of my heart," he said fiercely. "And that is what matters."

His words wrapped her up warm as his hugs. "But—"

"But nothing. Just because Ima didn't birth you doesn't mean you're not part of our family."

"So, who is my mother?" Arielle asked.

He smoothed the hair on her forehead. "We don't know. Someone left you at the entrance to our home. We're fairly sure you must be a Moabite, but there were no clues as to who your family was or where you came from."

"So my Ima and Abba didn't want me?" Arielle brushed a hand across her eyes.

"We don't know what the situation was," Abba said. "Maybe your Ima died. Maybe she was too sick to look after you."

"What about the rest of the family?"

"I don't know, my dove. There are many other reasons why a family can't raise a child."

"Like what?"

"Like poverty."

They weren't poor, but even if they were, she couldn't imagine that Naomi or Elimelech would ever give away one of their children.

"Maybe your parents gave you to us because they knew we'd share whatever we had and that we'd love you."

And Ima and Abba did love her. Even the boys did. They might be cross at her sometimes, but it wasn't because they didn't love her. Mahlon had once fought someone who had said something unkind about her. Ima was sometimes impatient if Arielle dreamed rather than helping around the house, but other times she allowed Arielle to help her cook. Still, it was hard not to be sad about her other Ima and Abba. Had they loved her, or were they glad to get rid of her like she was a piece of rotten fruit?

CHAPTER ONE

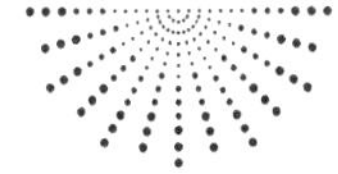

Moab, about ten years later

"What are we going to do with Arielle?"

The breath caught in Arielle's throat as she crouched below the level of the window. She'd bent down to pick up a tuft of wool, and now she couldn't straighten up without revealing her position.

"What do you mean, do with her?" Ruth, Arielle's sister-in-law asked.

"Would it be best to leave her here with one of our friends, or take her with us?" Naomi sounded conflicted.

What? They were leaving? Leaving Moab? Arielle's heart pounded. She'd never known any other place than this house, this town, this country. She'd assumed Naomi would stay here forever. After all, Naomi had been here for years. Her husband and sons were buried here. Why would she leave?

"Where would she go?" Orpah, Arielle's other sister-in-law asked. "We do not know who her relatives are. We don't even know if she has relatives."

Once Abba had confirmed that she had been adopted by himself and Naomi, Arielle had gone to Naomi and demanded more details. Naomi told her how she had been woken one morning by whimpering. Naomi and Elimelech had looked for the source of the sound and found a baby wrapped in sopping wet clothes at the front entrance. There was no explanation and no clue as to who she was. They'd washed her and wrapped clean cloths around her and searched for answers, but none had ever been found. Arielle had lived with them as a member of the family ever since, assuming Mahlon and Kilion were her much older brothers. But from that time on, Arielle began to think of her adopted Ima as "Naomi". Out of respect for raising her, Arielle still called her Ima, but secretly she hoped to find the mother who had given birth to her someday.

"We can't leave her here," Ruth said. "It's too dangerous."

Listen to Ruth, Arielle urged inwardly, sweat prickling along her hairline. *Listen to Ruth.* Moab was a dangerous place for a girl, not yet a woman. Without protectors, Arielle would be prey for anyone around. She could be taken as a slave, or a second wife, or much, much worse.

Arielle's leg threatened to cramp. She carefully eased herself around to sit in the dust with her back against the outer wall of the house. Her people worshiped Chemosh. Chemosh the great and terrible. Chemosh with his scores of temple prostitutes. Arielle shivered. If a girl wasn't beautiful enough to attract attention, then she might be used as a sacrifice to propitiate Chemosh's anger ... and he was often angry since the death of Eglon, the once great and mighty king of their lands and conqueror of neighboring Israel.

"I don't think you understand our situation," Naomi said, her voice depressed. "We came full and we leave empty. We are three women alone with no men to protect us. Things will not be easy for us in Bethlehem."

"Ruth and I are strong and healthy," Orpah said.

"But you will be foreigners," Naomi said. "There are those who will think they are doing a good deed to deny you work or even to harm you. My people will say I am cursed and they will want nothing to do with us."

Arielle could understand why people might think their family was cursed. Her beloved adopted abba, Elimelech, had died of apoplexy, struck down in the middle of a heat wave. It still hurt to even think of the big hole his loss had caused. After his death their household had grown silent and the things of Yahveh had not been talked of for a long time. They'd been considered cursed after the first death, but the deaths of Mahlon and Kilion on a single day had been worse. And the thing about curses? People considered them contagious. No wonder the neighbors had mostly kept away since their losses.

Naomi had always said Yahveh was different from Chemosh and the Baals, but Arielle could not see it. Maybe if they'd made offerings rather than prayers, the menfolk would have been spared. Certainly, their prayers to Yahveh had been answered with a harsh no, like a gate slammed in their faces.

"Don't expect my hometown ..." Naomi snorted. "It's a village, really. Don't expect it to be like here. We won't be able to escape attention as easily as we can here in Ar. Everyone knows everyone's business in Bethlehem. The moment we arrive, they'll be talking about us."

"Do you still have a house in Bethlehem?" Ruth asked.

"If goats and pigeons haven't moved in." Naomi sighed. "One of our relatives should have checked it occasionally, but who knows?"

Arielle could picture Naomi scowling as she answered Ruth's question. Naomi had been drained of joy since the deaths of her husband and sons. Arielle missed the more cheerful woman of previous times. The woman who'd been the only mother Arielle had ever known. She could be strict, but she was always fair.

"But whatever home we have it won't be as roomy as this one, and it will probably need repairs." Naomi sighed again.

"Then we'll need all the hands we can get to help," Ruth said. "Arielle is a hard worker and she doesn't eat much. We'll manage."

And Arielle would work her fingers to callouses to prove that she was worthy of being taken with them. Although, even now, there was a tugging both ways in her heart. If they left Moab, how would she ever find out anything about her original family?

"I don't know," Naomi said. "We'll have to think more about it. Right now, we need to stop talking and get to work. Has anyone seen Arielle?"

Arielle shifted herself away from under the window. Once she couldn't be seen from inside, she pushed herself up to full height and hurried to the well. She was not going to be left behind. She would make herself so useful that they'd have to take her. She busied herself hauling water. One of Abba's last gifts to them had been digging this well. Arielle dashed a tear away from her eye. She missed him. He'd been so kind and always treated her as the daughter he'd never had.

"Arielle! Arielle! Where are you?" Naomi called from the front door.

"Here," Arielle called, picking up the full bucket and carrying it towards Naomi. "Just bringing the water."

She shouldn't have been wasting time thinking about Elimelech. If she was going to make herself indispensable, she needed to anticipate Naomi's every need so Naomi had no need to look for her. She'd get better at her tasks. She must. She'd been abandoned once, and she was not going to be abandoned again. Not if she could help it.

CHAPTER TWO

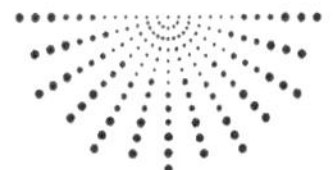

rielle walked towards the gate carrying the ripe figs that Naomi knew would be appreciated by the nearly toothless widow who lived across the lane. If Naomi was going to leave Arielle with anyone, it would be the widow. Arielle liked the woman, but she'd still fight to go with Naomi, Ruth, and Orpah.

Arielle opened the gate and was barely through it before someone grabbed her arm. She opened her mouth to shout.

"Be quiet!" a girl's voice commanded.

Kozbi! Arielle had only seen her occasionally since Tozbi's accident. And that had been a good many barley harvests ago.

Kozbi pushed Arielle back into her courtyard and closed the gate behind them. She leaned back against the gate and drew back her veil. Her pale face was ravaged with tears.

"What's wrong?"

"They've taken him," Kozbi choked out.

A cold fear gripped Arielle's heart. Kozbi must mean Tozbi, for no other person meant so much to her.

"Who has taken him and where?"

Kozbi looked intently around the courtyard and cocked her

head to listen for anyone passing outside. Then she leaned forward and whispered, "The priests. The priests have taken him."

The dread oozed into Arielle's belly. She couldn't think of any reason why the priests would be interested in Tozbi, but it didn't matter. Any mention of the priests made her skin crawl. They were corrupt, evil men, interested only in their own power.

"But why?"

Kozbi's legs seemed to have lost their strength, for she slid down beside the gate and buried her head in her arms. Her body shook with sobs.

Whatever it was, it must be bad. Arielle had only ever seen Kozbi upset once, and that was the day Tozbi had been crippled, a day none of them ever mentioned.

Finally, Kozbi took a gulping breath and used the inside of her veil to wipe her nose. "Father—" her voice wobbled. "Father said he was no use. That no one would ever want to marry him and he couldn't work in the fields."

"But he's clever," Arielle said. "There are many other things he can do."

"Father didn't think those were important. Said that Tozbi only had one use and that was to buy the favor of the gods."

The sour taste of vomit rose in Arielle's throat. What had Tozbi's father done? If Tozbi was no longer of any use to his father, she doubted the priests would consider him any more highly.

Kozbi reached out and gripped Arielle's forearm. "You must leave here. Immediately. Don't stay in this evil place."

Arielle was afraid to keep asking questions but not asking might be worse. "What has happened to Tozbi?"

Kozbi stared at the ground in front of her. "He's dead." Her voice was flat. "Sacrificed so Father's debts might be cleared."

Arielle scrambled to her feet and ran to the nearest tree where she vomited and vomited again until there was nothing left and she was left weak and spent. Tozbi was dead. Tozbi, who'd once laughed and teased. Tozbi, who had been very much alive despite his crippled leg.

Arielle looked across at Kozbi. She had wrapped her arms around her legs and was rocking back and forth.

Arielle went over to the water container, splashed water into her hand, and rinsed out her mouth. Then she walked back to Kozbi.

"Kozbi," she said gently. "I am more sorry than I can say." Anger surged through her. "And so angry."

"You think you're angry," Kozbi spat. "I will never forgive Father as long as I live. And I will never, ever serve Chemosh."

Kozbi might not have a choice. She would stay here and be married to a man of her father's choice to further whatever his plans were. If her husband worshiped Chemosh, he'd almost certainly insist his wife did too.

Kozbi glanced at the sun. "I must go, but don't forget what I said. You have the freedom to leave. Do it as quickly as you can."

Arielle watched Kozbi as she replaced her veil. It turned Kozbi into an anonymous woman, just one woman in a crowd. The veil hid all the anger and grief and pain from view. Would Arielle ever see her friend again?

* * *

"Whew, nearly finished." Arielle wiped her brow with the back of her arm, probably smearing her face and making it dirtier than it already was.

"The house looks much better." Ruth grabbed the opportunity to stand up straight and stretch.

Naomi wanted to get the best price for their home, so Arielle and Ruth had first repaired and wet the mud of their floor so it could be re-smoothed. Then they'd limewashed the walls.

Arielle dipped her brush made of tightly packed straw into the basin of limewash and patted it on the walls. It was satisfying to see the walls brighten up.

Arielle's nails were broken and dirty and her back and shoulders ached, but no one could ever say she didn't work hard. She had not heard Naomi, Orpah, and Ruth discussing her again. Maybe they talked when Arielle was running errands and unable to hear them. Arielle's news of Tozbi had prompted Naomi to get the house ready for sale.

"Has Ima said when we're leaving?" Arielle asked, the "we" deliberate to see if Ruth gave her a clue.

Ruth put her brush back in the basin and dabbed the wall. "When the house and furnishings sell, I guess."

When Naomi left, they'd only take what they could carry. There was no extra money to buy a cart.

Arielle sighed. Ruth hadn't given her the clue she'd hoped. Was Arielle going or not? She couldn't imagine Naomi leaving her behind unless it truly was the best option, but it would be nice to know for sure instead of losing sleep over the uncertainty.

Arielle looked at the two walls she'd worked on, checking to see if there were any spots they'd missed. The house looked much brighter with the white covering the earthy-colored mud bricks. They'd probably have to do this whole process again in Bethlehem, Naomi's home village. Arielle clenched her teeth. If, indeed she was permitted to go with them. Surely they wouldn't leave her behind. They were her family.

Naomi would never leave her in the hands of the priests intentionally, but what if that's where she ended up? The priests of Ar were always looking for more women to serve Chemosh. Serve him indeed! The priests just wanted slaves. Priests didn't get their hands dirty by actually working, as she and Ruth were doing.

"Are you nervous about leaving?" Arielle asked Ruth.

Ruth picked up the almost empty basin and carried it outside to rinse out. "I am a little. Ima is the only one of us who has ever traveled further than the next town." After washing the basin and turning it upside down to dry, she poured water over Arielle's hands and got Arielle to do the same for her. "We don't know how Ima's neighbors will treat us."

Even after all these years, Naomi was considered a foreigner. The neighbors here, apart from other Israelite migrants and the widow, had largely ignored them. Ruth and Orpah's fathers had done business with Elimelech but once Ruth and Orpah had married into the family, Ruth and Orpah had also been looked down upon.

Arielle shook the water off her hands. "Have you considered staying?"

"No." Ruth was emphatic. "I love my family, but there is little opportunity in this place to know and follow Yahveh."

It was odd, Ruth seemed to value Yahveh more than her own family. "What about Orpah? Is she planning to go?"

"I think she is, but leaving her family will be hard. Her parents had only two children and they depend on her help."

If Orpah stayed, it seemed more likely that Arielle could go. She'd worked hard to make herself indispensable, but had it been enough?

CHAPTER THREE

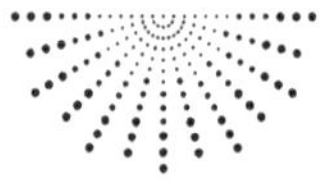

"Daughters, I need you to go out and buy us some more dried figs and raisins for our journey," Naomi said. "Whatever you do, don't get separated."

Arielle shivered. Naomi didn't need to say more. The priests of Chemosh were always on the lookout for more slaves, and they had become bolder in recent days. Naomi insisted they always walked with at least two others.

"And pray that I get a good price for the house," Naomi said. "Now the whitewashing is dry, some potential buyers are coming to view it."

"Don't you want one of us with you?" Ruth asked.

Naomi shook her head. "The next-door neighbor will be here."

They didn't know him well but he was an Israelite who'd arrived at about the same time as Naomi and Elimelech, married a Moabite and settled in the city.

Arielle put on her head covering and followed Ruth and Orpah out into the sunshine. Ruth gave them each a bag then picked up a hefty walking stick from outside the door. They were soon beyond their quiet alleyway and into the busier streets of the main town.

A chicken squawked and flapped across their path.

"No, don't go down there, Arielle. Let's stick with the main roads," Ruth said.

They walked with arms linked. All the roads of the town led into the vast circular road that went around the temple of Chemosh. It squatted like a bloated toad at the intersection of eight roads. Smoke belched out of the doorways and windows from the sacrifices and incense offered and the raucous blare of trumpets assaulted their ears. Arielle held tight to Ruth and Orpah.

They turned down one of the roads that led towards the market and here, Arielle loosened her grip on Ruth and Orpah. This area felt safer somehow, as though it was further away from the darkness of the temple.

Halfway down the road in front of them, a cart had obviously tried to turn and become stuck. Several people yelled at the driver, and he yelled back. There was no space for the three of them to walk abreast.

The driver of the cart yelled again. Arielle ducked through the narrow space at one end of the cart. She heard a swish behind her and all went dark. Her heart pounded as rough cloth scratched her face. Hot sticky fingers held her mouth shut. She struggled but she was so firmly held she could barely breathe. She was aware of being dragged backward. Then she was thrown over a man's shoulder—no woman could be this muscular—and carried further.

Was Ruth safe? And Orpah? Had the cart been a deliberate ploy to separate people? Arielle's heartbeat pounded in her ears and she struggled even though it was a waste of effort.

"Stop struggling," a man's voice growled. "Things will go better if you accept your lot."

Her lot? She was Arielle, adopted daughter of Naomi, and she was not going to give in without a fight. She struggled again. A blow struck the side of her head, leaving her ears ringing with sharp pain.

Yahveh, god of Naomi, if you're there, I need help.

It was stifling under the sack. Arielle attempted a deep breath and wheezed. Smoke.

The man stopped walking, swung her off his shoulder, and held her until she found her feet and stood, shivering with fear. What was next?

Footsteps came towards her and someone yanked off the sack. "What have we here?"

Arielle could barely see in the sudden brightness. After her eyes adjusted, she drew in a sharp breath. One of the priests was staring at her like he was buying a goat in the marketplace, seeking any flaw, grading her to see her quality.

"Well done," the priest murmured, lifting Arielle's chin to stare at her. "Well done."

Arielle dropped her eyes. *Please, Yahveh, send help.*

The priest smiled his false smile. "And what's your name, beautiful?"

Arielle buttoned her lips. This foul creature must not use her name.

"She's one of Naomi's brood," her captor said.

The priest stepped back as though she were a pile of dung.

"Polluted by worship of him I won't name."

If he was too scared of Yahveh to name him then Arielle would say the name. "Naomi is a daughter of Yahveh, creator of all."

"Pah," the priest spat on the floor. "Don't say that name."

"Yahveh," Arielle said again.

His hand came up so fast that Arielle couldn't duck. The sound of the slap echoed round the room but Arielle stood her ground despite the stinging pain across her cheek.

"Don't you defile this place with your talk."

He defiled the air he breathed.

There was a long pause and then the priest's scowl dissolved into a cunning smile "Let us not be hasty. You might be an unclean creature, but I could purify you."

Arielle felt like vomiting.

The priest nodded at Arielle's kidnapper and the man bowed himself backwards out of the room. Nausea swirled in Arielle's stomach. *Yahveh, are you there?*

"Much better on our own don't you think?" the priest said. "How can we get to know each other with that big clodhopper around?"

Yahveh?

"I have no interest in getting to know you," Arielle said.

"Do you know who you're talking to?" the priest said. "You're a nothing. With me, you have a chance to be somebody."

Arielle's head throbbed. *Yahveh?*

"I am perfectly happy with who I am already," Arielle said, wondering how her voice sounded so steady.

The priest drew himself up tall. "How dare you speak to me like this!" He swallowed. "But then ..." He reached out a hand to stroke her cheek.

Arielle flinched, her knees threatening to give way.

"Perhaps a little kindness is all you need." The priest licked his lips. "Yes, my pretty, kindness is like honey to a girl."

Yahveh? Are you there?

She clenched her fists to stop them shaking. "I have no interest in your kindness."

Again he slapped her. This time, a slap so hard she couldn't keep on her feet. Her head slammed against the wall. Blood trickled down her chin where she'd bitten her lip. She shook her head carefully to ward off the wooziness.

He leaned close. "I offer you the world and you prefer my fist. Well then, my pretty, I have other uses for you."

Running footsteps echoed outside the door.

"Who dares disturb us?" the priest snarled.

The door crashed open and a man erupted into the room. A big man, a very big man. Ruth's abba. In his hand he wielded the staff Ruth had taken for their protection. Ruth stood behind him, her face anxious.

Arielle used the wall to push herself to her feet then staggered over to stand behind Ruth's abba. Despite his size, Ruth's abba was usually as gentle as a lamb. He brandished the staff and they all backed out of the room, Ruth holding Arielle's arm, before the priest could protest.

Once back into the main room of the temple, Ruth's abba lowered the staff and used it as a walking stick. "Don't run. Just walk towards the side entrance."

Arielle felt her knees begin to buckle, all the fake strength she had mustered now fast abandoning her. Ruth's abba put his hand under her elbow and propelled her forward. "Almost there," he murmured. "Ruth would never forgive me if we lost you now."

They walked against the current of people flowing into the temple to present their offerings and beg Chemosh for health or wealth or the right marriage partner. Did they condone the evil that happened in Chemosh's name? Or did they simply ignore it, intent instead on bettering themselves and their situation?

Once they were well away from the temple, Ruth threw her arms around Arielle. "I was so scared."

"I thought no one would come," whispered Arielle, holding back tears.

"It took us a while to work out what must have happened," Ruth said. "Thankfully we had caught a glimpse of the man who took you when he was lounging near the cart."

"We had nearly given up finding you when we saw him coming out of the back rooms of the temple." Ruth held on to Arielle's arm as though she'd never let go.

Arielle turned to Ruth's abba and thanked him profusely.

He held up a hand. "Don't thank me. I would never have dared to do that without Ruth's clever plan. She said I only had to look threatening and it should be enough."

"You scared me until I recognized you."

"Come on," Ruth said, tugging Arielle's arm. "We must get home."

"What about the dried fruit?" Arielle asked even though she had no desire to go to the market.

"Abba will bring us some later," Ruth said. "We need to find Orpah and leave as soon as possible."

So Orpah had not dared to join the rescue. Would she have the courage to go with them to a foreign country?

CHAPTER FOUR

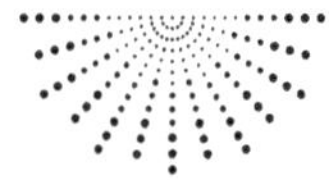

A rielle turned over for the umpteenth time. Her head still ached from the events of the day before.

"Will you please stop wriggling," Orpah whispered through the pre-dawn darkness. "I've barely slept all night."

"Sorry," Arielle muttered.

In the hours since she'd been rescued from the temple, Arielle had been trying to capture a thought that hovered on the edge of her mind. There was something important. Something for the journey they would start today toward Naomi's hometown.

When Naomi had heard about what had happened to Arielle she'd given a decisive nod. "That's it. We leave tomorrow. Arielle, make sure you've got all your things ready to go."

Presumably the sale had been made, for Naomi wouldn't leave without that business sorted out.

Arielle had still not captured the elusive thought before her eyelids closed.

"Wake up, Arielle."

Someone was shaking her. Arielle groaned. Having at last fallen asleep, she would have loved to have slept a lot longer.

A cock crowed and suddenly the thought Arielle had been chasing all night was there. Ruth's abba was a gentle giant, but the priest hadn't known that. His size and the staff he'd brandished had convinced the priest not to mess with them. They would be four women alone, vulnerable, and easy prey for any ill-intentioned travelers. But could they trick people into leaving them alone?

Arielle got out of bed and gathered her spare tunic and the leather sandals Elimelech had made for her. She joined the others as they ate a little bread dipped in olive oil and a few dried figs.

"Ima, where is that old clothing you were going to leave behind?" Arielle asked.

Naomi narrowed her eyes. "We haven't got time to go sorting through those things again."

"I think we can use them to make ourselves look less defenseless," Arielle said. "The extra cloth can go around our middles to make us look bulkier. We can each carry a staff, and I can make bows and arrows."

"But we can't use a bow," Orpah said.

"I don't think it matters. We just need people who see us from a distance to think we are armed." Arielle looked around the group. "We need to look like a group of warriors, not a group of women."

Naomi indicated her short stature. "I'm not sure it can be done."

"We can't do anything in town because people will ask questions, but once we are well away I'm sure I can make us appear taller and bulkier," Arielle said.

"You're welcome to try." Naomi leaned down towards her bundle of possessions.

"Shouldn't we ask for Yahveh's blessing before we go?" Ruth asked.

Naomi stood upright again. "You pray, Ruth. I don't have the heart."

"I'm not sure I know how," Ruth said. "It ought to be you."

"You heard Elimelech pray often enough. You'll do fine," Naomi said.

Ruth raised her hands and ducked her head. She'd always been shy. Maybe she was regretting her boldness in taking the lead on this matter.

"Yahveh, we are setting out today to return to Bethlehem." Ruth took a breath. "Please keep us safe as we go and lead us back to Ima's home."

It sounded easy, but they would have to walk for many days and it was not certain that Naomi's old home would still be livable. Still, Arielle's stomach churned. Some of it was excitement at the thought of seeing new places and maybe making new friends, but some of it was regret that she was leaving Moab where she might still have family. How could she ever find out more if she lived in faraway Bethlehem?

They picked up their cloth-wrapped bundles. Each woman also had a full waterskin. Naomi and Ruth took stout walking sticks. Arielle and Orpah would look for one each along the way. Arielle gathered several lengths of flax she could use as bow strings. She knew a tree that would provide suitable pliable branches. The shape of a bow was distinctive from a distance and might work as a warning.

Naomi walked out of their home without looking back. As Arielle looked over her shoulder, she noticed Orpah also glancing back. According to Naomi, Arielle had been placed on that very threshold. What kind of mother did that? Abandoned her child on a stranger's doorstep. Arielle clenched her fists. No, she was not sad to be leaving Moab. Not at the moment. One day, she'd be back. One day, she'd come looking for answers.

It did not take long to get out of the city gates. Once outside, Arielle kept her eyes open for the kinds of tree branches she needed to make the bows to deceive anyone who might want to harm them.

"Look for food as we walk," Naomi said. "I want to avoid going into any towns until we are well into Israelite territory."

Naomi had said that if all went well, they could reach Bethlehem in a week.

Arielle had never traveled much beyond the walls of Ar, but she had heard Moab was on a plateau which dropped down into a vast expanse of water. The Sea of Death, they called it, for no man or beast could drink of its waters and no plants could live close to its shores. She couldn't imagine such a vast sea, for water was scarce up on the plateau.

Remembering that long-ago day when Mahlon and Kilion had revealed that Arielle was not their sister, Arielle pointed. "Let's detour into that gully and get some of the willow."

"Will it take long?" Naomi asked.

"Not if we work together." Arielle scrambled down the path and selected the young and flexible shoots. She'd been thinking about how to make some headpieces while they walked, so it didn't take long to twist the first one. She placed the structure on her head and placed her veil over it.

Orpah snickered. "That's one way to finally make yourself taller."

"It only has to work from a distance," Arielle said. "To make us look more threatening." She handed some more willow shoots to the others and they quickly made crowns of some sort to fit each of their heads.

Leaving them to finish off their headpieces, Arielle selected three straight branches of willow as thick as her finger to make bows. Mahlon had shown her how to prepare the branches for bending by stretching them over her knee. Once the branch was ready, she attached the flax to each end.

"Could you really shoot an arrow with that?" Ruth asked.

"The boys did. It wasn't very accurate, but we aren't planning to fight. We just need to look like we're prepared to do so." Arielle handed one bow each to Ruth and Orpah. "If we can keep far away enough from people, it should fool them."

"Let's hope we have no need to fool anybody," Naomi said as she started back up the path.

Arielle hoped the same, but she wasn't leaving things to chance. She'd lost one and a half families already. She didn't intend to lose anymore.

* * *

Arielle helped Naomi to her feet after their first night.

Naomi groaned. "I'm too old to sleep on the ground."

Arielle gathered up her cloak and tied up her bundle of belongings. "How old were you when you came to Moab?"

Naomi wrinkled her brow. "Well, Mahlon and Kilion would have been about six and eight barley harvests old. They almost frightened us to death along the trip because they were so excited to explore anything and everything."

They broke their fast and were on their way before the sun rose, as they wanted to walk as far as possible before the sun climbed too high in the sky. They would find a clump of trees to rest under during the heat of the day.

"Why did you leave Bethlehem?" Orpah asked.

Naomi wiped the perspiration off her brow. "Our country was in the midst of a famine."

"I always heard your land referred to as the land promised to Avraham, a land flowing with milk and honey," Ruth said.

"That is what was promised," Naomi said. "But Yahveh also said that the land would be cursed if our people rejected Yahveh as king and turned to worship other gods."

"Are you saying the famine was because your people no longer worshiped Yahveh?" Arielle asked.

"That's exactly what I'm saying. Although some people of every generation have remained faithful, the majority of the people do as they like." Naomi sighed. "It has always been that way, ever since the death of Yehoshua, servant of Yahveh."

"Who was Yehoshua?" Ruth asked.

"I can see I have sorely neglected speaking of these things," Naomi said.

Stories had been one of Elimelech's gifts to Arielle. After he'd died, she hadn't asked for more, it would have hurt too much but Ruth had been hungry to hear and she'd heard stories from her husband.

Naomi took a deep breath. "You do know about Avraham, so we'll start there. He left the city of Ur in the region of the Chaldees following the promise and commands of Yahveh, who had promised to bless him and make him into a great nation. He took with him his wife, Sara, and Lot, his nephew. Lot settled on the plains of Canaan and Avraham remained in the hills."

Listening to Naomi talk distracted Arielle from focusing on the painful spot where her sandal rubbed against her heel.

"Lot's descendants were the Moabites and the Ammonites," Naomi said.

"Which means we are all related," Orpah said.

"We are," Naomi said. "We are also related to the Edomites, through Esau, one of Avraham's grandsons."

"Aren't Edom, Moab, and Ammon all about the same distance from Bethlehem?" Ruth asked. "Why did you go to Moab and not towards Edom or Ammon?"

It was a good question. Elimelech had once drawn a map in the dirt to explain where all these lands were.

"I'm not really sure," Naomi said. "Maybe it was because Yahveh had allowed Eglon, your king, to overrun some of our land to your north. It was safer to travel here and some of our neighbors had already come. It's always easier to go somewhere you already know people."

Arielle, Ruth, and Orpah knew no one in Israel and Naomi had never been fully accepted in Moab. Would it be the same for them in Israel? Arielle's shoulders tensed. Would she have to continue through life as an outsider, never belonging anywhere?

CHAPTER FIVE

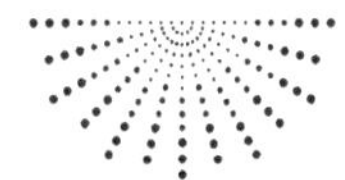

"I never knew such places existed," Arielle said, chest tight and keeping well back from the edge.

Below them, there was a precipice at the side of a wide gorge and far away cliffs of equal height rose up on the far side. The setting sun glinted off the water in what looked like a deep river.

Arielle shivered because she couldn't swim. Few Moabites could, for there were few lakes or rivers in which to learn.

"It's the Arnon Gorge," Naomi said. "The natural northern border of Moab." She waved her arm to the north. "Although King Eglon crossed it and pushed far into Reubenite territory."

"Reubenite?" Arielle asked.

"The Reubenites are one of the twelve tribes of Israel," Naomi said.

Arielle raised her eyebrows.

"We have twelve tribes," Naomi said. "Named after the twelve great-grandchildren of Avraham, the sons of Avraham's grandson, Yaacov."

The names sounded familiar, but although Abba had told Arielle many stories, over time they'd become a bit jumbled in her mind.

"It looks uncrossable," Orpah said.

Naomi indicated towards where the sun rose. "We have to go further towards the edge of the eastern desert. The cliffs aren't nearly as high, and there is a path down into the gorge and up the other side."

Orpah shuddered. "It makes me feel strange even looking down that far."

"Come further from the edge then," Naomi said, leading the way. "I will feel safer once we have crossed into Reubenite lands."

Naomi might feel safer across the gorge, but if these lands had switched hands many times, they might not be as safe as Naomi wished them to be. Every step they took towards Bethlehem was a step away from Ar and all Arielle had ever known. If she left Moab, how could she ever discover more about the parents who'd given her away? She wasn't naive enough to assume that finding them would make for a perfect life, but she did want the chance to know where she came from. Somehow, when she was older, she must return and try to find out what she could.

They set off towards the point that Naomi had indicated. For two days, they had only seen people at a great distance. The nearer they got to the crossing, the more likely they were to see people. People who could be innocent travelers but who also might not be.

The ground was rough. Naomi stumbled on feet that must be aching from the unaccustomed walking.

"Ima, would you like me to carry your bundle so you can use my stick as well?" Ruth asked.

Naomi stopped and rubbed the hip that had been bothering her since the day before. "I can manage."

"I'm sure you can manage, but it might be easier to only have yourself to carry."

Naomi smiled gratefully as she handed over her bundle. "I don't remember it being this hard last time."

Last time, Naomi had been considerably younger and she'd had her husband and two lively boys to keep up her spirits.

"Look." Orpah pointed with her chin. "Someone's coming."

Far ahead, a series of heads had popped above the edge of the gorge. Four, five, six at least and with several camels too.

"They're probably merchants, but we would be wise to get further off the path," Naomi said. "Far enough away so our disguises work."

Heart pounding, Arielle followed Naomi as she walked diagonally away from the edge. They would then be able to pass the merchants while remaining at a distance.

"Slow down a bit," Naomi said. "And stand up straight, as if we have nothing to fear."

The straighter they stood, the taller they'd appear. They'd added an extra layer of cloth around their middles that morning, to make them appear bulkier. Arielle adjusted the position of her bow so it was more visible to the approaching strangers.

"They're probably as suspicious of us as we are of them," Orpah said in a low voice.

"Let's hope so," Ruth said. She was muttering to herself. It looked like she was praying but Arielle wasn't sure which of the gods she was asking for help. Maybe Arielle should follow her example, but she was certainly not going to pray to Chemosh. Tozbi's fate and her own fright at the temple had scared her well away from such a god.

"Pull your cloaks forward so our faces are in shadow," Orpah said. "And don't move. We surely walk like women and tired ones at that."

Arielle stifled a nervous giggle. She straightened her back and stood in the confident manner that Kilion used to stand. She took her bow and added a fake arrow, as though she was ready for action but not aggressively seeking a fight.

The group continued to move towards them. Arielle took a deep breath. Were the travelers innocents like themselves, or people intent on taking what they could get from anyone they encountered?

They could now hear the jangle of the camels' harnesses, but there was not a sound from the group. They'd bunched together but continued to walk forward. Arielle held her breath.

"It's alright," Orpah said from beside her. "The leader trades with my father, and I recognize two of the other men."

Arielle let out a whoosh of air and let her bow rest on the ground. They watched as the group passed by.

Orpah stepped forward. "Greetings Mesha, son of Balak."

The man leader stopped and his group stopped with him. He turned towards them. "Who calls me by name?"

"Orpah, daughter of Husham," Orpah said.

"You should have let them pass," Naomi said in an undertone.

"Maybe," Orpah said. "But they are my last connection with home."

Was Orpah having second thoughts about going to Bethlehem? If so, she might yet endanger them for they only had her word that these people were safe.

"Where are you off to?" the man said. "You and your companions."

Orpah stepped forward. "I am accompanying my mother-in-law to her home."

"So you are leaving Moab?" the man asked.

"We are," Orpah said. "What of the road ahead of us?"

"It is much safer nowadays." He indicated a cluster of rocks and some stunted trees ahead. "We were about to camp for the night. It might be safer to join us. Then you should be able to complete the crossing of the gorge in the morning. It is a tough scramble."

Orpah turned to Naomi. "We would be wise to listen to him. He does this journey often."

"You trust him?"

"I do. He would never do anything to harm his trade with my father."

Naomi moved towards the travelers. "We will gladly accept your offer. Is the water of the river safe to drink?"

Even drinking sparingly, their water supplies were low as they had not found a well so far from the towns.

"It is safe enough, especially if you fill your waterskins from one of the side channels. The main channel runs too swiftly."

"Is there still a bridge?" Naomi asked.

"There is. It has had to be repaired several times after its initial destruction by those ruffians who murdered our king."

He talked to the man next to him then said, "Let us set up first. Then we'll find space for you."

Arielle waited for the men to move away. "We'd better get back to our normal height and weight. Hopefully our loose clothing hid what we'd done or there might be some awkward questions."

Ruth laughed. "Why don't we hide our extra clothing and weapons behind this rock and pick them up tomorrow?"

When they reached the temporary camp, places were found for them. Soon they were eating fresh bread with herbs and onions and a tasty goat's cheese. Orpah chatted, but Naomi was unusually quiet. Perhaps she was just tired.

Later, in the darkest time of night, Arielle heard Naomi sit up. She rocked back and forth with her arms around her knees and her head bowed. What was bothering her? Was she regretting their journey? Or worrying about their future? A future where they could well have less than Naomi had expected. The neighbors had known they were in a hurry to leave and they'd made low offers for their home and possessions. The Israelite neighbor who should have helped had not. Naomi admitted she should have found someone else to ask, because his loyalties were divided. He was married to a Moabite and planned to remain in Moab.

* * *

*T*he next day, Arielle rubbed her arms to get warm in the crisp early morning air. She went to make use of the water available for washing her face and hands. As she returned to where they'd slept during the night, Naomi spoke to Orpah and Ruth. "Come aside and talk with me."

What was going on?

Arielle followed them as the other women moved to a small hillock.

"My daughters," Naomi said. "I have been thinking long and hard during the night."

She'd not just been thinking. Arielle was sure she'd heard Naomi crying. Arielle's stomach felt like it was full of jumping ants. Something wasn't right.

"Go back, each of you, to your mother's home," Naomi said.

Go back! They'd only just started on this journey. They couldn't go back.

"May the Lord show you kindness, as you have shown kindness to Mahlon and Kilion and to me. May the Lord grant that each of you will find rest in the home of another husband."

Why was Naomi breaking their family even further apart? *Don't listen to her,* Arielle's heart cried. *Don't leave us alone.*

Naomi reached out and kissed Ruth and Orpah, who also had tears running down their faces. Arielle bit her lip to stop herself from joining in their tears.

"No," Ruth said. "We will go back with you to your people."

But Naomi shook her head. "You must return home." She indicated the merchants with her chin. "Here is a safe way to do so, with companions for the journey. Why would you come with me? Am I going to have sons who could become your husbands?"

Arielle had wondered how Orpah and Ruth would get married again, for marriage was the way to security and protection.

"Return home. I am too old to have another husband. Even if I thought there was still hope for me—even if I had a husband tonight and then gave birth to sons— would you wait until they grew up? Would you remain unmarried for them?"

Arielle could see the sense in Naomi's words but still her heart cried, "No, no, no!" She could not lose more of her family. Arielle would go with Naomi to Bethlehem because she had nowhere else to go, but she didn't want to go without Ruth and Orpah.

"It is more bitter for me than for you, because the Lord's hand has turned against me!" Naomi continued.

Arielle hugged her arms around her body as Ruth and Orpah and Naomi wept together. After a long time, Orpah kissed Naomi and walked back towards the camp to gather her things together.

No! Don't go! Arielle wanted to cry out to Orpah. It was unlikely Arielle would ever see Orpah again. Would they lose Ruth too, now that Orpah was going?

Ruth still clung to Naomi. Naomi straightened and held Ruth by her shoulders. "Look, your sister-in-law is going back to her people and her gods. Go back with her."

Did Naomi want Orpah to return to the gods of her youth? Arielle had always thought Naomi wanted them all to follow Yahveh. Who would teach Orpah to follow Yahveh now?

Ruth shook her head. "Don't urge me to leave you or to turn back from you. Where you go I will go, and where you stay I will stay."

Arielle lifted her head, a surge of hope filling her. Of her two sister-in-laws, she'd been closer to Ruth than Orpah. Orpah had done her duty, but she obviously hadn't thought that included befriending Arielle. In contrast, Ruth had warmly embraced Arielle as an extra sister.

"Your people will be my people and your God my God. Where you die I will die, and there I will be buried." Ruth's voice was steady. "May the Lord deal with me, be it ever so severely, if even death separates you and me."

Joy bubbled through Arielle. Ruth wasn't leaving. Ever since the death of Elimelech, the man Arielle thought of as her abba and missed more than anyone, she'd been closest to Ruth. Mahlon and Kilion had each other and never thought of her as more than an annoyance. Ruth had treated her as a younger sister. If Arielle had had to choose only one person to be with, then she would choose Ruth.

CHAPTER SIX

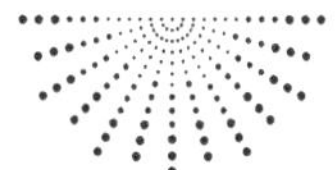

Watching Orpah leave was horrible. The merchants were almost packed by the time Naomi, Ruth, and Arielle collected their meagre belongings. The leader agreed to take Orpah along with them without much fuss.

Arielle and Ruth stood on either side of Naomi, their arms around her, as they watched Orpah leave. Several times Orpah looked back at them as she grew smaller and smaller in the distance. Was she already regretting her decision to leave?

Naomi sighed, shrugging herself free of Ruth and Arielle's embrace. "Well, we can't stand here all day. We need to get down the cliff before the day gets any hotter."

"And we still have to collect the weapons and things we left at the rock," Arielle said. "Let's leave the headpieces behind. We can't carry too much down that cliff."

Naomi picked up her staff and tied the bundle to the top. "Yes, you'll need one hand free so you can steady yourself on the wall of the cliff."

They were soon at the edge of the descent. This portion of cliff was much lower than where they'd first encountered the gorge, but it wasn't a place for anyone who was afraid of heights.

Naomi took a deep breath. "Slow and steady. Don't look over the edge. Just put one hand on the cliff and look at your feet."

"Do you want me to go first?" Arielle asked. Heights had never bothered her. She'd climbed trees and scrambled down ravines her entire childhood, always desperate to keep up with Mahlon and Kilion and earn their approval.

Ruth nodded, looking pale. "Let's put Ima in the middle."

Arielle listened closely but couldn't hear anyone coming up the path. She took her first steps downwards. The path zigzagged back and forth down the cliff. On some of the corners there were places where people could pass each other.

"Are you alright, Ima?" Arielle asked as they made their way down.

"Better than I expected. It is not so tiring going down. I'm not looking forward to going up the other side."

"We'll help you," Ruth said as they negotiated yet another zigzag turn. "Ima, I thought I heard the merchants mention that we're walking the King's Highway. Why is it called that?"

"I don't really know, but it is the road to follow through Edom and Moab and into Reuben's territory. I do know that Mosheh asked permission to travel on it with my ancestors, and they paid in silver for their food and drink. Yahveh instructed them not to provoke Edom or Moab or go to war with them because we were related."

Arielle navigated her way around the next switchback. "So did your ancestors travel near Ar?"

"They did indeed. They also crossed this gorge." Naomi stopped and leaned against a convenient rock. "Let's have a short rest and a drink."

They each took two mouthfuls of tepid water.

"When Mosheh crossed this very gorge, he sent messengers to

Sihon, king of the Amorites, offering peace. 'Let us pass through your country. We will stay on the main road and will not turn aside to the right or to the left. Sell us food to eat and water to drink for their price in silver. Only let us pass through on foot—as the descendants of Esau, who live in Seir, and the Moabites, who live in Ar, did for us—until we cross the Jordan into the land the Lord our God is giving us.'"

"Did they accept the offer?" Arielle asked.

Naomi shook her head. "They were fools. Yahveh had already stirred up Sihon to be stubborn, for Yahveh planned to give the Amorites' land to Mosheh and the Israelites."

Ruth took another swallow of water. "Did the Israelites win?"

"They did. They destroyed Sihon's army and wiped out the Amorites, then took all the plunder for themselves. Later, Sihon's lands became part of the tribes of Reuben and Gad's inheritance. Further north, Og the king of Bashan also thought he could beat the Israelites. He too was totally defeated, and all his sixty walled towns and his territory given to the half tribe of Manasseh."

"You'd think the Amorites would have remembered that Yahveh had already helped Mosheh defeat the Egyptians." Ruth got to her feet and peered over the edge. "We'd better keep going. Not far to the bottom now."

When they reached the bottom, Arielle and Ruth took turns carrying Naomi's bundle and gave her two sticks to lean on, for the gorge was full of rocks and debris from past floods.

Arielle looked ahead to where they could see the road winding up the far wall of the gorge. "Someone's coming."

"Let's get across the bridge, then go to the side stream and fill our waterskins," Naomi said. "If we take no notice of them, hopefully they'll leave us alone."

They hurried on and crossed the bridge. It was obvious it had been repaired many times but it seemed sturdy enough. Below them, the grey-green water rushed over a tumble of rocks.

"I wouldn't want to drink from the main river," Ruth said. "Too much silt. The side stream is much slower and the water clearer."

The group approaching was still distant, but Arielle made sure her bow was visible and tried to make her stride look manly. She probably didn't succeed, but it made her feel better. They filled their waterskins and waited until the other group crossed the bridge and moved towards the Moabite side of the gorge.

"Let's keep walking until we reach that clump of trees. Then we can have something to eat before we tackle the uphill bit," Naomi said. "We need to get out of this gorge today. I think it will be safer to skirt Dibon, since it is often still claimed by Moab, and go to Heshbon, which is still thoroughly Israelite."

* * *

*M*uch later, after their slow ascent of the cliffs, due to the many rests needed, Naomi stopped and pointed to a hill in the distance. "There she is. Mount Nebo, where Yahveh took Mosheh to show him the whole land that had been promised to the descendants of Avraham, Itzchak, and Yaacov."

Nebo rose to the west. Arielle would have liked to see the view from the top, but Naomi would never make it. She was already walking more slowly and needing more frequent rest. "Mosheh died on the top of the mountain. He was one hundred and twenty years old. Then Yehoshua took over as leader."

"That seems a bit unfair, letting Mosheh see the land but not enter it after leading your people for so long," Arielle said.

Naomi was silent for a long moment. "Yahveh did not permit Mosheh to enter the land as punishment for something he'd done earlier."

"What kind of wrong would merit that punishment?" Arielle asked.

"It's complicated." Naomi pursed her lips. "The easiest way to explain is to say that Mosheh had seen Yahveh do great miracles. Miracles which finally battered Egypt into a state of complete submission so that Pharaoh expelled my ancestors from Egypt. Then Yahveh opened a path through the sea and provided food and drink for all the people, every day for forty years."

Arielle would ask Naomi for more stories once they were settled in Bethlehem. Since Elimelech had died, Naomi had seldom spoken of her old life or told her peoples' stories.

"Even more important than the miracles, is the fact that Mosheh had talked with Yahveh on Mount Sinai and been given Yahveh's laws. Laws that, when obeyed, mean all foreigners are welcomed and the weak looked after so no one goes without."

"Israel sounds like paradise," Arielle burst out.

"I wish I could say it was," Naomi said. "But you will discover there can be a big gap between knowing what is right and actually putting it into practice. Indeed even Mosheh did not fully trust Yahveh, despite having seen so many miracles and knowing more of Yahveh than anyone else."

Arielle was still puzzled. "I cannot think of a sin so terrible that would make Yahveh prevent Mosheh from going into the Promised Land."

"Ah, there was one particular time when the people were grumbling and complaining as they often did. They asked, 'Why did you bring us up out of Egypt to this terrible place? It has no grain or figs, no grapevines or pomegranates. And there is no water to drink!' Mosheh went to Yahveh and was told to speak to a rock so that it would pour out water for the people to drink." Naomi shook her head and sighed. "But in his frustration, Mosheh struck the rock to produce the water."

"And?" Arielle asked. "I don't see the problem."

Naomi turned to Ruth. "Can you see why Yahveh might have been angry?"

Ruth pursed her lips for a moment. "Was it because striking the rock made it look like Mosheh had produced the water rather than Yahveh?"

"Something like that is probable," Naomi said. "Yahveh said Mosheh had stolen the glory that rightfully belonged only to Yahveh. Mosheh should also have learned after one hundred and twenty years that he must obey fully and not add his own ideas."

Arielle stared at the ground in front of them. Why was Yahveh's glory so important? The priests of Chemosh promoted themselves rather than the god they said they worshiped. They never hesitated to take the place of honor in festivals. Sometimes it seemed as though the gods were just an excuse for the priests to step forward and exert control.

* * *

The next day, Arielle pointed to an enormous mountain of stones and mud bricks. "What was there?"

The three of them halted and looked around.

"That is Jericho," Naomi said. "Have you not heard what happened at Jericho?"

Arielle shook her head. It seemed that there were stories about all the places they were passing as they crossed these lands. They had just waded through a ford across the Jordan River. The water had come up to their thighs but the current had not been very strong. As they crossed, Naomi had told them the story of the Israelites crossing the river when it was in full flood. Yahveh had stopped the waters upstream so that a wall of water had formed and allowed the people to cross with dry feet.

"Jericho occupies a strategic spot, so why hasn't it been rebuilt?" Ruth asked. "All the building material is right there for strong walls."

"Yehoshua laid a curse on it. If it was rebuilt, the foundation would be laid at the cost of the builder's eldest son and when completed, the youngest son would die."

"I can see why no one has rebuilt it," Arielle said. "But why was it razed to the ground in the first place?"

"It was the first place Yehoshua conquered on this side of the Jordan," Naomi said. "Why don't we sit under those trees and have a meal? I'll tell you the story. My feet would welcome the rest."

Hers weren't the only hurting feet. Arielle spread out her cloak on the ground and helped Naomi to sit before placing one of the bundles behind her back. It didn't take long to hand around the bread and cheese they'd bought on the outskirts of Heshbon. To Arielle's disappointment, Naomi had decided not to risk entering any town, so Arielle hadn't had the chance to see if an Israelite town was any different from Ar.

Naomi ate first before speaking. "The Israelites had already conquered Sihon and Og. They were camped somewhere over there, across the river." Naomi pointed back the way they'd come. "Yehoshua sent two spies across the river and they went into Jericho seeking weaknesses in its defenses. While in Jericho, they met Rahab. She was an extraordinary woman, for she had heard what happened in Egypt and knew Yehoshua had been commanded to kill every man, woman, and child within the borders of Canaan."

"What had they done to deserve that?" Arielle asked.

"It is not easy for an outsider to understand." Naomi brushed some crumbs off her lap. "Four hundred years earlier, Yahveh had promised Avraham that his descendants would live here in Canaan, but Yahveh also said that the sins of the Canaanites had not yet reached their full measure."

Arielle raised an eyebrow but said nothing. She was pretty sure that Naomi would explain these puzzling words.

"Yahveh meant that the peoples of these lands were not yet evil enough to be completely wiped out. He'd give them four hundred more years of opportunities to repent and turn to him."

"And did anyone ever repent?" Ruth asked.

"There may have been many. We know that Rahab was one, let me tell you more about her."

Arielle settled herself to listen.

"Rahab protected the two Israelite spies when the soldiers of Jericho came looking for them. She told the soldiers that the spies had escaped to the hills but really she had hidden them. The soldiers believed her and left. Rahab threw a scarlet cord out of her window for the spies to shimmy down. Before Rahab let the spies down, she begged for her life. 'I know what Yahveh did in Egypt and a great terror has fallen on all of us so we are melting in fear. Yahveh is lord of earth and heaven above and I know Yahveh has given you this land.'"

Ruth stared at the site where Jericho had once stood. "So Rahab was one who had risked trusting Yahveh. Did the spies protect her?"

"They did. They told Rahab to gather her family together into her home which was right in the city wall. Then she must leave the scarlet cord hanging out her window so it could easily be seen by the approaching army."

Arielle nodded towards the mounds of rock. "I still don't see how the city ended up like that. What kind of army could reduce a city to piles of rubble?"

"Ruth, do you remember this story? I once heard Mahlon telling you about this battle."

Ruth frowned. "I don't remember the details, but it was something about marching around the city. Was it once a day for six days and then seven times on the seventh day?"

"You have a good memory," Naomi said.

It was the weirdest battle strategy Arielle had heard of. "But how could marching in a circle achieve anything?"

Naomi nodded. "That's just it. It would normally achieve precisely nothing. For the first six days, the people of Jericho probably stood on the walls and laughed at them. The Israelites were commanded to be silent as they circled the city. When they finished the seventh circling on the seventh day then they were commanded to shout—and shout they did. It was then that Yahveh caused the walls of Jericho to fall down." Naomi indicated the rubble.

There was a long silence as they looked at the remnants of the destruction. Then Naomi pointed to the sole remaining section of the city wall. "But Rahab and her family were rescued from their home and her descendants live among us to this day."

Arielle wasn't sure what she thought of this god. His judgments were fierce and his power beyond anything she had experienced. Ruth seemed to trust him. But was he worthy of trust? Did he care about someone like her, a girl who was likely a Moabite but one whose own parents had abandoned her? Or was he like the gods of Moab: distant, cruel, and implacable?

CHAPTER SEVEN

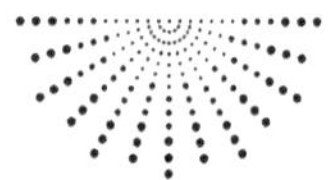

"Poo, what is that terrible smell?" Arielle asked.

"Pigeons." Ruth pointed as one flew out the door of Naomi's old home. "They've moved in while the place has been empty. Ima, please sit in the shade while we see how bad the situation is."

As they'd entered Bethlehem, they'd seen locals but no one had approached them. Now Arielle and Ruth moved towards the front doorway of what had once, Naomi assured them, been a lovely home. Weeds filled the entranceway, growing towards the light. The same abundance of growth spilled out each window. Arielle's heart sank. There'd be a lot of work ahead.

Ruth put her hands around the stalks of the closest plants and gave a tug. They didn't budge, so she planted her feet and gave another pull. "Help me, Arielle."

Arielle added her hands to the plants and together they heaved. They staggered back as the plants came out by their roots. They repeated the process five times until finally they could push their heads in the door.

The smell inside was worse, much worse. Although there wasn't enough light to see the birds roosting inside, there was a chorus of coos somewhere above their heads.

"Maybe it will be easier to shoo them out if we can clear all the plants," Ruth said. "We certainly can't share the house with birds."

"Girls, this is tomorrow's job. Let's stay out here tonight," Naomi called. "We'll need water, and the closest well is only a short walk away."

They left Naomi lashing twigs together to make a broom and followed her directions to the well. They waited in line but no one spoke to them, although behind their backs, there seemed to be a lot of chattering about them. It wasn't as if she and Ruth looked any different from the other women. They had the same dark eyes and hair, the same skin color, but somehow everyone knew they were foreigners. Perhaps it was just because they obviously didn't know how things worked here.

On the way home with their full waterskins, Ruth said, "That was awkward but perhaps if Ima introduces us it might be better. Presumably she knows some of these women."

Arielle giggled. "They probably haven't had outsiders draw water from their well since Yehoshua's days."

"It's a small town," Ruth said. "I wouldn't be surprised if someone comes to find out who we are as soon as the news spreads around town that there are strangers here."

They only had time to clear a space outside to sleep that night when a tall woman peered over the wall. "Naomi, is that you?"

"Don't call me Naomi anymore. Call me Mara, for El Shaddai has made my life bitter. I left full but have returned empty."

"Empty?" the woman said.

"Yes, El Shaddai has seen fit to take not only my husband but my two sons as well."

"Little Mahlon and Kilion?"

"They weren't so little when they died, but yes, those boys. The light of my eyes."

They'd been the light of all of their eyes. It was the first time Arielle had heard Naomi talk about them since they died.

The woman indicated Ruth and Arielle. "But you are not alone. Who are these women who have come back with you?"

"My daughter-in-law, Ruth, and my adopted daughter, Arielle," Naomi said.

"And which tribe are you from, dear," the woman said to Ruth, although she must have known they were outsiders.

"Tribe?" Ruth asked.

"Surely you know your tribe. We Israelites always know our tribe."

"I am a follower of Yahveh from Moab," Ruth said with dignity.

"Oh," said the woman. "I was not aware that you could follow Yahveh if you were a Moabite."

"I believe he accepts everyone who will follow him."

"Perhaps," the woman said but the curl of her lip suggested she doubted it. She backed off. "I must be going. My husband's meal won't cook itself."

Arielle doubted they'd see this neighbor again. What would she report to the other women of the town? Likely nothing kind or welcoming. They watched the woman walk away.

"I'm sorry, my daughters," Naomi said. "She's one of the worst gossips in town, but I didn't want to offend her."

"I fear my very existence offends her," Ruth said. "But no matter. We don't have time to worry about what others think. We have a home to repair, and we'll need to be up early to get started."

* * *

"*D*on't be afraid, Arielle. They're only pigeons," Ruth said the next morning.

"I don't like them flying at my head," Arielle said. "And they have made a disgusting mess of the floor."

"Now that all the plants are gone, we need to borrow some tools to dig out the floor," Ruth said. "Maybe Ima could go and ask a neighbor."

By the time Naomi returned with two hoes, the pigeons had all been shooed out.

"How will we keep them out?" Arielle asked.

"Maybe they'll stay outside if we're inside." Naomi held her nose. "But we couldn't possibly live inside at the moment."

Ruth leaned on her hoe. "Let's see what the smell is like if we dig out half a hand-width of soil. It will make a good base for our garden."

"Then we'll have to get more dirt from somewhere else, to keep the floor level."

"You're good girls," Naomi said. "I don't know what I'd do without you."

Every day, Arielle was thankful that Ruth had come with them. Things would have been very different without her, for Naomi no longer had the energy for heavy work and Arielle would have found it hard to do the work alone.

Ruth put her hands on her hips. "Let's go and look at the place where we'll plant our garden. It would make sense to clear there first and dig out the clean dirt we can put in the house."

"And pile it over there?" Arielle pointed to a spot by the house door.

Ruth nodded.

A girl about Arielle's age, nearly marriageable, walked past. She stooped to pick a flower, and Arielle stifled a sigh. If only she could wander around the small town picking flowers, but another back-breaking day was ahead. Her hands were already blistered from pulling out all the plants inside the house the day before.

Ruth lifted her hoe and headed towards the back of their land. "Do you prefer to pull out the plants we don't want or dig?"

"We'd better both start with clearing, then I'll dig." Arielle picked up her hoe and followed Ruth around the back. It was a mass of shrubs, grass, and vines.

"We can pull up that vine." Ruth pointed. "But the other one might produce something if it gets more sunshine."

Arielle followed Ruth's instructions and untangled the two vines before pulling out the rejected one. They worked forward, sorting what might be useful and what needed to be pulled out.

At last, Ruth put her hands on the base of her spine and leaned back. "We've cleared enough for you to start digging. Just push the dirt into a pile. We'll keep the basket for carrying the pigeon droppings."

They only had one basket tough enough for these kinds of jobs. Arielle lifted the hoe and swung it. It landed awkwardly and made the merest of indentations in the soil.

"Let me show you," Ruth said. "My abba taught me."

Ruth demonstrated how to lift the hoe and then handed it to Arielle. "Put your hands here and here before you swing it."

Arielle swung the hoe again. This time, she made more of an impact. She found her rhythm by the fourth try, but she was going to need a lot of rest. Mahlon and Kilion would have been so much more useful, but they weren't here. She and Ruth would have to do it themselves. The ache of missing them returned with a heaviness beneath her ribs.

They worked until every other part of her ached as much as her heart.

Ruth touched her shoulder. "Rest a while, Arielle. We won't finish today."

Arielle rubbed her wet forehead with the back of her forearm. "I wish we could hire a few brawny men to help us."

"Well, we can't, and don't say anything to Ima. She's got enough to worry about."

Maybe things would have been easier if Naomi had come back on her own. Only one neighbor, an elderly woman, had dropped in to talk. She'd brought some freshly baked bread and dried fruit. Arielle had been hungry enough to snatch them out of the woman's hand but hadn't. Knowing Naomi would be horrified with such rudeness, she'd gone back to work.

What were people afraid of? She and Ruth were just young women. Women who'd never hurt anyone in their lives. The whispers whenever they went to the well stung, but Ruth just squeezed Arielle's hand and looked straight ahead.

"Why don't I go and dig a basket load from inside the house to put in the hole you've made? That way, we're making progress on all three tasks at the same time. It would be better if we could get inside if it rains."

Arielle looked up at the sky. It didn't look like rain, which was good, as the barley fields were ripe. They were pushing to get the house ready before the harvest started so they could go and glean in the harvest fields. Naomi had said that Yahveh's law made provision for the poor. Farmers were supposed to leave the corners of their field unharvested so those who needed the grain could come and gather it themselves. Naomi had winced when she'd said the word "poor" for, as she told them, "We were never poor, and I never expected to be in this situation."

Arielle narrowed her eyes as she considered the work they'd completed that day. If they could keep up the pace and if nothing went wrong, they might be able to finish the digging in three to four days. But then they'd have to clean the house and limewash the walls. Her whole body groaned in protest, but the work had to be done. It was clear that none of the neighbors were going to help, and they needed to glean grain. Without grain, there would be no bread. Without bread, they'd starve.

CHAPTER EIGHT

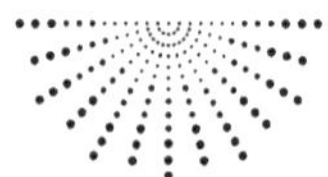

The birds were singing and there was a murmur of voices in the predawn gloom. For a moment, Arielle thought it was Elimelech and Naomi. Listening to their early morning chats was one of the sounds of her childhood. But no, Elimelech had left them and Arielle was snuggled up in her cloak on the roof of their newly renovated home.

Arielle slowly opened her eyes. Above her, an owl glided by on whisper-soft wings. Ruth and Naomi must already be up, for she was alone on the rooftop.

"Now the house is livable, we must think about work outside the home." That was Naomi's voice.

"At least to feed us until the fruit trees produce their crop and we can get the garden going," Ruth said.

Arielle's palms had hardened with the daily use of the hoe. The garden was now fully cleared and ready to receive new plants. Now it only remained to beg what seeds and cuttings they could from neighbors. As they'd dug out all the pigeon droppings, Naomi remained on guard with a long leafy branch, swishing at any pigeon trying to reclaim its place back inside. A few days ago, they spent a day treading down all the new soil for the internal floor. It wasn't a task Arielle had ever done before.

"We need grain for bread. Then we can forage something to go with it," Ruth said.

Arielle's stomach growled. She had gone to sleep hungry the night before, as all the hard work had made her ravenous.

"Arielle is too young to go, too vulnerable," Ruth said.

Arielle bristled with indignation but kept quiet as she knew she shouldn't be eavesdropping.

"I will go," Ruth said.

"I hate for you to have to, but my stiff back is simply unsuitable for such work," Naomi said.

"I would never expect you to go out to work," Ruth said.

"Instead I will do my best to help Arielle whitewash our inside walls."

Arielle let out a sigh. If Ruth was going out to glean, then Arielle would have to do most of the whitewashing on her own. They had found a store of lime in a safe place under the tangled vines in the garden. Whitewashing on her own in Bethlehem would not be nearly as fun as whitewashing had been in Moab. Working with Ruth meant singing and jokes along the way. And whitewashing wasn't the only task for the day. Naomi's stomach was upset so Arielle would also have to go and ask the neighbors for seeds, plant cuttings, or seedlings. The thought made her stomach ache too. Naomi had tried to warn them about the gap between what people ought to do in keeping Yahveh's law and what they actually did. The gap was wider than Arielle had believed possible.

"Arielle, come and eat," Naomi called up the outside stairs.

They ate a handful of dried fruit and some not-quite-ripe berries they'd found in a corner of the garden.

"I'll try some of the closer farms first so I don't have to carry the grain too far," Ruth said.

"Be careful," Naomi said. "If there is danger, leave and come home. I'd prefer to starve than have you come to harm."

Arielle's chest tightened. She hadn't even considered that gleaning might be dangerous, but of course it could be. If someone wanted to harm Ruth, who would stick up for her? So far, no one had shown them any kindness except the one woman who'd brought them the dried fruit and had told Naomi she was blessed to have two such hard-working companions. Her kind words had warmed Arielle's heart. If only there were more women with her kind spirit.

* * *

Heart pounding, Arielle approached the first house she'd chosen. "It's just some seeds," she murmured to herself, but her words didn't slow her heartbeat.

Arielle opened the neighbor's squeaking gate and lifted her chin as she walked towards the main entrance. They were only people, so why was she so afraid?

She'd not yet reached the door when the woman of the house peered out. "No, thank you. We don't want anything."

"I was hoping you might have some s-seeds you could s-spare," Arielle said.

"No, nothing," the woman said.

It had taken so much courage to come and ask that Arielle wasn't going to give up so easily. "Or some s–seedlings or cuttings?"

"No, nothing," the woman said, turning her back on Arielle.

Arielle swallowed and retreated back across the courtyard and through the gate. She didn't believe the household had nothing to share. They just didn't want to share with a despised foreigner. Well, so be it. She'd ask someone else.

The next house was the same as the first, except the second woman didn't even wait for Arielle's second request. The third gave her some seeds, but Arielle got the impression the woman was just trying to get rid of Arielle as fast as possible. No matter. The main thing was that she had some seeds and she'd get more, even if she had to steal them.

At the next house, she went around the back and found some cucumber plants growing over the wall. Plants growing outside the wall were available for everyone, weren't they? Arielle wasn't going to ask. Using the sharp-edged stone she carried, she collected a series of cuttings.

She debated whether to leave what she had outside the gate of the next place but thought that if it looked like other neighbors had given her seeds, it might convince the next person to give her something too.

The next woman glanced over her shoulder and whispered, "I see others have been generous. If you go to the back gate, I'll put something outside for you." She put her finger to her lips, and Arielle did as instructed.

She waited for a while but there was no sign of the woman or the promised seedlings. Then she heard someone coming along the inside of the back wall. The gate was flung open and a man glared at her. "Oho, so this is why my wife is sneaking around. What do you want?"

"Only a few s-seedlings." Arielle barely got the words out, despising herself for being intimidated.

"There are no seedlings for someone like you … Take yourself home. Back to Edom or wherever it is you're from."

"Moab. I'm from Moab," Arielle muttered as the back gate was slammed in her face.

"Woman, you keep away from that girl," the man growled from the other side of the wall.

Arielle listened, breathing a sigh of relief when she didn't hear the sound of a hand striking flesh. It would be horrible if someone got in trouble because of her. Why couldn't people treat others like they wanted to be treated? Had Naomi and Elimelech and the boys had similar experiences in Moab? She hadn't been aware of anything until that last day, when Naomi was cheated out of the proper price for her house. Was that because she was an Israelite, a defenseless widow, or simply because she was a woman?

Seeing a few more plants hanging over the wall, Arielle took a few more cuttings. If no one gave things willingly, she'd harvest them herself.

At home, Naomi took one look at Arielle's face. "You look like you've had a tough time of it."

Arielle nodded, afraid to speak in case she cried. She laid down the cuttings and Naomi gave her a rare hug. "I'm sorry our neighbors are so unwelcoming. It's not fair that they should give you and Ruth such a hard time."

"Did my people do that to you when you first moved to Moab?"

Naomi looked thoughtful. "The majority just ignored us, but there were some that took advantage or said hurtful things. A few eventually became friends."

Arielle sniffed. "How did you handle it?"

"I kept telling myself that it was their loss. They lost the opportunity to know our family and make new friends and have their understanding of the world expanded."

"Did that help?"

"Sometimes," Naomi said. "And I was blessed with a good husband who comforted me and made me laugh."

"Would you show me what to do with the cuttings?" Arielle asked.

"It's easy enough. We will stand them in water. Once they've grown strong roots, they'll need to be transplanted into the garden."

"I'll get the dish." Arielle scampered into the house. She must never do anything that would make Naomi think she wasn't useful. After all, if Naomi didn't have Ruth and Arielle around, the neighbors would likely treat her a lot better.

* * *

"What's wrong, my daughter?" Naomi asked as Ruth limped in at the gate.

"I fell. That's all," Ruth said.

Naomi narrowed her eyes. "You're not usually clumsy."

Ruth perched on the wall. "It wasn't any clumsiness on my part. The day was a total failure."

"Was there no grain?" Arielle asked.

"I went to four different farms, and none of them were leaving grain in the corners. When I finally found one that didn't harvest the corners, I was pushed out of the way and told, 'This grain is for Israelites, not for the likes of you.'"

Naomi placed a hand on Ruth's shoulder. "I am so sorry, and I'm sorry to hear that so many farmers are no longer following Yahveh's law. Just before we left for Moab, a high place was built to the south."

"A high place?" Arielle asked.

"We Israelites were commanded quite clearly that there was only to be one place of worship for the whole land."

"Only one?" Arielle couldn't keep the surprise out of her voice. Even in Ar, there were a myriad of temples and altars at which people could worship.

"I know it's unusual," Naomi said. "But Yahveh knew that if worship places proliferated, then people would worship whatever and however they wanted."

That was certainly true in Moab. Sometimes Arielle had suspected that people just made up the name of a god and appointed themselves priests so they could live on the offerings of their followers.

"Where is that one place?" Ruth asked.

"Shiloh. Before you ask, it is about a three day walk that way." Naomi pointed even further away from Moab. "We're supposed to gather there three times each year, but I don't know what the state of the priesthood is."

Ruth rubbed her knee. "What do you mean?"

"As I've said previously, there are twelve tribes. The tribe of Levi is designated to serve us all as priests. Their job is to look after the Tabernacle, the tent of meeting, and the whole sacrificial system."

Sourness filled Arielle's mouth. Not more sacrifices. She thought she'd escaped all that.

"It's complicated. I will eventually teach you what I know, but it is impossible in the time we have this evening."

"So is Shiloh in the land allotted for Levi?" Arielle asked.

"I told you it was complicated. The Levites are the only tribe that don't have their own lands. They've been allocated cities within different tribal allotments." Naomi smoothed the hair back from her forehead. "I guess they're supposed to be a kind of yeast that grows and spreads throughout all our lands. The priests are to teach us Yahveh's law—the law that was given to Mosheh on Mount Sinai when my ancestors left Egypt and began the journey towards this land that was promised to Avraham. By being spread out, the priests should also be models to us of what it means to be a follower of Yahveh—"

"But?" Ruth said. "I sense a hesitation."

"But unless things have changed since I've been away, many priests are no better than the rest of us. They've often failed to be good models, or to teach us Yahveh's word, or even treat the sacrifices properly. They might not lead the way into worshiping the gods of Canaan, but they certainly haven't prevented it happening or spoken against it." Naomi sighed. "As worship of the Baals and Asherah has increased, so have the injustices that you've experienced. People go their own way, so they no longer care for the poor or the widows and orphans."

Naomi sighed. "But we can choose to be different. Let's all go and wash. It's nearly sunset and we must celebrate Shabbat," Naomi said.

"But we haven't got anything to celebrate the Shabbat with." Arielle remembered back in Moab, when Shabbats were times of plenty with other Israelite friends and fresh bread, curds, and herbs.

"Then we will bring a sacrifice of thankful hearts and enjoy a good rest."

The problem was Arielle couldn't eat thankfulness. It seemed they had a lot more to complain about than to be thankful for.

CHAPTER NINE

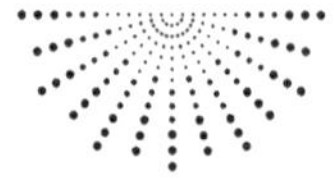

"Look, Ima, Ruth has returned and she is bringing something home," Arielle said.

"It looks to me like she needs your help," Naomi said.

Arielle dashed out the gate and ran towards Ruth, who was bent over and struggling along the dusty path.

"Careful," Ruth said. "My cloak is nearly ripping."

Arielle took one side of the cloak, careful not to pour its contents on the ground. It was much heavier than she'd expected. "What have you got?"

Ruth beamed at Arielle, her face burnished from a full day of work outside. "Barley, and lots of it."

"How did you manage to glean so much?"

"You'll have to wait until I've washed, then I'll tell you both. Yahveh has heard our prayers."

Inside the gate, they placed the grain in clay jars, left in the house from the early years of Naomi's marriage, to keep it safe from rodents and any pigeons who still considered their place home.

"There's clean water ready at the back, daughter," Naomi said. "We'll have a drink waiting for you."

In Moab, they'd had a goat for milk. Here, they were a long way from affording any animal. Water was all they could provide, but at least it was cool, for it had been lying in the shade all day.

It seemed an age until Ruth was finally seated in the shade.

Ruth let out a sigh of exhaustion. "Ah, sitting here feels good. What have you been doing all day?"

"I'll tell you later," Arielle said. "We want to know why you have so much grain."

"Yes, daughter, whose fields were you in today?" Naomi asked.

"The man's name was Boaz."

"Boaz?" Naomi clapped her hands. "Praise Yahveh."

Naomi obviously knew the man, but Arielle had never heard of him. Even Ruth looked confused.

"The Lord bless him!" Naomi said. "He has not stopped showing his kindness to the living and the dead. That man is a close relative, one of our guardian-redeemers."

Guardian-redeemers. That was not a term Arielle had heard before, but she didn't get a chance to ask as Naomi leaned forward. "How did you end up in his fields?"

"I had been to all the farms close to Bethlehem and I was getting desperate. Boaz's farm is well outside Bethlehem. I was a bit late, but it was obvious that Boaz is a farmer who still honors Yahveh's laws, for the harvesters left generous corners. The other workers and I had been working all morning when the man I now know as Boaz arrived and greeted the harvesters by saying, 'Adonai be with you.' The harvesters answered with a hearty, 'Adonai bless you,' so they were obviously used to this kind of greeting."

"And did he speak with you?" Naomi asked.

"Not immediately," Ruth said. "I'd been working in the corners of the field all morning and had already gleaned a reasonable amount of barley. Boaz talked with his overseer, but I didn't hear what he said. Soon after, Boaz came over and spoke to me. 'My daughter, listen to me. Don't go and glean in another field. Stay here among the women who work for me. Follow the women as they follow the harvesters. I have told the men not to lay a hand on you. Whenever you are thirsty, go and get a drink from the water jars the men have just filled.'"

Arielle hung on every word. Finally here was an Israelite who actually followed Yahveh's law. "What happened next?"

"I bowed and asked, 'Why have I found such favor in your eyes that you notice me, a foreigner?'"

"And what did he say?"

Ruth laughed and ruffled Arielle's hair. "Even you would have been amazed. Boaz said, 'I've been told all about what you have done for your mother-in-law since the death of your husband—how you've left your father and mother and your homeland and come to live with a people you did not know before.'"

Arielle's eyes moistened. Such kind words.

"I told you everyone knows about everyone here," Arielle said. Just being part of the scenery was one of the things she most missed about Ar. Here in Bethlehem, everyone thought they knew all about them and chose to turn their backs.

"I am delighted to hear that someone recognizes your worth," Naomi said. "Not that I'm too surprised. Boaz was always an exceptional man. He is greatly respected among the followers of Yahveh, although some of the farmers think he is a fool."

"Why is that?" Arielle asked.

"Because he is generous to the poor and always looking out for the foreigner."

Ruth flushed. "Boaz also blessed me."

"What did he say?" Naomi asked.

"'May Adonai repay you for what you have done. May you be richly rewarded by Adonai, the God of Israel under whose wings you come to take refuge.'" Tears shimmered in Ruth's eyes.

After all the rejection, the blessing was beautiful, just beautiful. The words brought a lump into Arielle's throat. She loved the picture of sheltering under Yahveh's wings, although somehow she doubted he actually had wings.

"And it didn't end there," Ruth said. "I said to him, 'May I continue to find favor in your eyes, my lord. You have put me at ease by speaking kindly to your servant—though I do not have the standing of one of your servants.'"

"Well done, Ruth," Naomi said. "Boaz is an important man from Elimelech's clan and a member of the town council." She chuckled. "Though that is mostly because he is too wealthy to ignore, rather than through his ancestry."

His ancestry? What was wrong with his ancestry? Naomi obviously didn't think this was the time to explain.

"At lunchtime," Ruth continued, "he called me over and offered me bread and invited me to dip it in wine vinegar. He also gave me roasted grains. I've brought some of that and the bread home for us to eat."

"See, Arielle," Naomi said. "Yahveh has provided us with fresh bread just in time for Shabbat."

"And after Shabbat, I'll grind some of the barley, and we can make fresh bread of our own," Ruth said with a smile.

Naomi narrowed her eyes. "But even with all that kindness, you still gathered a lot more grain than I'd expect."

"I wondered about that. After lunch, there were more stalks of grain than before lunch. I watched the harvesters and I'm sure they were pulling out extra stalks and leaving them on the ground for me. By the time I went to thresh at the end of the day, I had collected about an ephah." Ruth rubbed her lower back. "No wonder I nearly didn't make it home."

Arielle giggled. "Maybe you should have asked Boaz to bring you home in his cart."

Ruth threw her headscarf at Arielle. "He'd already shown such kindness, I couldn't ask for more. Although he did do more. He suggested I remain in his fields, not only for the barley harvest but for the wheat harvest that follows."

Naomi stood up and hugged Ruth. "I am greatly relieved. Boaz is a good man. He will watch out for you."

Could Ruth's good fortune also be an answer to prayer? Since they'd returned to Bethlehem, Naomi had been praying again, every morning and evening. Perhaps Naomi's faith had been stirred by Ruth's growing trust in Yahveh and the remembering of all the stories of Yahveh's faithfulness in the past.

CHAPTER TEN

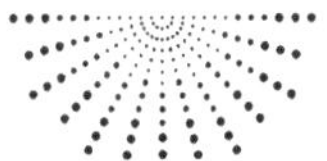

*A*rielle stretched. She really should get up a little earlier, for she was sure she'd just heard her name mentioned. What were Naomi and Ruth saying about her down there? Arielle rolled out of bed and crawled towards the roof's parapet.

"Ima," Ruth said. "Would it be alright for Arielle to join me in Boaz's fields?"

Please, Naomi, listen to her. Arielle was tired of seeing Ruth go off alone each day.

"But what about all the gardening and things to be done around the house?" Naomi asked.

"I think it will work out better if she comes with me."

Arielle strained her ears to listen. Ruth's voice didn't carry as well as Naomi's.

"If there are two of us gleaning, half a day should be enough. Then we can come back together and do the household tasks."

Arielle could picture Naomi nodding her head as she thought about Ruth's suggestion.

"I'd be much more at peace, because there'd be two of you walking to and from Boaz's fields. I have been worrying about that,"

Naomi said. "Have any of the men behaved …" She hesitated. "Inappropriately?"

Ruth wasn't beautiful, but she had a pleasant face and a willowy gracefulness. Naomi wasn't the only one worrying about Ruth's safety. Since the incident in the temple, Arielle had become suspicious of other men, keenly aware that not all men were honorable like Elimelech, Mahlon, and Kilion.

"Boaz has made it quite clear that none of that sort of behavior is acceptable among his workers. That's why the other gleaners prefer his fields over anyone else's."

"But you aren't protected when you walk to and from his fields," Naomi said.

"No, but so far I haven't had a problem. I walk as quickly as I can, but having Arielle with me would make us less likely to be approached."

Arielle grinned. Ruth's plan would allow Arielle to get out a little more, and she'd have someone to work with in the afternoons. She'd missed having someone to work with. Naomi did most of the cooking, but it could be lonely in the garden.

"Arielle," Naomi called up the stairs. "Time to get up."

"Coming," Arielle said, trying to sound like she'd just woken up and hadn't been eavesdropping while her elders organized her life. She shook out her bedding and laid it to air over the parapet. One of the many tasks Naomi had lined up for them was to build a shelter on the roof in case it ever rained. Not that it did much at this time of year.

Downstairs, Naomi explained what she and Ruth had decided, and Arielle did her best to respond as if it was the first time she had heard it. She and Ruth ate something, kissed Naomi, and headed off with their gleaning bags.

Ruth looked across at Arielle. "I don't know why I didn't think of this earlier. I have felt so lonely out in the fields."

"Won't anyone talk to you?" Arielle asked.

Ruth sighed. "They seem to have decided I'm not worth talking to. I've been praying someone would have the courage to reach out."

Arielle looked to check no one was around. "Do you think praying actually works?"

Ruth pursed her lips. "I do, but sometimes it is hard to explain why I think that."

"Since others looking at us might assume that Yahveh doesn't care about us at all," Arielle continued.

Ruth walked on. "We can look at what we haven't got or we could look at what we have. I'm choosing to focus on all the gifts we've been given. We may not have any menfolk, but we have each other. We have a home, and a garden which is starting to produce good things."

Last night, they'd eaten some cucumbers from a vine that had been covered up. Once they'd cleared the weeds and allowed the plant to receive sunlight, it had produced flowers almost immediately.

"And," Ruth continued. "We were directed to Boaz's fields."

"Do you really think you were directed?" Arielle asked.

"I do," Ruth said with an emphatic nod. "After my first few discouraging experiences, I was praying hard to find a safe place and I eventually went out of my way. Now we have plenty of grain, and the wheat harvest starts soon. Naomi has said we will be able to exchange the wheat for salt and oil and other things we need."

Perhaps they did have much to be thankful for. Arielle looked around. It was still early but already the dew was disappearing but the day promised to be hot.

* * *

"Who have you brought with you?" one of the women asked Ruth.

Ruth was startled. "Arielle is my sister. Sort of."

"What's a sort of sister?" the woman asked.

"I am Naomi's daughter-in-law, and Arielle is Naomi's adopted daughter."

"Why did Naomi adopt a daughter?" the woman probed.

"You'll have to ask Naomi," Ruth said. "But Arielle has been the best kind of daughter a woman could want."

The woman clicked her tongue and moved off.

Arielle took a deep breath. Naomi had told her she must not take people's rejections to heart but it still hurt, every time. People judged them and moved on without bothering to see if there was a person worth knowing behind the Moabite label.

Ruth squeezed Arielle's hand. "Stick close to me."

Arielle followed Ruth as they moved to the corner of the field the harvesters had just finished.

"The easiest way is to pull up the whole stalk and then discard the straw." Ruth demonstrated. "Boaz has promised to bring some of the straw to us later."

Boaz certainly seemed to be taking extra care of their family. Was he just a kind man, or did he have other motives? Was he the kind of man who used kindness and later demanded other favors? Arielle shuddered. Please no.

They finished gleaning the first corner and moved towards the second. No one talked to them, but they looked. Looked as though she and Ruth were creatures from somewhere in the deepest seas. Something they'd never seen before and were too afraid to approach. It made Arielle plain angry. How were she and Ruth ever going to fit in if no one ever talked to them? She blew out an angry harrumph.

Ruth looked across at her. "Don't let the others bother you."

"But it does bother me."

"We've just got to give them time. Maybe if they see us work hard and get as red in the face as they do, they'll eventually bridge the gap."

Maybe. But it didn't look like it would be happening anytime soon.

At lunchtime, Ruth led Arielle over to the shade created by a small tree. The regular gleaners sat apart in the shade of a well-placed awning. Soon they were laughing and joking. Arielle munched in silence but inside her gut was churning.

"Oh, you know Moabites," a voice cut through the air. "All Moabites are thieves."

"And liars," another voice added.

Arielle was on her feet.

"No," Ruth said as she grabbed for Arielle's hand and missed.

"And as for their morals, they're worse than dogs."

"What would you know?" Arielle said, breathless from her dash across the space dividing them. "You won't even talk to us. Ruth is the best woman I know."

Ruth was beside Arielle now and gently tugged her arm. "Don't waste your breath."

Arielle shook off the restraining arm. "She's loyal, and fun, and endlessly patient. You treat her like the dirt beneath your feet, but she's worth ten of you."

There was nervous laughter in the group and the women looked away.

"Come on," Ruth said. "Come back and rest."

Arielle turned her back on the group and allowed herself to be led back to the shady tree. "They make me so angry," Arielle whispered.

"I love that you defended me, but I don't think it will do any good."

Arielle sniffed. "But what they say isn't right."

"No, but I'm not sure we can stop them saying it."

Arielle grimaced. "And now they'll call us hotheaded as well."

The corner of Ruth's mouth tilted up. "Maybe, but there are worse things."

"Yes, like being a gossip. Or just plain mean."

"Which is something we will not be." Ruth sat and offered Arielle a drink of water. "We can remain who we are and not stoop to their level. Let's finish the last corner of the field. Then we can go home."

Home to where they could see the results of their labors and be welcomed.

* * *

The group of boys was hidden behind a pile of rocks.

Arielle and Ruth had left a little later than usual because today was the last day of the barley harvest. Tomorrow, there would be no barley left to glean.

Ruth turned to go back as the boys appeared from behind the rocks, but it was already too late. There were youths behind them as well. Arielle's heart pounded in her ears. Youths were worse than men, for they lacked wisdom and restraint.

Ruth grabbed Arielle's hand. Arielle could feel Ruth shaking. The boys behind herded them closer to the ones who'd been hidden behind the rocks.

"C'mon. Give us a kiss," said the closest youth of the group in front.

"Never," Arielle said.

"Ooh, she's a feisty one," said another. "I like them feisty."

"Let me do the talking," Ruth said out of the corner of her mouth.

Arielle was happy to let her, for the words she'd uttered had only stirred the youths up.

"Come on boys, who's with me?" the leader asked. "Moabites are free and easy."

Arielle's hand was sweating in Ruth's grasp. These cowards wouldn't behave like this with their own people, but they thought they could get away with it towards foreigners. They were probably right, for even if there were Israelites about, no one in Bethlehem would bother to defend two Moabite women.

Ruth drew herself up as tall as a short woman could. "What would Yahveh think of your behavior?"

"Leave Yahveh out of it," the leader said.

"Why?" Ruth asked. "Yahveh is my protector and he sees all."

"Leave them alone," one of the youths at the back suddenly squeaked.

"Why should I?" the leader's tone was belligerent.

"Because if you don't, you'll have to deal with me," said a deep voice behind them. Arielle and Ruth turned around. A man stood there with a staff in his hand and he looked like he could use it.

"Boaz," the leader said. "We were just messing around."

Arielle's shoulders relaxed. If it was Boaz, then they were safe. Ruth had assured Naomi that Boaz was a kind man, even if now, the lines on his face were hard and the expression stern.

"It is not the kind of messing around that I appreciate. These women are virtuous. Now, be off with you. Go back to your homes."

Arielle moved closer to Ruth. She could feel her shaking.

The first of the youths took off at a run.

"And you," Boaz said to the leader of the group. "You no longer need to report to work in my fields."

"But sir ..."

"There are no buts. You should have thought about the consequences before you opened your big mouth and threatened these women. You knew they were under my protection. Do you understand now?"

"Yes, sir."

"Then why are you still here?" Boaz asked.

The leader of the gang and his closest supporters turned and took off at a run.

Ruth sank onto the nearest rock. "Thank you."

Boaz leaned on his staff and chuckled. "Did you see the speed at which he ran off? He looked like a frightened hare." He smiled. "There's no need to thank me. I am disappointed that such a thing should happen in Bethlehem." Boaz sighed, casting his eyes around the surrounding hills. "It's a tragic reality that many of my people are followers of Yahveh in name only. Their hearts are far from him."

Arielle took a shaky breath and sat down next to Ruth. How did one follow Yahveh with one's heart? Whatever it meant, Ruth seemed to be such a follower.

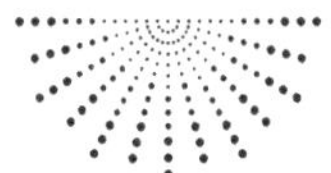

"Phew." Arielle rubbed her neck. "I am not sad that the barley harvest is finished and we only have to work in the garden. My body needs a rest."

Ruth stretched her shoulders. "You're not the only one. A few days' rest and a change of pace before the wheat harvest starts will do us good."

Every late afternoon, after gleaning in the fields, they had labored in their garden. The herbs and vegetables were already doing well. They'd exchanged some of their excess barley for fruit and then dried the grapes and dates on the bare earth at the side of their house.

Naomi came out from inside the home. "Hurry and wash. The sun will set soon. After we have enjoyed our Shabbat, I have something special to tell you."

"Why can't you tell us now?" Arielle asked.

"You'll have to wait," Naomi said, a smile peeping through as though she was brimming over with some sort of inner excitement.

"Come on, tell us," Arielle begged.

Naomi shook her head. "Not until Shabbat is finished. Shabbat is not the time for plans and busyness."

Arielle's first memories of Shabbat were of annoyance that it interrupted her daily tasks or play. Since they'd come to Bethlehem, she'd begun to appreciate the rest. The time to slow down and not have to cook or clean or glean. Time to trust Yahveh to grow their garden without any help from them. Time to sit back and enjoy their garden and the sense of accomplishment its fruitfulness brought. It was much easier to be thankful if they actually spent a day sitting in the garden and being quiet. It was also a day for Naomi's special fruit bread, and that was not something to be missed.

* * *

"What is the special something you have to tell us?" Arielle asked. She'd found it hard to properly rest during Shabbat when it was obvious that Naomi had some secret or other.

"Tonight is the winnowing of the barley," Naomi said.

That was nothing secret.

"But we are not part of that," Arielle said.

"No," Naomi said. "But I have a plan. It is a risky plan, but I believe it will work."

Ruth stood quietly, waiting for Naomi to continue.

"Ruth, I have thought long and hard about how to find a home for you and make sure you are well provided for. As you know, I cannot provide a son for you to marry, but I can perhaps, if Yahveh grants us favor, find you a husband."

"How, Ima?" Ruth asked, brow furrowed.

"Wash and put on your best clothes. I have made some perfume. I want you to go to the threshing floor. But carefully, so no one knows you are there."

Had Naomi taken leave of her senses?

"Wait until Boaz has finished eating and drinking and watch where he lies down. Then once all is quiet, go and uncover Boaz's feet and lie down."

Arielle shivered. Lie down in the dark near a man's feet! It sounded more than risky to her. "Surely Boaz already has a wife." He was not young.

"That is what I assumed," Naomi said. "For how could such a man not have a wife? A neighbor told me he does not. It is most unusual."

"Do you know why he isn't married?" Arielle asked.

"I am sure there is a good reason." Naomi turned to Ruth. "But whatever the reason, Boaz is our guardian-redeemer."

"You said something like that before," Arielle said. "But I don't know what it means."

Naomi rubbed her eyebrow. "Sometimes I forget that so many of our ways are new to you. A guardian-redeemer is another of Yahveh's provisions, one he made in the law he gave to Mosheh on Mount Sinai. Yahveh's law covered almost every situation you can imagine. We are all benefiting from the laws which allow gleaning, and there are also other laws that benefit widows and their families." She paused for a moment as if to gather her thoughts. "If someone's husband dies, then the nearest male relative is to marry the widow to ensure the continuance of the family line. Since I don't have more sons, there are others who carry out the responsibility. They are called guardian-redeemers."

"Why are you bringing this up now?" Ruth asked.

"Because, like you, I assumed Boaz was married, and I didn't want you to be a second wife. Once I heard he was unmarried, I was almost sad because I selfishly want you around for my sake." Naomi cupped Ruth's chin in her hand and tilted her face up. "But that wouldn't be fair to you. You should have the chance to be married."

No! The last thing Arielle wanted was for Ruth to be married. Even as her heart rebelled, Arielle chastised herself. Ruth couldn't be expected to help them forever. They'd have to learn how to survive on their own.

"What do you think of my plan?" Naomi asked.

Ruth blushed. "It sounds awfully forward to me."

"My daughter, I wouldn't suggest such a plan except that I know Boaz is a man of the best character who honors Yahveh in all he does."

"Then," Ruth inclined her head. "I will do everything you say."

"But, Ima, so much could go wrong." Arielle's dinner stirred unpleasantly in her stomach as she pictured the leer of the priest in the temple of Chemosh.

"It could," Naomi said. "So we will accompany Ruth to the edge of the fields and watch her settle into a safe place to wait for the right time."

* * *

"You look beautiful," Naomi said as Ruth adjusted the hang of her embroidered dress, one of her wedding gifts. "The sun is dropping in the sky, so let us be on our way."

"Shouldn't we pray first?" Ruth asked, a slight quaver in her voice.

Naomi chucked Ruth under her chin. "You are right as always, my dear. This is too important to neglect committing the night to Yahveh."

Naomi reached out a hand each to Arielle and Ruth and they stood together in a tight circle.

"Great Creator, Yahveh, provider of all things."

Arielle couldn't remember the last time she had heard Naomi take the lead in prayer. Was it before the death of the boys? Maybe.

Although Naomi had never rejected Yahveh after their deaths, she had clearly found it difficult to be thankful and praise him.

"Thank you that you have cared for us in the move back to Bethlehem. We can't pretend it has been easy, but we have never starved. We thank you for the kindness and protection Boaz has given to Ruth and Arielle. Tonight, we are taking a risk, and we ask you to protect Ruth again. Protect her from those who could harm her. Prevent them from even seeing her. May Boaz not misunderstand what we're asking. May he fulfill his role as our guardian-redeemer and be willing to be a man of honor."

"Yes, may it be so," Ruth murmured.

Arielle released her hold of Ruth and Naomi.

Naomi looked at Ruth, "Ready?"

"As ready as I'll ever be."

Outside, the shadows were lengthening and the orange glow burnished the leaves and the tall grass. They saw no one as they approached Boaz's fields and stopped out of sight the moment they heard the sound of chatter. The workers were over near a clump of trees, between the two piles of grain.

"We'll watch you until you're safely out of sight." Naomi leaned forward and planted a kiss on Ruth's brow. "Be assured of our prayers."

Ruth set off, walking slowly in a wide loop around the workers. There was little danger of her being noticed yet, for laughter and loud talking filled the air along with an occasional burst of song. Boaz obviously made such events into a party.

"Yahveh, don't let them be drunk," Arielle muttered.

Once Ruth reached the far side of the group she paused, almost invisible among the shadows of the trees. Then she moved slowly between the trees, pausing next to each.

Don't let her be discovered.

Ruth reached the end of the row of trees. She must have waited there to assess the best way to go, because Arielle almost missed it when Ruth left the shelter of the trees, bent low and moving in a smooth glide.

Don't let her be discovered.

With the last few steps Ruth slipped behind the large pile of grain. The tension in Arielle's neck eased. Ruth was safe for now, but it might be a long wait until the merrymakers went to sleep.

Naomi touched Arielle's arm. "Now we go home and wait. I won't get much sleep tonight."

Neither would Arielle. She'd pray for Ruth's safety, but it looked like she'd lose Ruth no matter what happened. She was tired of losing people. As she and Naomi walked home, the moon peeped out from behind a cloud. Arielle rubbed a tear from the corner of her eye.

When they reached home, Arielle laid out their sleeping mats and lay looking at the myriad of stars above. So many patterns and colors. Were they created by Yahveh, as Naomi and Ruth claimed? And if so, did the god who'd made everything really care about someone as insignificant as a Moabite lying on a rooftop in Bethlehem? Ruth always treated Yahveh as if he was personally interested in her, but Naomi had seemed bitter since her husband and sons had died. This had only changed recently. Maybe anger and bitterness created distance between a woman and her god just as it did between a woman and her husband.

Naomi was sitting on her mat not far from Arielle. Arielle rolled over to face her. "Ima, do you miss Abba?"

"Every day," Naomi said. "Sometimes I wish he could come back, even for just one day. Then I'd say all the things I should have said when he was still with us." She sighed. "No one expects to lose their husband so suddenly. He was still healthy. Too often I got impatient with his plodding ways when I should have been grateful for his kindness and patience. I never heard a cross word from him."

Abba had indeed been a patient man, and it hurt Arielle to know she would never see him again.

"He taught me a lot about loving others." After a moment or two, Naomi continued, "I guess I was angry when he was taken from us. Angry that Yahveh didn't know how much we needed him. I got angrier when the boys were taken as well." She turned her head towards Arielle. "But it is only since we set out to come back to Bethlehem that I have realized that Yahveh hasn't left us. Seeing Ruth's trust in Yahveh has been both a rebuke and an inspiration."

Arielle raised an eyebrow. "Rebuke?"

"That a foreigner who knew nothing of Yahveh when she married Mahlon could have such a strong trust in him now." Naomi gestured to the neighborhood. "Especially when so many Israelites only give allegiance to Yahveh occasionally and only when it is convenient."

"But isn't that the way of most people with their gods?" Arielle asked.

"It certainly was in Moab. Most of our neighbors participated in festivals because it was expected of them or because they loved the noise and excitement."

"And most Moabites are afraid that if they don't make offerings, then the gods will be angry and bring bad luck. How is that any different from worshiping Yahveh?"

"I am so sorry that most of the people you've seen, both the Israelites in Moab and here in Bethlehem, are not worshiping Yahveh in the ways he desires."

"How does he want to be worshiped?"

"For who he is, a great god who has rescued his people and wants them to live with the blessings of serving him." Naomi sighed. "It is so frustrating. I want you to see Yahveh, but most of his followers, including myself, give you such a distorted picture that it is easy to dismiss Yahveh as being just like other gods.

Arielle had hated Chemosh because of those who claimed to serve him, but she'd never considered that someone like Boaz might be the way he was because he followed Yahveh.

"Boaz is the only local who has impressed me," Arielle said. "I only hope it is not for show."

"Do you think I would be doing what we're doing if I had any doubts about his character? On the days that you were both in the fields, I went to visit some of my old friends."

"Those same friends who never came to see you?" Arielle heard the sarcastic edge in her words.

"Your sarcasm is understandable, but please don't get bitter. It only harms the one who lets the bitterness take root." Naomi touched Arielle's shoulder. "Some of them wanted to come but didn't dare because their husbands or other family members wouldn't let them. Not everyone has courage. I wonder what I would have done in their situation. I like to think I would have been different, but I am less confident in myself than I used to be."

It was unsettling to hear an older person admit to faults. If Ruth married Boaz, Ruth would leave them. Then Arielle would be alone with Naomi, and they would have to learn to live and work together.

"None of the village folk had anything negative to say about Boaz." The corner of Naomi's mouth rose. "They often thought him odd for following the law to the extent he did, but no one could deny he kept it." She chuckled. "And a lot of the women were peeved that he remained unmarried, despite their best efforts."

It was certainly puzzling as to why such a man hadn't married, but good to hear he was worthy of their Ruth.

CHAPTER TWELVE

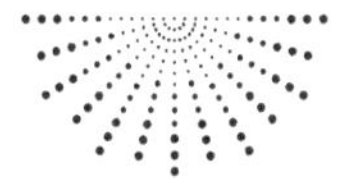

"Arielle, wake up. Ruth is coming," Naomi said.

Arielle sat up and rubbed sleep from her eyes. She had finally dropped off to sleep sometime in the early hours of the morning. Naomi drew her cloak around herself and walked down the stairs, steadying herself against the wall. Had she slept at all?

Arielle jumped to her feet and headed after Naomi. She was just in time to see Naomi throw her arms around Ruth and draw her close.

"Is everything alright, my daughter?" Naomi asked.

Ruth hugged the bundle in her shawl. "Yes, Ima. Boaz will come here to see you as soon as possible. Then he will go to the elders."

"I knew the man could be depended on. He will not rest until the matter is settled. Let me get you a hot drink."

"And we want to hear everything," Arielle said.

Ruth showed them the six measures of barley Boaz had given her. Arielle stored it away from the mice. Ruth was soon seated with her hands clutching a beaker of warmed water.

Arielle settled herself where she could see Ruth's face. "How long did you have to wait in hiding?"

"Why don't we let Ruth tell us in her own words," Naomi said.

Arielle wanted to hear Ruth's account, but she couldn't help being aware that she might be losing Ruth—and soon. Was it only a few days ago when she'd been so happy that their small family had finally settled into a rhythm, doing better than simply surviving?

"The scariest part was reaching the safety of my hiding place behind the grain pile. I was terrified that someone would look up and see me. For most of the time, I didn't actually know if Boaz was even there."

If Boaz hadn't been present, there was no knowing what the workers might have done if, having had too much to drink, they had then seen Ruth.

"As I lingered in the final stand of trees, I heard Boaz's voice." Ruth took a sip of her drink. "It was a relief. I was much less scared once I knew he was there." She flushed. "He's never given me any reason to be afraid."

"How long did you have to wait?" Arielle asked.

Ruth laughed. "You do like to keep repeating the same question."

"Well, you haven't answered it yet!"

"No, I haven't, but I'm not really sure. It seemed a long, long time until the meal finished and people began to look for places to sleep. I did get a fright when it looked like someone was headed towards me to relieve themselves. But Boaz called out, 'Not near the grain please' and redirected them towards a pile of rocks."

"That was a lucky escape," Arielle said with a grin.

Ruth finished her drink. "Eventually everyone lay down and went to sleep. I had to fight sleep myself. It turns out that a pile of grain is not as uncomfortable as I expected. Once it had been quiet for a long time, I crept out of my hiding place and went and lay at Boaz's feet." Ruth yawned. "I didn't dare to sleep. During the darkest part of the night, I got a terrible shock when Boaz kicked out and woke up to find me there."

Arielle leaned forward. "What did he do?"

"Well, of course, he asked who I was, and I said what Ima had instructed me."

"Which was?"

"I am your servant, Ruth. Spread the corner of your garment over me, since you are a guardian-redeemer for our family."

These Israelites certainly did things differently. "Then what did he say?"

Ruth half-closed her eyes. "'The Lord bless you, my daughter. This kindness is greater than that which you showed earlier. You have not run after the younger men, whether rich or poor."

Boaz was rather old, closer in age to Naomi and Elimelech than to Ruth and Arielle. Such a good man should have been married long ago and have a crowd of children. Perhaps even grandchildren.

"He told me not to be afraid and that he'd do what I'd asked."

"Daughter," Naomi asked gently. "Did he say anything about you personally?"

Ruth nodded and there was a slight flush to her cheeks. "He said that all the people of Bethlehem know I am a woman of noble character."

Arielle couldn't help a little snort shooting out her mouth. If they thought such things, why had the townsfolk ignored them all?

"But Boaz said he is not the closest guardian-redeemer." Ruth turned looked at Naomi. "Is that true?"

Naomi's brow furrowed. "There is one more man, but he's married. I didn't want him for Ruth's husband, even though he is younger."

"What happened next?" Arielle asked, wanting to get back to Ruth's account.

"Boaz told me to stay at his feet for the night. I actually slept until he woke me before dawn. He told me that no one must know I'd been there, and he gave me the barley as a gift for us all."

"The man has been nothing but generous. We can expect him

any moment. Girls, we must get moving." Naomi clambered to her feet.

Ruth yawned again. "Once he is gone, I will try to sleep."

Arielle doubted Ruth would succeed. Naomi was too excited, and her excitement was infecting them all.

* * *

"Here he is, girls," Naomi said.

Arielle hurried out the doorway, smoothing her hair and then her skirt. Naomi ran an approving glance over Arielle, then helped Ruth tuck in a stray curl of her hair.

"Arielle, go and lay out the dried figs and the milk. Boaz and I will talk. You must stay outside until I call you."

Arielle nodded and scurried to do Naomi's will. This was not the time to be asking questions and distracting Naomi from her task. She laid out the refreshments, although it was really too early in the morning for such things.

"Naomi, Ruth, may Yahveh smile on you both," Boaz said from the front of the house.

Arielle went out into the back garden as ordered. Did Naomi know that she'd probably be able to hear everything from the garden? Maybe. But perhaps she wouldn't mind if Arielle overheard, for surely this impacted Arielle as well.

"Come in and sit down," Naomi said.

Ruth would serve the refreshments. Ruth wouldn't say a word, but Arielle knew she'd be listening to every word as she quietly did her tasks.

"I am sorry for your losses," Boaz said.

"They have been great," Naomi said. "But I have also had gains, and Ruth is one of them."

Boaz laughed. "Direct as ever."

"I like to think of it as sticking to the important things," Naomi replied.

"And today we have important things to discuss. I know how precious Ruth is to you, and I am deeply touched by you asking for me to step in as guardian-redeemer. But, as you know, there is a closer redeemer than me."

"But he is married. I assumed you were too, or I would have acted earlier."

There was a long silence. Arielle strained her ears to make sure she didn't miss anything.

"I guess you want to know why I am not married," Boaz said. "And since you are wanting to entrust Ruth to me, you deserve to know."

Arielle held her breath. Not marrying was unheard of when you were a landowner, and fit and healthy.

There was a pause while Boaz presumably worked out how to start.

"At first, it was more to do with my mother. You know the background and why it was a sticking point for so many."

Bother! Naomi obviously already knew the story, and Boaz wasn't going to go into detail. What was so mysterious about his family?

"While my mother was still alive, no one was willing to allow their daughter to marry into our family." Boaz was silent for a long moment. "I found that rather unforgivable. Yahveh accepted my mother and gave her a new start, but those who claimed to be Yahveh's people were not nearly so kind. My mother was never accepted here except by a very few people, your family being one of them."

"And your neighbors were the poorer for it," Naomi said. "Your mother was an inspiration. I learned a lot from her about what it means to trust Yahveh."

"She laid the solid foundations in my life and taught me every story of Yahveh that I know."

"She was a fine woman," Naomi said. "She was very proud of you."

It sounded like Boaz was an only child and that his mother had died some years ago. Presumably his abba had died even earlier, for he had not been mentioned.

"Neither of my parents were farmers. My abba was one of the generation who'd wandered in the desert with Mosheh and then fought with Yehoshua. My ima was a city girl. They made many mistakes on their land."

"Which you have rectified," Naomi said.

"I'm still learning, but I have found that it is as the Law says. When you honor and obey Yahveh, he blesses."

"Didn't that change people's attitudes towards you?" Naomi asked.

"It's difficult to know. Certainly, people were more willing for me to marry their daughters once I became prosperous, but I didn't want just anyone. I wanted someone with the faith of my ima and that—" Boaz sighed. "That has proved almost impossible."

Until now, thought Arielle.

"Until now. Ruth impressed me from the moment I met her. I know how hard it is for an outsider to live in Bethlehem. I know what it's like to be ostracized for simply being a foreigner, yet she chose to come here out of love for you and for Yahveh."

"And I'm so thankful she did," Naomi said. "But I knew if she came, then it lessened the chances of remarriage for her."

"I have watched Ruth while she has worked in my fields, and I've never been anything but impressed. I will be happy to have her as my wife, for at last I have found someone who matches my mother in faith and dignity."

"And I believe that I have found someone worthy of her, for I would not part with Ruth for any less than the man I believe you to be."

"The elders will soon be gathering at the gate," Boaz said. "I must go and talk to the man who is a closer guardian-redeemer than I am and present my case."

"Go with Yahveh," Naomi said. "We'll be waiting."

Arielle heard the rustle as Naomi and Boaz stood.

Naomi and Ruth would be praying, but Arielle's heart was divided. If Ruth married either of the men, Arielle would be left as the sole outsider. This marriage would provide for the whole family, but what about her? She was unable to return to Moab, yet didn't fit in here either. Would anyone ever be willing to marry her?

CHAPTER THIRTEEN

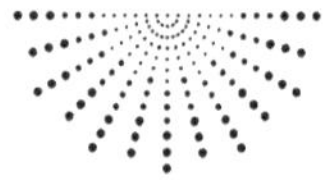

Ruth came out into the back garden where Arielle was weeding and Naomi followed.

"Well, my daughter, how are you feeling?" Naomi asked Ruth.

"To be honest, I'm a little nervous. What if the other man says he wants to act as redeemer?"

"We do not have to accept him," Naomi said. "But I'm guessing he will be happy for Boaz to solve the problem. He spoke out strongly against us going to Moab in the first place."

Naomi didn't say anything more about the other man, but she didn't really need to. The man was a relative yet he hadn't come to visit them once since they'd come back. Perhaps he was another person who believed foreigners should stay in their own countries, as far as possible from Israel. There seemed to be far too many people with that attitude. Surely, if Yahveh was so great, they'd want as many people from amongst the nations to worship him as possible. Instead, they seemed to want Yahveh to be exclusive to them, as though that somehow meant they'd get all the benefits from Yahveh and wouldn't need to share them with outsiders.

"Could we pray together?" Ruth asked. "Then I must keep myself occupied."

"We could all do with being occupied," Naomi said. "But we shouldn't have to wait too long. Boaz is considerate. He'll do what needs to be done and come back to tell us as soon as he can."

Once again, Naomi drew them into a small circle, a circle of belonging and acceptance. A circle that pulled strongly on Arielle's heart. Why could things not stay the way they were? Arielle would have been content just to be the three of them forever, but she wasn't so young and naive as to think that such things were possible. Abba, Mahlon, and Kilion had already left them. Now Ruth was likely to leave as well. Naomi was no longer young. One day they'd lose her, too. Then what would Arielle do? She had no one else. It would be almost impossible to return to Moab, yet the people of this place didn't want her either.

Ruth concluded a prayer that Arielle had not heard a single word of. Naomi squeezed their hands. "Yahveh, although you are great and mighty, you see us here."

Did he really? Why would a god care for people of such little significance?

"You know how hard it has been for us all and what Ruth has given up. Please give Boaz wisdom and grant him success today with the city elders."

Ruth wasn't saying much, but what did she feel about all these plans? Was she willing, or simply being an obedient daughter? Arielle would wait until Naomi went inside to prepare the bread dough before she asked Ruth.

"Blessings upon Boaz, blessings on Ruth, and blessings on Arielle and myself," Naomi concluded. She reached over and kissed Ruth on the brow, then Arielle.

"You go and rest Ima. We'll do some gardening and pick a few more cucumbers to go with our meal," Ruth said.

Once Naomi had gone, Ruth handed the basket to Arielle. "I know you like to do the picking."

Who wouldn't? It was so satisfying to see the vegetables they'd planted and tended produce what they would eat today. Arielle began to search the vines for cucumbers ready for picking, while Ruth knelt to continue the weeding.

"Ruth, are you happy to be marrying Boaz?" Arielle asked.

"Why do you think I ought to be happy?" Ruth asked.

"I thought you seemed happy with Mahlon."

Ruth sat back on her haunches. "I was in the process of becoming happy. I barely knew him when we married. We were adjusting to each other."

"But Boaz is, you know, old," Arielle said.

Ruth chuckled. "Oh, I think he still has plenty of life."

"But do you love him?" Arielle asked, thinking of the tenderness she'd witnessed between Naomi and Elimelech throughout her childhood.

"Who's been filling your head with nonsense?" Ruth said. "Ask Naomi. She'll tell you most women don't love their husbands when they marry them, for they barely know them. They grow to love them. When I listen to Boaz speak and see his obedience to Yahveh and the way he seeks to honor him, I am not worried about not being able to love him. As we follow Yahveh, we will grow together."

"You sound so sure," Arielle said. She didn't know if she wanted this kind of marriage. She'd once imagined loving Tozbi, but that dream had been a child's dream abruptly destroyed by his father's cruelty.

"Ima hasn't looked at outward things. Things that fade, like good looks and good teeth. She's looked for characteristics that last. Things like integrity, generosity, and kindness. Boaz has an abundance of those characteristics. We already get along. I am not worried." She flushed. "I have prayed, and Yahveh has given me a deep sense of peace."

Arielle didn't understand, but she could hear Ruth's sincerity in her voice. Maybe she would understand when her own time came.

* * *

"I see him, Ima," Arielle called from the front door. Boaz was striding along the track towards their home with the step of a man younger than his years. She took a shaky breath. It looked like he'd been successful.

"Go and watch the last of the bread while I welcome him," Naomi said.

Arielle went around the back of the house to where they cooked their meals. She spread out the dough until it was flat and tossed it on the hot rock they used for making flatbread. It sizzled and she willed the bread to cook quickly, for she didn't want to miss out on anything.

Straining her ears, she only heard the sounds of greetings. Arielle flipped the last bread. As soon as it was cooked through, she put it into the basket and left the fire to slowly burn itself out.

Boaz had been given the seat of honor under the grapevines. Ruth placed the fresh cucumbers, olives, and yogurt with herbs in front of him. Arielle walked across and put down the basket of bread.

"My abba always said that nothing beats the smell of fresh bread," Boaz said. "Thank you for your hospitality, but you must be dying to hear my news." He looked around at the three women. "All is well. If you allow me to have a few mouthfuls of this delicious food, then I will tell you what happened."

Naomi signaled for Ruth and Arielle to join them, and Arielle took a seat at a suitable distance. She nibbled on a cucumber.

Boaz tore the flat breads and handed some to each woman. "If we are to be family, you must eat with me."

Arielle glanced at Ruth. She appeared calm, but there was a slight flush around her throat. She must be anxious to hear what Boaz had to say.

Boaz took a few mouthfuls and then laid down his bread. "I arrived at the town gate in time and sat down to wait for the other guardian-redeemer to come along. When he did, I said, 'Come over here, my friend, and sit down.' He joined me and then I invited ten of the town elders to join us. Then in front of all of them I said, 'Naomi, who has come back from Moab, is selling the piece of land that belonged to our relative, Elimelech. I thought I should bring this matter to your attention in the presence of the elders, so I could suggest you buy it. I wanted you to have first chance for you are closest in line, even closer than I am, to Naomi.'"

"What did he say?" Naomi asked.

"'I will redeem it.'"

No! Arielle's heart sank. Hadn't Boaz said that everything was alright? Maybe he was relieved to get out of the responsibility.

"But I said, 'On the day you buy the land from Naomi, you also acquire Ruth the Moabite, the dead man's widow, in order to maintain the name of the dead with his property.'" Boaz chuckled. "He changed his mind quickly at those words and said, 'Then I cannot redeem the land because I might endanger my own estate. You can redeem it if you want to.'"

Arielle's shoulders relaxed. Boaz had been clever.

"I must admit I had been praying for this exact outcome," Boaz said. "And ten of the elders had heard the man's words. He took off his sandal, which is our custom for legalizing such transactions, and he handed it to me with the words, 'Buy it yourself.' So, I announced to all the elders and others standing around, 'Today you are witnesses that I have bought all the property of Elimelech, Kilion, and Mahlon. And I have also acquired Ruth, Mahlon's widow, as my wife, in order to maintain the name of the dead with his property, so his name will not disappear from among his family or from his hometown.'"

Arielle could imagine the scene and Boaz's voice ringing out to make sure that nothing was hidden from view.

"Then all the elders and people at the gate said, 'We are witnesses. May Yahveh make the woman who is coming into your home like Rahel and Leah of old, who together built up the family of Israel. May you have standing in Ephrathah and be famous in Bethlehem. Through the offspring the Lord gives you by this young woman, may your family be like that of Perez, whom Tamar bore to Judah.'"

Naomi had tears in her eyes. "Yes, may it be so." She turned to Ruth, took her hand, and joined it with Boaz's. "May you both be blessed as you follow Yahveh together."

Boaz bowed his head. "May it be so."

"Is there any reason to wait for the marriage to take place?" Naomi asked.

"The timing is up to Ruth." Boaz turned to Ruth. "Would you and the family like to come out to my home and look it over? I have lived on my own for some years. I'm sure you will see some things that need to be repaired or tidied. I will follow anything you suggest and freshen it up. Then we can be married. It is time this town accepted your family."

But would the townspeople accept them? Would Arielle one day be invited to weddings and festivals? Would people actually talk to her, instead of merely about her?

Yes, Boaz was respected, but could he change people's hearts and attitudes?

CHAPTER FOURTEEN

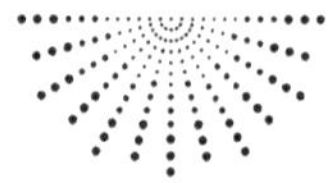

$\mathcal{A}$rielle speared the ground and dropped her hoe.

"What's wrong?" Ruth asked.

"Nothing," Arielle muttered as she picked up the hoe and attacked the ground again.

"There's obviously something," Ruth said.

Not something Arielle wanted to talk about. She was supposed to be happy, happy, happy and she simply wasn't.

"I know this must be hard on you," Ruth said. "You've had a life-time of losses and it probably feels like you're losing me too."

A tear trickled down Arielle's cheek and she wiped it away with the back of her hand.

"I'm not going far away."

"It feels a long way to me," Arielle said, a sob close to the surface. "Everyone leaves me."

Her parents had dumped her on a doorstep as if she meant nothing to them. Then Elimelech had been snatched away. He'd understood her better than anyone and had always been her encourager. She'd loved to sit on his lap, her head on his shoulder, and talk about the concerns she'd had when she was a little girl. Probably boring to him but big happenings for her. Mahlon and Kilion had always had each other, and she hadn't been able to keep up with their running or throwing or climbing. She was always trailing behind them calling "Wait for me." Now they too were gone, gone somewhere she could never find them.

"Come here," Ruth said. "It sounds like you need a hug."

They both stood up and Ruth drew Arielle into a hug. When Ruth had come into the family, Arielle had been hugged more than ever before. Each hug was a warm embrace, but they never quite filled that empty hole in Arielle's middle.

"You'll always be my sister," Ruth said into Arielle's ear.

Arielle broke out of the hug. "But I'm not. That's just it. I'm not your sister. I'm probably no one's sister."

"You might not be my sister by blood, but there are other kinds of sisters."

"Such as?"

"Such as sisters of the heart, sisters we choose. Those sisters can mean more to us than the sisters we grew up with."

It sounded lovely, but would it ever be enough?

"I've been praying for you," Ruth said. "I'm concerned that in your desire to belong and have a family, you latch on to one person or another to fill that emptiness you feel inside."

It was true. First it had been Elimelech. Now it was Ruth. Arielle had also tried to latch on to the boys, but they'd always resisted.

"I felt that emptiness until recently too," Ruth said.

What? Arielle had thought Ruth had always had everything, at least until Mahlon died. "But you have a family who loves you and soon a new one too."

"I don't think the emptiness has anything to do with what we have or haven't got. It seems to be the condition of all people. When I look back now, I think it happens when we don't know our

Creator, for the emptiness went away when I submitted myself to him."

Arielle raised an eyebrow. Yahveh had always seemed somewhere far out there to her.

"I can see I'm not explaining myself clearly. Let me see if I can do better." Ruth looked around her, then unpegged her spare tunic from the line of clean clothes flapping in the breeze. "If I was to rip this tunic in half, it would always be missing something. Half a tunic is not much use for anything. I often felt like I was missing half of me." Ruth pursed her lips. "Do you remember the story of A'dam and Havah in the garden?"

"Of course."

"They walked and talked with their Creator."

Arielle hadn't really thought of the details of the story. It had just been an interesting story that Elimelech told her, not something that was connected to her.

"Back then, A'dam and Havah were given the responsibility of caring for Eden and naming all its creatures. They were the Creator's children, and he presumably spent much time with them. Then came the snake—"

"And he tempted them to go their own way."

"Which they did, rejecting Yahveh as their ruler." Ruth lifted the garment again. "That rejection is when Yahveh and his people were torn apart." Ruth shook her head. "And ever since then people have felt empty, dissatisfied—"

"As though something is missing," Arielle murmured.

"Exactly."

"I thought I was the only one who felt that way," Arielle said.

"That's part of the problem. We don't voice our emptiness to other people so everyone thinks they're the only one feeling empty."

Arielle kneeled and pulled out some weeds. She'd never imagined Ruth felt anything but joy in her life. "When did you decide to submit yourself to Yahveh?" The word submit felt cumbersome on her tongue, yet Ruth had used it to describe her choice to worship Yahveh instead of the gods of her ancestors. What did submission to Yahveh even mean? Submission to Chemosh meant terrible things, but Ruth used the term as if it was a positive.

Ruth kneeled down next to Arielle. "It came on gradually. I hadn't really known anything about Yahveh when I joined the family, but Naomi took the opportunity to tell me many things." She paused. "Mahlon used to pray, and I listened closely to what he said because his prayers were so different from any I'd heard before."

"How so?"

"For a start, they weren't pleading prayers asking for wealth or other benefits for himself. And they weren't bargaining prayers, 'If I do this, will you do that?'"

Like most people prayed.

"In fact, most of his prayers were praising Yahveh for his goodness or repenting of harsh words or impatience." Ruth sighed. "Even when he got sick, his prayers were more for the rest of the family than for himself."

Soon Mahlon had been too sick to pray at all. Both he and Kilion had descended into the confusion of high fevers.

"If I had to say exactly when I trusted Yahveh though, it might have been that moment when Orpah said she would return to Moab. Suddenly I knew I couldn't. I didn't want to go back to a place where people worshiped Chemosh and thought nothing of offering a child in the flames to achieve their own selfish desires."

Arielle's throat narrowed as she remembered Tozbi.

"I knew that I wanted to stay with Naomi and be around someone who trusted Yahveh."

Arielle frowned. Now Ruth spoke of trusting Yahveh as if trust was the same as submission. Submission to Chemosh never meant trust. Trust was what you offered a friend, family member, or business partner. Someone you knew had your best interest at heart. Arielle trusted Ruth, and she trusted Naomi. Chemosh was more like a powerful king, to be submitted to because it was safer to be his servant than his enemy. Trust was not a factor in this submission.

Arielle pushed the pile of weeds she'd pulled up to the side. "Why do you think Yahveh is worthy of your trust?"

Ruth put her head to one side. "That's a really hard question. I think my trust has grown gradually, much like trust grows in a marriage. First I knew about Yahveh from the history of his dealings with people. Then I learned to pray and as he answered, I grew in trust."

"How did he answer?"

"Often in small ways at first: help to do a task or remembering something. The big challenges came after Mahlon's death. I asked Yahveh to help me see joy again and he did so." Ruth touched Arielle's hand. "You were part of the answer to my prayers, for you bring me joy."

A smile curved the corner of Arielle's mouth. The thought that she brought joy to Ruth warmed her belly. "And how have things been different since you decided to trust Yahveh?"

"The difference has mainly been inside me. I feel like my heart has been put together again. Yes, I'm still sad about losing Mahlon, but I also feel a sense of confidence that Yahveh is in control and has plans for me in this place."

"It seems he has, with Boaz."

"Maybe. But I don't need to be married to feel complete. That completeness was there because I am following Yahveh. Anything else is a bonus."

Submit, trust, follow.

Ruth used the words as though they were interchangeable. Ruth had followed Naomi away from her family, her homeland. Such following did require deep trust. Yet Naomi was worthy of this trust, fiercely ensuring Ruth was provided for by pursuing Boaz to be her husband despite all odds. In the stories that Elimelech and Ruth and Naomi told, Yahveh was great and powerful. He even cared for people like the woman who was saved from Jericho.

It all sounded too good to be true.

"But Yahveh isn't just for me or the Israelites." Ruth leaned forward, reaching for more weeds. "He's waiting for you to follow him too."

Could it be true? Could Arielle have whatever it was that Ruth had? Ruth's contentment, her joy, and her feeling that she was complete wherever she was? Or was the whole thing just made up? If Arielle just looked at Ruth, the choice was easy. Or if she looked at Boaz or Naomi. But looking at anyone else in this town, she doubted their god could be as Ruth described.

"What about all the people in this town?" Arielle asked. "If they follow Yahveh, then I want nothing to do with him."

Ruth sighed. "Yes, they've been a great disappointment to me. I thought when we moved here that we'd leave all the evil of Moab behind us. Then when we arrived, I discovered how many people are Yahveh-followers in name only. They don't submit to him or love his words. It is just an outward show while their hearts chase after their own ways."

"There are high places to worship the Canaanite gods all over the place."

"I asked Naomi about those. She said the reason Yehoshua was commanded to totally wipe out all the inhabitants within the borders of Canaan was to make sure the Israelites wouldn't be influenced by the Canaanites and worship their gods."

"Well, that didn't work," Arielle said.

"'Because the Israelites didn't follow Yahveh's instructions. They did a half-hearted job of the conquest and have lived amongst Canaanites and their gods ever since."

"Are you saying that if the Israelites had fully obeyed, then they would be much more likely to follow Yahveh wholeheartedly?"

Ruth nodded. "But because they didn't obey, their hearts were easily led astray. Naomi says there are always some who are faithful, but more are unfaithful and it pollutes the whole country. It is a great sadness. Do you remember hearing that King Eglon invaded and ruled over parts of Israel for eighteen years?"

"Elimelech explained that to me. How they expanded their territory and ruled the areas north of Moab's current boundaries."

"I think King Eglon was able to conquer Israel because Yahveh allowed it."

Arielle raised an eyebrow.

"Yahveh promised that if the Israelites obeyed him, then he would bless them abundantly. But if they didn't, then Yahveh would punish them by making their crops fail and allowing other nations to come and rule over them. Recently it has been the Midianites."

"How is that different from any other god? Worship them and they'll be blessed and if not, they'll be cursed?"

Ruth put her head to one side, the way she always did when she was thinking hard.

"Firstly, I don't think that the other gods are consistent in their dealings with their followers. Tozbi's father sacrificed him because he'd made some unwise decisions and had large debts."

Arielle drew in a strangled breath, as she always did when she thought about Tozbi.

"The family never received any blessing despite everything they'd sacrificed. Yahveh couldn't be more different from those gods. He is like a mother hen who gathers his people under his wing. He always works for their good, and he is not inconsistent or cruel."

Arielle had seen mother hens protecting their chicks. Just the thought of a god as powerful as Yahveh who was also caring made her skin tingle. If she were ever to follow a god, that's the kind of god she wanted.

"So how does one choose to follow Yahveh?" Arielle asked.

Ruth laughed. "There is no particular way. You could always tell him, although he reads your heart anyway."

If Yahveh was what Ruth claimed, then having her heart read sounded comforting rather than threatening.

"Would you like to tell him now?" Ruth asked.

"Now is as good a time as any," Arielle said. She'd heard Ruth pray often enough not to need any instruction with how to pray. Ruth normally prayed while standing.

Arielle stood up and Ruth reached out her hand and took Arielle's dirt-smeared one in her own. If Yahveh was currently reading her heart, he'd know it was beating fast.

"Are you alright praying on your own, or would you prefer me to help you?" Ruth asked.

"I'll do it," Arielle said. It might not be smooth but as Ruth said, prayer was more about the heart anyway. She didn't know how to start, so maybe she'd just treat Yahveh like she'd treat someone superior to herself.

"Yahveh, Ruth tells me that you are not only powerful but good." Arielle licked her lips to give herself time to think of the next line. "Since Ruth has been following you, she has been so much happier and more content. I want that."

Ruth squeezed her hand. Encouraged, Arielle continued, "I don't really know what it means to follow you, but I'm willing to give it a try."

If Yahveh was so great, he might not like her attitude.

"I don't mean to be rude, but I don't know you well yet. Ruth has told me that you know me because you made me."

Arielle turned to Ruth. "I don't know how to end."

"Perhaps just tell him thank you," Ruth said.

Arielle's face burned. Elimelech would have told her off for forgetting that. "Thank you, Yahveh. Teach me to follow you."

Ruth turned and enveloped Arielle in a hug.

Arielle savored that hug, for there might not be many more in the future. How she was going to miss this sort-of sister of hers. Why did people have to get married? Ruth wouldn't be far away, but it would be so different from waking up next to her every morning.

CHAPTER FIFTEEN

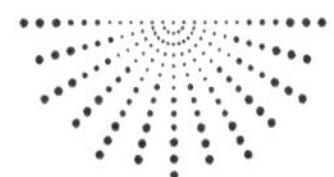

$\mathcal{A}$rielle looked around her, amazed. Boaz's house was so spacious. Perched on a small hill, it had a wide view across his land. Boaz had shown them through all the rooms and now they were seated on a deep verandah. No need to sleep on the roof in the hot weather here.

"Is it acceptable?" Boaz asked, looking at Ruth.

Unbelievably, he seemed nervous as he waited for Ruth's answer.

"Acceptable? It's beautiful," Ruth answered.

Boaz beamed. "The fresh whitewash does make it look better, and I'm happy for you to make any suggestions you'd like."

Arielle doubted Ruth would make any suggestions. It was so much better than anywhere she'd ever lived before. It even had a separate kitchen, away from the house, to prevent cooking fires from threatening the main house.

"My abba made the house to Ima's design. Abba wanted the house built down there, protected from the elements." Boaz pointed to a dimple in the hills. "But Ima said she'd cope with the weather if she could have the views." Boaz laughed. "She'd always had views from her home in Jericho's city wall."

Oh! Was his mother the woman in the story Naomi had told them as they had passed the rubble of Jericho? What was her name? Something beginning with R.

Even before they'd settled themselves on the verandah, a servant had come in answer to a silent summons and laid out refreshments of cold goat's milk, dried apricots, pistachios, fresh bread, and cheese.

Arielle's eyes widened, but she quickly averted them from the food, trying not to look greedy for things she hadn't eaten since they arrived in Bethlehem.

Enoch, the steward, had told her that everything they ate was grown on the farm and there'd be plenty left to sell. Everything on the property proclaimed Boaz as meticulous and prosperous. Even the outside area around the house was swept and raked and clear of debris. Would Ruth find enough to do here? She'd always said she liked working. It gave her satisfaction to see neat rows in the garden and a row of plants tied on to the stakes.

Boaz took one of the loaves of bread and held it up. "Let's pray and thank Yahveh for this day."

Naomi and Ruth raised their hands. Arielle followed their example. It felt good to be part of this Yahveh-following family, but had anything else about her life really changed since praying with Ruth? Maybe she'd expected something mysterious. On reflection, she wasn't sure what she'd expected. Maybe a flood of peace or joy. She'd asked Ruth that morning, and Ruth said she didn't know what was normal. For her, it had just been an absolute conviction that she was making the right decision.

"Great and mighty Creator, we thank you for all the gifts you bring, for bread and the fruits of our labor. Thank you for these, my soon-to-be family. Help us to keep our eyes focused on you and remain grateful for everything you've blessed us with."

Lowering his hands, Boaz broke the bread into pieces. Then he offered them the food, first to Naomi, and then Ruth. Arielle was content to wait her turn. Boaz would not forget her.

Arielle closed her eyes in delight at the flavors of the food. The bread was flavored with herbs she had not tasted before. She had to restrain herself from stuffing her mouth.

After the meal, Boaz gestured behind him towards the walls of the house. "Abba wanted to make a beautiful house for Ima since she had suffered so much hardship, first in Jericho then once she came to join the Israelites."

Arielle broke off another piece of warm herb-dusted bread to nibble, quietly hoping Boaz would talk more about his mother. "Your ima did not deserve the way she was treated here," Naomi said. "Anyone who knows Yahveh would have recognized her worth."

"That is true, but as you have seen, few of the Israelites actually follow Yahveh. They claim loudly that they follow him, but their feet run after other gods and the things their hands have made. It breaks my heart. I long for their hearts to turn back to Yahveh."

"Do you think that will ever happen?" Ruth asked.

"I pray it does. Each time Yahveh raises up a leader, the people repent and return to Yahveh. But when the leader dies, they quickly drift away. It happened far too quickly after Yehoshua died, and was repeated after each judge, like Othniel and Ehud."

Arielle vaguely remembered these names.

"My father told me of Othniel when we saw his tomb at Hebron," Naomi said. "Abba had known him well and respected him."

"He came from a godly heritage, for his father was Caleb's younger brother."

"The Caleb who was one of the spies with Yehoshua?" Ruth asked.

More people Arielle did not know.

"The very same," Boaz replied.

Ruth leaned over and touched Arielle's arm. "Don't worry. We'll introduce you to all these people and places."

Arielle gave a tight smile. She had much to learn about this nation's history.

"I think it is important that you know about my ima," Boaz said. "People will judge you for marrying into this family. Abba was constantly criticized and Ima was made to feel people's displeasure."

As they had all felt since the moment they'd arrived.

"Boaz," Naomi said. "You don't need to tell your story. I could tell Ruth and Arielle at home."

He shook his head. "No, I'd prefer they heard it from me. Otherwise, they will hear it or be judged by it from the mouths of others. I am not the least bit ashamed of Ima's story, for she was a wonderful woman of faith. I believe you know that she and a few members of her family were the only ones saved from Jericho."

"We saw her house in the only remaining bit of wall," Arielle said.

"I thought you might have come that way. Did Naomi tell you about Yehoshua's conquest of Jericho?"

Arielle nodded. "She was a brave woman to trust her life to the two spies and go against her own people."

Boaz nodded. "She was certainly brave but she had a hard life. She grew up in a fairly ordinary family, but her abba made a very unwise choice of bridegroom for her. The man turned out to be a gambler. When he had run out of things to sell, there was only his wife left." Boaz sighed. "Ima always said her beauty was a curse. If she'd have been ugly, then she might have lived out her days as the ugly wife of a poor man instead of being sold to the highest bidder. When that second man tired of her, he used her to earn riches for himself."

An image of the priest in the temple and his leering smile

flashed through Arielle's mind. Her throat tightened. Men could be evil. She forced herself to replace the image of the priest with the earnest face of Boaz. He impressed her at every turn.

"Ima helped me to understand the evils of this world." Boaz's voice hardened. "And to fight them at every opportunity. Many people—especially women—face injustice through no fault of their own." He turned towards Ruth. "That's why, when you came to my attention, I made sure to look out for you. Ima might no longer be around, but she taught me to care for the widow and the fatherless."

Arielle swallowed. She might not be a widow like Ruth, but she was fatherless twice over. Sometimes, when she woke in the night, she'd think about who her father might have been. Was he even alive? Or was she placed on Naomi's doorstep because her parents were dead? At least they hadn't placed her at the door of the temple.

"One of the things I love about following Yahveh is his concern for those that others look down upon. His law is full of instructions on how to protect the weakest members of society. He must have a special heart for them, and I work at making sure my heart is in line with his."

"This is why I thought of you for our Ruth," Naomi said. "We would not want her to marry anyone who was less worthy. Maybe I considered the match because she reminded me of your mother. Two women who passionately pursued Yahveh."

Boaz smiled at Ruth. "That is the kind of woman I want for my wife. When will you do me the honor of marrying me?"

Ruth flushed but her eyes were dancing. "Whenever Naomi thinks we can be ready."

"I think we can be ready by the time of the full moon." Naomi looked from Ruth to Boaz, clearly pleased with both.

"Well, if Ruth and Arielle can entertain themselves for a while, I would like to discuss details with Naomi."

Naomi stood, and she and Boaz wandered down towards a much smaller building on the edge of the hilltop.

"What do you think they're talking about?" Arielle asked.

"Probably just wedding details," Ruth said. "Boaz knows we have no riches to bring as a dowry. He will have to provide everything, and he is talking to Naomi on her own so she is not embarrassed in front of us. She blames herself for the poor price she accepted for the house in Moab and the state that left our family."

"But it wasn't her fault. The neighbors took advantage of her," Arielle said.

"We know that, but Naomi finds it easy to blame herself."

Arielle looked at the view shimmering in the heat haze. "Ruth, are you happy about this?"

Ruth smiled. "I am trusting that Yahveh knows exactly what he is doing, and I don't think I could have found a better man to be my husband. Yes, it will be a big adjustment, for we are from two different backgrounds, but he will be more understanding than others because he is half Canaanite."

Ruth seemed so calm, but was she as calm as she seemed? Arielle would be afraid to have to leave her family. If only things could stay just as they were, with Naomi and Ruth and herself in their little house and the garden that was beginning to produce their daily needs.

CHAPTER SIXTEEN

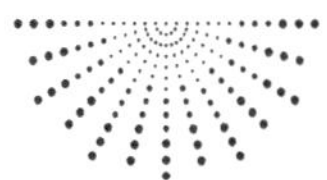

A cock crowed, and Arielle was instantly awake. Today was Ruth and Boaz's wedding day! She looked over at the dark mound next to her. This day Ruth would leave them to enter her husband's home. Arielle would not dwell on that, for it was Ruth's day and she deserved to be happy.

Arielle stood and peered out in the darkness. A faint orange line gilded the horizon. Above, the stars sparkled in the heavens, sprinkled in patterns only the Creator understood. A breeze ruffled the leaves in the garden.

"Is it morning?" Ruth whispered.

"Soon," Arielle replied as she padded back on bare feet and lay down. They should let Naomi sleep a little longer. She'd been so exhausted with all the preparations that they'd had to help her take off her sandals last night and rub her feet.

Ruth's eyes glinted but she remained quiet. Was she excited or frightened or a mix of both? Maybe she had some of the emotions that churned in Arielle. Boaz had spoken with Naomi to ask if she wanted to move into the small house on the edge of his property. Naomi hadn't accepted immediately but had come and spoken with both Ruth and Arielle, for she said the last thing she wanted to do was to get in the way of Ruth's marriage. Ruth had told her not to be silly and that she'd be delighted to have them nearby. So, for Arielle and Naomi, these were their last weeks in their little house. They'd give Ruth and Boaz a chance to adjust to each other and then move themselves.

Boaz had already prepared their house according to Naomi's instructions. Yesterday, he'd sent over their wedding clothes. Oh, Arielle couldn't stay lying down on such a day. It was all too exciting. She'd go down and stir up the fire and get Naomi a drink and something to eat.

* * *

*N*aomi patted Arielle's hair. "You look beautiful. A worthy companion to Ruth."

Ruth, Naomi, and Boaz had discussed the wedding several times. On one hand, Boaz wanted to make it a big celebration to both express his joy and to honor Ruth, but he'd also been concerned that people might turn down their invitations and hurt Ruth or turn up just to stare and gossip. In the end they'd chosen to have a smaller wedding with people who would be genuinely happy to celebrate with them. He'd had tents set up around the main house to accommodate guests from outside Bethlehem, mostly other farmers and relatives who were faithful to Yahveh.

"Now help me dress Ruth," Naomi said. "It's going to need two pairs of hands to drape all that material."

Boaz had sent Ruth the most beautiful wedding gown. Ruth had gasped when she'd seen it. It was made from finely woven linen and must have cost a fortune.

"Careful," Ruth said as they helped her into the dress. "I will never wear such a dress again."

112

"And you look like the queen you are," Naomi said, kissing her brow.

Ruth gnawed her lip. "Do you think it a fitting match?"

"I think you couldn't have found a better husband," Arielle said. She had not heard a cross word from Boaz directed toward herself or Ruth, and the more servants she'd talked to, the more he'd sounded like what he appeared—a man of integrity. The servants had all agreed that Boaz would grow angry at any injustice, unkindness, or cruelty, as he had at the boys who had threatened her and Ruth.

"He's probably more nervous than you," Naomi said. "After all, he's never been married before."

Naomi fixed Ruth's hair, then dabbed the expensive perfume Boaz had sent as a gift on Ruth's hair and neck. She leaned back and considered Ruth. "Perfect."

"You're too kind, Ima. I hope I won't disappoint." She flushed. "You know."

"Are you worried you won't be able to have a child?" Naomi asked.

Ruth didn't lift her head. "Well I never did with Mahlon."

Naomi put her arms around Ruth. "We don't know that you can't have children. Let's leave that to Yahveh, shall we?"

Ruth nodded.

Naomi ended the embrace. "Now, Arielle, go and get the clothes that Boaz sent us."

Arielle scurried to obey. She could hardly wait. The linen cloth was finer than anything she'd ever worn. After the wedding she'd put the dress away. Maybe she'd get to wear it again at her own wedding. Not that a wedding looked likely, as men like Boaz were rare. Besides which, Naomi needed her.

Naomi and Arielle helped each other dress. As they finished, they heard the music approaching.

"He's coming," Naomi said. "Are you ready, Ruth?"

Ruth nodded, gnawing her lip.

"It will be alright, my sweet," Naomi said as she adjusted Ruth's veil then took her arm. Arielle stood on Ruth's other side and they moved to the door and outside.

Boaz was surrounded by his entourage, but he paid them no attention as he gazed at his veiled bride. Was he frustrated that he couldn't see her? It was an interesting custom to veil a bride but it meant Boaz would only see Ruth once they were in the privacy of their own home.

* * *

Once they reached Boaz's home he helped Ruth, Naomi, and Arielle down from the cart he'd used to transport them. Then he led Ruth towards the tent set up under a large tree. Arielle stood beside Ruth as her attendant as Ruth and Boaz were married in the sight of Yahveh and his faithful people. Guests had come from as far away as Shiloh, guests who were delighted to see their friend married at last.

After the ceremony and prayers, the guests each came forward to bless the new couple. Then the feasting began.

Arielle found herself being introduced to a stream of people, most of whom even Naomi didn't know. She stayed close to Naomi.

"And are you Ruth's sister, dear?" asked an older woman.

"No," Arielle said. "Although we're both from Moab, I don't believe we are related. I was adopted by Naomi and Elimelech."

"And that has been a blessing," Naomi said. "I don't know what I'd do without her."

Arielle blinked back tears. Emotion was close to the surface today. She had to keep reminding herself of Ruth's words that following Yahveh meant she was accepted and loved. Ever since she'd made her decision to follow Yahveh, it seemed like Ruth was even more like her sister, as though following Yahveh meant she'd joined a new family. A family that now included Boaz. A Boaz who was enthusiastically introducing Ruth to his friends.

"Why don't you go and remove Ruth's veil?" one of those friends asked.

"I thought it was custom to keep it on," Boaz said.

"It might be custom," said the woman. "But I know at my wedding it was stifling and frustrating not to be able to meet the guests properly." She turned to Ruth. "What do you think?"

"I am new to your customs," Ruth said. "I don't want to do the wrong thing, but I would like to get to know the guests better."

"It has always seemed like a man-made custom to me," Boaz said. "We're deprived of seeing you and you are cut off from us." He took Ruth by the hand. "If you're happy to let me free you from the veil, then I'm happy to do it." He turned towards Naomi. "What do you say?"

"It's your wedding. I'd love to have Ruth participate more fully."

"Then let me help you up, my love," Boaz said. He helped Ruth up and took her behind the tree. They soon reappeared, and Ruth was all shy smiles for her guests.

She did not look at all unhappy with her new husband and Arielle knew she would not see her now for many days. And, soon Arielle and Naomi would move into their new home just below the crest of the hill, neither too close nor too far from the main house.

Yahveh, may Ruth be richly blessed in this new marriage.

It was hard at this time not to think about Orpah. What had happened to her after returning to Moab? Was she happy in her choice? Did she remember what she'd learned of Yahveh?

CHAPTER SEVENTEEN

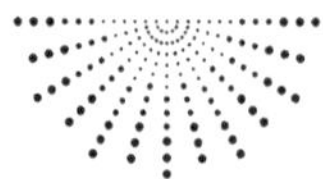

"Ima, now things have settled down after the wedding, I'd like some help." Arielle said, sitting down with a sigh of contentment on the main house verandah between Naomi and Ruth. "You and Ruth and Boaz seem to know all the stories of Yahveh, but they're just a mixed-up mess to me. I don't know what comes first and what happened more recently."

"You know more than you realize," Naomi said. "I often heard Elimelech telling you stories." She leaned forward and touched Arielle's hand. "I'm sorry I neglected to continue telling you stories after he died." She dabbed her eyes. "I couldn't do much after he left us. Looking back, I can see I really struggled to believe that Yahveh still cared after all my losses."

"But you do know he cares now, don't you?" Ruth asked.

"I do. Your faith strengthened mine, and having Boaz as a son has strengthened it further. Yahveh truly guided you to work in his fields. I am so happy you found him."

"Me too," Ruth said, flushing.

Arielle was sure Boaz would answer likewise. She often heard him whistling as he strode off to his fields in the mornings.

"I know you have heard the story of A'dam and Havah and their sons, for I have heard Ruth telling it to you," Naomi said.

"I have heard that one several times, but then I get confused after that."

"I have an idea," Ruth said. "You know that deposit of clay at the back of the hill? We will get the house steward to have some brought up so we can make a little figure to represent each story. Then we can lay them out in order and use them to prompt us for the next story."

Naomi frowned. "Let's not make figures. I would hate visitors to think we were making Canaanite figurines for worship or cursing others."

Ruth's eyes widened. "That would indeed be terrible. Maybe we should make a series of plaques and scratch the designs on them."

"That would be much less idolatrous and quite fun to do," Naomi said.

Ruth called Enoch the steward and he sent someone to the clay pit. Ruth found some boards to put on their laps and Arielle collected some sticks with which they could scratch their designs.

By the time Arielle returned, Ruth had squares of clay ready.

"Let's all do a design for creation and one for A'dam and Havah's story. We don't have to keep all three designs, just the one we like the best." Ruth took the pointed twig Arielle offered.

Arielle took a portion of clay and flattened it. Should she just draw one summary picture to represent Yahveh's creation of the world, or should she try and convey more? She thought back to the story that both Elimelech and Ruth had told her and drew something round with fuzzy edges in the middle to represent the sun. Each day of creation she then engraved around the sun, for everything relied on sunlight to live. She had the most problems with the sea creatures, because she had never seen the sea or what lived in it.

"You are quite skilful at this," Naomi said, peering at Arielle's effort.

"Do you remember this story well enough to tell us?" Ruth asked, looking at Arielle.

"I'll try as long as you help me." These stories were important. Something urged her to tell them accurately. Arielle thought back to when Elimelech had first told her this story. He'd woven a picture of chaos and darkness in her mind. "In the beginning, the earth was formless and dark. But the spirit of Yahveh hovered over the waters and he said, 'Let there be light,' and there was light. He separated the light from the darkness and said, 'That's good,' and there was evening and there was morning, the first day."

"Good memory," Ruth said, still working on her clay. "Keep going."

Arielle pulled the story up from the depths of her memory and spoke of each day of creation, ending each day with the chorus, "And Yahveh saw that it was good and there was evening and there was morning on that day."

"Good," Naomi murmured. "Good."

Arielle stumbled over day five by trying to add the creation of the animals on that day instead of day six, but Naomi corrected her and she was able to finish her story.

"Well done," Naomi said.

The praise warmed her for Naomi had always been sparing with her praise. Although since Ruth's marriage, Naomi had become more full of life each day.

"Is everyone finished?" Ruth asked.

They each looked at each other's work.

"It's amazing how different they are," Ruth said. "Each unique and special, like Yahveh's creation." She looked at Arielle. "Shall we tell the next section of the story and draw another picture?"

Arielle nodded, and Ruth told the story of the snake tempting Havah and A'dam and all that resulted from them trusting his word. As Arielle drew in the clay, she couldn't help wishing Havah had not gone her own way. Would the Moabites and all the other people have known and followed Yahveh if Havah and A'dam had made a better choice? She'd asked Ruth once. Ruth had said if Havah and A'dam hadn't rebelled against their Creator, another of the earliest people would have. It seemed to be the way people were, always prone to rebellion and making foolish decisions.

"You've told me the story about when A'dam and Havah's son murdered his brother, and I know the story of Noach," Arielle said. "I guess we'd better draw a picture to represent those stories, but I have another question. I have often wondered about where languages came from. I know the Israelites and Moabites speak the same language, although the Israelites use words I'm unfamiliar with."

"The differences are mostly to do with matters of worship," Naomi said. "When I moved to Moab, it surprised me how much of my vocabulary and theirs had to do with words like sacrifice, but they talked about divination as well."

"What do you mean?" Arielle asked.

"My neighbors went to diviners to decide names for their children, good days for marriage, and days to avoid for funerals. While I turned to Yahveh in prayer, they turned to diviners to ask their questions about life."

And the diviners would tell the people they needed to sacrifice to Chemosh.

"Arielle, do you want to draw something to represent Noach's story? And Ruth, do you remember the story about the tower of Babel? That will answer Arielle's question about languages."

"Why don't you tell that one?" Ruth said. "But let us draw Noach's story first. This one should be fun."

They busied themselves with drawing. Arielle stole glances at the others' drawings. Ruth drew competently, but Naomi kept sighing and restarting and ended up with an ark that was too small and didn't have enough room for animals.

Once they were finished, Naomi said. "I am just going to tell the story of Babel and leave the drawing to you ladies. I don't think drawing is my strength."

Naomi put down her stick and closed her eyes for a few moments. "Now in the days after Noach, the peoples of the earth still had one language. They kept migrating east until they found the vast plain of Shinar and settled there. They learned to make bricks and said, 'Let's build ourselves a city with a tower that reaches to the heavens, so that we can make a name for ourselves. This will prevent us being scattered over the face of the whole earth.'"

This wasn't the answer Arielle had been expecting. In fact, it didn't seem to have anything to do with language at all, but she dutifully drew a city with an enormous tower with its head wreathed in clouds.

"Adonai came down to see the city and the tower and he said, 'If they have done this as one people speaking the same language, then nothing they plan will be impossible for them. Let us go down and confuse their language so they will not understand each other.'"

There was the link to Arielle's original question.

"So Adonai scattered the peoples of the earth and they stopped building the city." Naomi leaned back. "And that is why the place was called Babel, for there the languages of the earth were confused."

"I don't really understand," Arielle said. "This sounds like one of Moab's myths about how the camel got its hump. What was wrong with the people building the city and tower?"

Naomi looked across at Ruth. "Do you have any thoughts?"

Ruth finished the last stroke of her drawing and laid down the twig. "Do you think the problem was that the people wanted to build to make a name for themselves? They wanted the glory for themselves rather than living their lives seeking to give Yahveh the glory?"

Naomi nodded. "That's what I've always thought. The tower was a symbol of pride in their achievement, and Yahveh didn't want them working together to set themselves up against him."

"As A'dam and Havah had done," Arielle said. "It seems to me that Yahveh cares a lot about our attitudes. He wants willing hearts that follow him. Those willing hearts then spill over into appropriate words and actions. You can speak false words and do fake actions, but he looks under the surface and demands a trusting attitude from hearts that completely follow him."

Naomi nodded and smiled.

It was so good to see her smile after knowing that she had been overcome with bitterness for too long.

There was the sound of footsteps crunching over the gravel. Boaz came into the shade from the glare of the hot sunshine. "What have we got here?"

He looked over their shoulders to the clay rectangles across the tables.

"You should judge which is best," Ruth said.

He shook his head. "How could I do that? I would be torn between choosing those of my treasured wife, the mother who chose me for you, and the sister who shared her best friend with me."

"Can you work out what we're doing?" Ruth asked.

Boaz leaned forward and peered at the damp clay. He pointed. "That one is obvious. It's Noach's ark." He peered again. "Is that group different representations of creation?"

Ruth nodded. "We're telling the stories in order so Arielle understands the whole sweep of Yahveh's interactions with his people. The pictures are to remind her and us of the stories."

"It's a great idea. We could try firing the clay so it is preserved."

"Then it would be here to help the workers remember the stories as well," Ruth said.

Boaz nodded. "I love that you are always thinking about how we can introduce Yahveh to others and remind those who already know about him, so that they remain true and don't stray."

If Arielle's drawings could help others follow Yahveh, she'd be honored. Tomorrow she'd ask for the next stories in the series.

CHAPTER EIGHTEEN

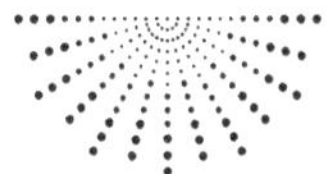

$\mathcal{A}$rielle reached up for the ripe pomegranate. With a tiny tug, the red fruit came off in her hand. She checked it over and put it in the basket for non-split fruit. This was one that could be kept for many moons in their cool cellar. Boaz had a policy of selling the split fruit immediately and releasing other fruit for sale slowly. If he could keep them and sell them in a few moons time, there would be few others available, and he could sell them for higher prices.

Arielle continued around the bush, selecting the riper fruit and leaving the ones that were not yet easy to pull off. Once a branch was fully harvested, she pruned it. The more compact the bush, the easier it was to manage, and the more fruit it produced.

Boaz had told them there was no need to be involved with the harvesting if they didn't want to, but Ruth and Arielle wanted to take part. Naomi remained at home to assist the cook so there'd be a meal ready after they'd finished for the day.

The grape harvest had finished and Boaz had turned more than half the crop into raisins. They too were stored in the cool of the cellar in pottery urns with wooden lids.

As the figs ripened around the same time, Arielle alternated between picking figs one day and pomegranates the next. The next two pomegranates were split so they went into the appropriate container to be sold immediately. The sun warmed her back and Arielle used the cloth tucked in at her waist to wipe the sweat from her cheeks and forehead.

"Is Boaz happy with the harvest?" Arielle asked Ruth, who was picking on the other side of the tree.

"Very happy," Ruth answered. "Some of the other farmers ask Boaz what magic he uses to get such plentiful harvests. He just laughs and says that if farmers would follow Yahveh's law, they would see such harvests too."

"It does seem strange that although Boaz is so generous to the poor, allowing them to harvest from the corners of the fields and a portion of all his fruit, he still ends up with more than the farmers that refuse to obey Yahveh in these matters."

"Not very strange," Ruth said. "Yahveh promised to bless those who obey. If you look around us you can see those blessings."

Arielle had often looked out from Boaz's verandah and commented that his property looked quite different from his neighbors. It was green and lush compared with others. Just last week, a new spring of water had gushed out exactly where it was most needed.

They continued down the row of trees, picking the fruit that was ready and leaving the rest for another day. Each morning, Boaz would do a tour of his trees and specify which ones were to be harvested.

"If Yahveh blesses people for obeying him, why don't more people obey?" Arielle asked.

Ruth laughed. "Good question! You'd think it would be so simple. Obey Yahveh and be blessed, or disobey and lose the blessing."

"Does that mean if we obey Yahveh fully, we'll never suffer?" Arielle placed a few more pomegranates in her baskets.

There was a long pause before Ruth answered "I don't really know, but I wonder if the promise is more to the nation as a whole. There are two mountains which face each other a little north of here, Ebal and Gerizim. When Yehoshua led the Israelites across the Jordan River and into Canaan, he took them to these two mountains. Half the tribes went up one mountain and proclaimed all the blessings that would come if the people obeyed Yahveh. The rest of the tribes went up the other mountain and proclaimed the curses for disobedience."

The name Yehoshua meant so much more to Arielle after they'd completed the history of the Israelites. Boaz had found a spot for their plaques, and Arielle often found herself going to look at them and remind herself of the history they represented.

"I asked Boaz about why Yahveh commanded the Israelites to do this," Ruth said as they both moved on to the next tree after pruning the previous one.

Some of the workers on another row yelled back and forth. Arielle picked a little more fruit and waited until it was quiet enough to talk. "What did he say?"

"He took me back a few steps to explain Yahveh's purpose in blessing his people. Let's see if I can get it right." Ruth pruned a few branches then stood still. "Yahveh wanted to bless his people to make the nations of the world envious. They would see the blessings and say, 'No other people have such a wonderful God. We want to know him too.'"

"So the Israelites were to be a sort of light in the darkness?"

"A light to the nations." Ruth nodded vigorously.

"That purpose was so important that rather than just issue a command, Yahveh had the twelve tribes act it out on the two mountains."

Arielle was quiet. The Moabites couldn't see anything different about the Israelites. "They haven't done a good job of it since Yehoshua died."

"Not only was it a strong memory for that generation but every time people see those twin mountains they are supposed to remember what happened there. Speaking of which, Boaz wanted me to suggest to you and Ima that we all go together to the Tabernacle in Shiloh. From there, we should be able to see the two mountains."

Excitement bubbled in Arielle's stomach. Although she loved living here on Boaz's farm, she would also love to travel elsewhere, especially if they were traveling in a group. Then they wouldn't need to worry about safety.

Naomi had mentioned that Shiloh was the central place for all worship in the Promised Land. If Boaz was willing to take them, then Arielle was more than willing to go.

CHAPTER NINETEEN

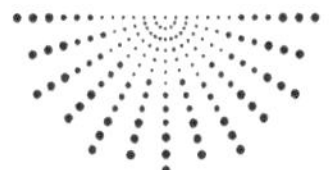

$\mathcal{A}$rielle and Naomi tended to have their first meal of the day in their own house. Tucked in the hollow near the crest of the hill, it had both views and protection. The farm manager had once lived here, but he had seemed happy to exchange houses and move to their old home. It probably gave him and his family more rest as he could leave his work behind after he finished each day.

"What do you think of Boaz's idea to travel to Shiloh at the end of the harvest?" Arielle asked Naomi.

"If I go, he'll have to travel more slowly," Naomi said.

"I asked him how far it was and he already said we'd take it slowly for you. It's four days walking each way. If you don't want to walk, he's willing to take a cart."

"I'm considering it," Naomi said. "I would love to celebrate Sukkot properly again."

"What's Sukkot?" Arielle reached for some goat's cheese.

Naomi looked across at her. "I keep forgetting you don't know very much about our festivals. They were hard to celebrate in Moab. Sukkot celebrates the end of the harvest and is only five days after Yom Kippur, the day of atonement.

"You've lost me again," Arielle said with a laugh.

"I'm sorry. Two unfamiliar names of festivals so close together is unfair of me. We stuck to stories when we did our timeline. It will be much easier to explain the law and festivals as we live them."

Shabbat had become a precious day for Arielle, a time to go slow, enjoy the beauty around them, and praise Yahveh for the blessings he'd given them. Boaz led their prayers and praise with great joy.

"There are seven festivals," Naomi said. "They are mainly in two clusters, one cluster at the beginning of the planting season and one at the harvest. You already know about Passover, on the fourteenth day of the first month. Then there are three festivals in the seventh month—the festival of Trumpets, the Day of Atonement, and Sukkot, the festival of booths."

Were the festivals clumped like that to focus on the bounty that Yahveh provided? It meant they could work hard during the peak farming and growing seasons. Then, once the harvest was collected, they could rest and rejoice.

"The feast of booths starts on the fifteenth day of the seventh month and lasts for seven days. It is to commemorate our wilderness wanderings and remind us how we lived during those times, dependent on Yahveh's provision. We live in booths made from palms or willows or any leafy trees, and we celebrate everything Yahveh has provided."

"It sounds like fun unless it rains," Arielle said.

Naomi stroked her chin. "I used to go most years with Elimelech and I don't ever recall it raining."

"Can we go then?" Arielle asked.

Naomi nodded. "It will be good for you to learn more of our beliefs."

Our beliefs. Arielle liked the sound of that. Looking back, Arielle had really decided to follow Yahveh because Ruth did. She hadn't wanted to be left out and she could see how much Yahveh meant to Ruth. Her initial prayers had been quite skeptical not just about whether Yahveh had the power but whether he'd answer the prayers of a young Moabite woman. Ruth had encouraged her to make specific requests. They weren't always answered with a "yes" but when the answer wasn't what Arielle had wanted she was beginning to trust that Yahveh knew best.

* * *

*A*rielle paused as they came close to Shiloh.

"Isn't it beautiful, Ima?" Arielle swept her arm back towards the way they'd come. The pace of their four days of walking had left them plenty of time to enjoy the scenery. The vineyards were just turning red and orange, and warm days were followed by cooler nights with just the tiniest bite in the air. The whole way they'd stayed with Boaz's friends. Families who were also faithful to Yahveh and who'd been at the wedding. There'd been much prayer and encouragement. Though through it all, a question had been growing in Arielle's heart. "What about the Moabites?"

If Yahveh truly was the only God and all other gods were false because they prevented people coming to know Yahveh, then her people were in danger. It wasn't a question she wanted to dwell on, for it was unsettling. She had had many opportunities to hear about and get to know Yahveh, but she wouldn't have had those opportunities if she'd remained in her birth family, whoever they were.

"It has been a wonderful journey," Naomi said. "I'm glad I came."

"We're nearly there," Boaz said. "You can just see the Tabernacle on that raised area ahead."

It would have been impossible to miss, as it was the biggest structure on the hillock. At this distance, they could see the squat structure of the Tabernacle behind the barriers.

129

"It looks somewhat strange," Arielle said. "I thought you said it had blue and red and gold curtains."

"In the wilderness, it was a tent that could be easily moved. Now that it doesn't need to be moved, there have been changes to the base. It is still a tent on top, but you're only seeing the outer layer of goat hair coverings. The beautiful colors are all hidden underneath."

Only Boaz would go to the Tabernacle, but all of them would live in their booth and spend time reflecting on the blessings they'd received from Yahveh's hand over the last moons of their being in Bethlehem.

"Who is that man over there?" Arielle asked, using her chin to point towards a rugged-looking man surrounded by other people.

"That's Ehud's son," Boaz said.

Ehud was a name Arielle had heard whispered in Moab, but she had never succeeded in getting anyone to tell her about him.

"His father judged our people for years," Boaz said. "I'll tell you more once we have set up our shelter."

Boaz led them through the crowds. Trees around the area were being stripped of their branches and young boys were standing next to piles of branches they were willing to sell. Smart. They must have come early, knowing many people would prefer to buy the branches needed to make their shelters rather than find their own.

"I always go to a friend's home and build my shelter in his court-yard. That way I can store the main posts at his place and use his trees to harvest the branches which we put over the top." Boaz laughed, a sound reminiscent of a much younger man. He had told them he loved coming to Shiloh at the end of the harvest and considered this a week of real rest.

Boaz looked around and then set off. "This way. My friend lives on the far side of the Tabernacle, away from the crowds."

They continued to push their way past donkeys and shelters. A child dashed across their path and Boaz reached down and scooped him up. "Not so fast, little man. Where's your Ima?"

"He belongs with us," a frazzled looking woman said. "I get distracted for a moment and he escapes." She reached out her hands and took her son back.

They continued on their way until Boaz stopped. "There it is."

Arielle gasped. Up close, the Tabernacle looked enormous. Arielle would have loved to have seen more, but she and Naomi and Ruth would stay outside. Only the men were permitted to go inside the enclosure and only the priests could enter the inner structure. She would have to be content with the descriptions of the Tabernacle that Boaz had given them from the descriptions in the law given to Mosheh. Under the dark goat skins would be cloths woven in red and blue. And gold covered altars and tables. Arielle's skin prickled with goose bumps.

If she had been born a man of the priestly family, she might have had the privilege of seeing the curtain that separated the Holy of Holies from sinful people. She could have glimpsed the place where the golden ark dwelt, holding the stone tablets of the law carved by the finger of Yahveh himself. A law she was increasingly seeing as good and loving in its protection of the weak and lowly. If only the Israelites would actually follow the law, then these lands would be a glorious place. A place where Yahveh reigned and the people he ruled lived in the benefits bestowed.

Boaz had said most Israelites either didn't come to the three great festivals or came more for the fun of a journey than an earnest desire to worship Yahveh.

"If we descend the hill here," Boaz said. "We'll soon be at my friend's place. They are also faithful believers."

CHAPTER TWENTY

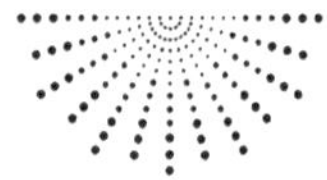

rielle held out her hands to the warmth of the fire Boaz had built in front of their shelter. They'd already eaten their meal when Boaz said, "I promised you a story. Are you ready?"

"I am," Arielle said quickly, in case Naomi tried to say this wasn't a suitable story for her ears.

"You do know that Ehud defeated King Eglon of Moab?" Ruth asked.

Arielle nodded. She knew that much. Ruth obviously expected her to identify with Moab and be upset at their defeat. Did Arielle still think of herself as a Moabite? She wasn't sure of anything beyond knowing the two women in front of her were her family. Being near them was the closest she had to a feeling of belonging.

Arielle settled herself into a more comfortable posture.

Boaz cleared his throat. "The history between the Israelites and Moabites has always been tense. Moab was a descendant of Avraham's nephew, Lot, and there seems to have been no connection between the families for close to four hundred years, until the Israelites approached the borders of Moab after they had left Egypt and before they entered these lands. Do you want me to tell the tale of Balak and Balaam, or only of Ehud?"

"Maybe the quick version of Balak and Balaam, then Ehud in more detail," Arielle said.

She closed her eyes and pictured the clay plaques along Boaz and Ruth's outer wall. If Balak was prior to the Israelites entering Canaan, then Mosheh would still have been the leader of his often-grumbling and complaining people.

"Balak, son of Zippor, the king of Moab was terrified of the hordes of Israelites. He hired a diviner called Balaam from over near the great Euphrates to come and put a curse on the Israelites."

Arielle raised an eyebrow. "I doubt that worked."

Boaz chuckled. "You're right. Every time Balaam was commanded to curse the Israelites, he ended up blessing them instead."

Arielle grinned. "How frustrating for Balak."

"It was. Sadly, the Israelites ended up cursing themselves because they committed adultery with Moabite and Midianite women and were led astray to worship their gods. Yahveh sent a plague on them as a judgment, and twenty-four thousand Israelites died. My abba could barely speak of it without getting angry about our people's lack of faithfulness."

It was strange to think that Boaz's father must have known Mosheh and Yehoshua, men who were now sleeping in the dust yet still living on in the stories of their deeds and the memories of their descendants. One day, Arielle too would only be a memory. But who would remember her? She was no one special. She would not be chosen by Yahveh to do great and mighty deeds like Avraham, Mosheh, or Yehoshua.

A log settled in the fire, sending a shower of sparks towards the star-spangled expanse of black sky above them. Boaz stood to add another log, pushing it into the coals.

"Eglon, king of Moab, formed an alliance with the Ammonites

and the Amalekites. They attacked the south-eastern areas of Israel and took possession of the area of Jericho, the City of Palms." Boaz settled back onto his mat.

Naomi leaned forward. "Perhaps we should say this is all part of a cycle that has been happening since the death of Yehoshua. Once his good influence was gone, our people quickly forgot Yahveh and were lured to worship the Baals. Yahveh would send the judgments he had predicted from Mount Ebal—"

Ruth leaned forward. "I've told Arielle about the blessings and curses recited from the two mountains."

Naomi waited until Arielle looked towards her again. "It saddened me to watch those in Bethlehem drift away. They soon became superstitious, feeling the need to placate the gods and spirits just in case. Yahveh first judged us with lack of rain and poor harvests."

"You'd think that people would ask why this was happening, and remember the blessings and curses they'd recited.'" Arielle had sometimes forgotten things when she'd been a child. The Israelites were adults. Adults were supposed to remember the important things.

"Surely that was why Yahveh made them climb the two mountains," Ruth said. "To help them remember."

"It should have been easy to work out what was wrong. We simply had to ask, 'Have we drifted away from Yahveh?'" Naomi shook her head. "But I am a fine one to talk. When Yahveh saw fit to take my menfolk, I grew sullen and refused to talk with him."

"Isn't that normal?" Arielle asked.

"Normal, yes, but it is also foolish and wrong. Yahveh has been my rock all my life. But when things didn't turn out how I wanted them to, instead of trusting him, I doubted him. I doubted that he really cared for me." Naomi clicked her tongue. "I added resentment and bitterness on top of my grief and insisted on walking my own way, without Yahveh's help. I made things much more difficult for myself."

And for the rest of them. They'd been three women grieving the same men but with their faces turned away from each other instead of reaching out in comfort and support.

"If the Israelites didn't respond to Yahveh's lesser judgments, he had said he'd allow other peoples to oppress us. That is exactly what King Eglon did," Boaz said. "Yahveh allowed him to oppress the south-eastern area of our lands for eighteen years, but we eventually cried out to Yahveh for a deliverer. He sent Ehud, son of Gera, from the tribe of Benjamin to rescue us."

Arielle hugged her knees with her arms.

"Ehud went to Eglon, king of Moab, to deliver our regular tribute. Ehud made a double-edged sword almost the length of his thighbone. He strapped it on his right thigh under his clothing." Boaz looked up at Arielle. "If he strapped it to his right thigh, what does that tell us about Ehud?"

Arielle mimed drawing the sword with both her hands. "He must have been left-handed as drawing it with the right would be too awkward."

"Well done! You have guessed Ehud's secret!" Boaz leaned in and added more fuel to the fire. "The Benjaminites have many left-handed warriors. It gives them an advantage, as people do not expect an attack to come from their left hand."

"Don't stop there," Arielle said.

"Ehud and the other men presented the tribute, then went back the way they'd come—"

"Oh," Arielle said, disappointed. "I thought Ehud was going to be the deliverer."

"Have patience, young lady. At the stone images at Gilgal, Ehud went back to King Eglon on his own and told him he had a secret message for the king. The king ordered all his attendants to leave the room."

Arielle unclasped her hands and quirked an eyebrow. "And?"

"Ehud said he had a message for the king from Yahveh. The king was so interested that he heaved his bulk—he was a very fat man—out of the seat. Ehud reached with his left hand, drew his sword, and stabbed him."

Mahlon and Kilion had talked about this tale. She'd heard them say the blade went in so far that King Eglon's rolls of fat hid it. When the boys had seen her, they'd shushed each other and refused to respond to her begging to hear more.

"Once the king was dead, Ehud locked the doors of the upper room behind him and left via the porch. King Eglon's servants saw the closed doors and were reluctant to try and enter the upper room in case the king was doing his private business. After a long wait, they unlocked the doors and discovered him dead inside."

"Clever Ehud," Arielle said. "He gave himself plenty of time to get away."

"Once he got back to the hill country of Ephraim, Ehud called out the Israelites to follow him and attack Moab."

"Ten thousand of our men were struck down," Ruth said, voice low. "Ten thousand who never had a chance to follow Yahveh."

Arielle hugged her knees, rocking back and forth. The tale had sucked her in. Until Ruth's comment, she'd forgotten they were talking about real people. Real Moabites who had lived and breathed and worked in the fields and marketplaces of Moab.

The flames in front of her flickered and hissed around a drop of sap. Orpah had been given a chance to know Yahveh because of her marriage to Kilion, but had she chosen to follow him? And she was just one woman. There were countless other Moabites who spent their days worshiping Chemosh, who never had Orpah's opportunities to hear that there was another God. A God who loved them and cared for them and who did not demand their children in sacrifice with no guarantee of any blessing in return.

Yahveh, it's not fair. How will the Moabites hear of you? How will they escape the darkness from which I was delivered?

CHAPTER TWENTY-ONE

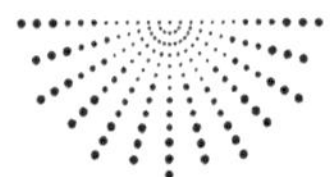

week later, as Arielle walked south towards Bethlehem, the questions still lingered in her mind. Ruth had family in Moab. Did she worry that they were still enmeshed in worship of gods other than Yahveh? Was it possible that Arielle had family in Moab? Did she have a mother and father? Brothers and sisters? Did they worship Chemosh? Arielle shivered. And what about Orpah? Had she remembered what she'd learned of Yahveh in Naomi's household? Or had it all been forgotten once she returned to Moab? She was probably married again, as she had the clear skin and upright posture much admired by Moabites.

A stone was kicked up by Arielle's sandal and skittered off the path. She turned towards Ruth, who was walking alongside her.

"Ruth, both you and Orpah heard the same stories and had the same opportunities to learn of Yahveh, but you made opposite choices," Arielle said.

"Uh-huh," Ruth said. "I've never forgotten Orpah's face as she looked back at us. She was torn by her decision. Did she ever regret it?"

Naomi dropped back to join the conversation. "I regret encouraging Orpah to return, but I wasn't thinking of the loss of her opportunity to learn about Yahveh. I was focused on making sure she didn't suffer mistreatment in Bethlehem and making sure she had another chance to marry."

Boaz turned and looked at them. "Yet Ruth trusted in Yahveh and chose to join you." He grinned. "You'll have to ask her if she has any regrets."

The beauteous smile Ruth bestowed on her husband answered any doubts. Not that Arielle doubted, for she had witnessed Ruth blossom within his care and heard Ruth thank Yahveh every day in her prayers for the miracle he had worked on her behalf.

"What made you choose to come with Naomi?" Arielle asked. "You were close to your family. It must have been hard to leave."

Ruth nodded. "It was very hard, especially when my mother pleaded with me to stay with tears running down her face."

Arielle's throat tightened. She'd longed all her life for a mother who cared like that. Ruth's mother hadn't put her on a doorstep and walked away. Yet Ruth had chosen to walk away from her mother. Why?

"In the end, I wanted to stay with Naomi and have a chance to know more of Yahveh. I was willing to pay any price to know him. If I'd stayed in Moab, I'd be totally isolated, trying to follow Yahveh on my own and without anyone to teach me." She gestured at the fields around them and the nearest village. "Here, even if most of the people are not faithful to Yahveh, there are still plenty of people who are and I can easily find more." Ruth sighed. "I pray a lot for my family back in Moab, and for Orpah and her family. Back before I married Boaz, I had thought about whether I should go back and tell them what I have learned."

Naomi drew in a sharp breath. "That would be terribly dangerous."

"Ima, do you think danger really matters if people receive the blessing of following Yahveh? If my family had the joy and peace I have, I would be willing to die in the attempt," Ruth said.

Boaz turned and came and took her in his arms. "My beloved. You are the woman I searched my whole life for. Someone who sees Yahveh as more precious than any king's treasures. If you must return to speak with your family, we can go together."

Ruth blushed, placing a palm to her stomach "I might not be able to travel again for a while."

Boaz's eyes widened. "Are you saying you're expecting a child?"

Arielle's heart leapt for joy and then fluttered with worry. Would Ruth allow Arielle to come alongside her each day to help raise her child, or would Arielle slowly be pushed aside? It might not be deliberate, but children would demand more of Ruth's time.

Ruth nodded several times. "I'm fairly certain."

"You shouldn't have come with us on such a long walk," Boaz said.

"It's done me good. Anyway, I wanted to see the Tabernacle. But I'm willing to stay at home now." Ruth turned to Naomi. "Ima, you guessed, didn't you?"

"I was hoping," Naomi said. "But I was hesitant to say anything."

Boaz was not young, and Mahlon had not given Ruth a child in the years they'd been married. Naomi had probably worried that Ruth was barren.

"Let's not be afraid," Boaz said. "Let's pray. Come and stand in the shade."

Arielle couldn't suppress a grin. Already the man looked taller, as though joy and pride had made him stand up straighter.

They gathered in a circle, with Boaz holding Ruth and Naomi's hands on one side, and Arielle between Ruth and Naomi on the other. *Please don't let children break up our intimate circle.*

"Great Yahveh. You truly are the God of miracles. Who would have thought an old man like me might one day be a father. Please protect our precious little one and bring Ruth through to a safe delivery. May our child be one of the faithful ones. We will do everything we can to teach him or her to follow you and bring you honor. May our child be a blessing to many."

"Amen." Naomi didn't bother wiping the tears off her cheeks. "Amen."

"I am very grateful that we were taking the journey slowly." Boaz brushed Ruth's cheek. "We'll stay with another friend tonight, and definitely no carrying heavy things for you. I'll carry that extra water bag."

He slung the extra load over his shoulder and strode forward, whistling.

* * *

Arielle stood in safety in the middle of an island in the middle of a lake. All the shores of the lake were aflame, as far as she could see. A woman Arielle somehow knew was from Moab stood on the shore and called, "Come and save us. Come and save us."

Arielle didn't want to go. She wanted to stay on her nice, safe island and enjoy its bounty. Everything and everyone she loved was here.

"Come and save us," the woman called again. A hot wind whipped the woman's veil and allowed Arielle to see a scar across the woman's cheek. The woman wasn't someone Arielle knew. Just a strange Moabite woman in danger.

"Chemosh, Chemosh," the woman said, bowing down. "Rescue us."

"No!" Arielle tried to yell but nothing came out of her mouth. "Chemosh won't save you," she yelled, but again her voice wouldn't work. Why didn't the woman walk into the water of the lake? It was as though she couldn't see the water that could save her from the fire. With one more cry, the woman spun on her heel and plunged into the fire.

"No!" Arielle screamed after her.

"Arielle! Arielle!"

Someone was shaking her.

"Wake up."

Arielle forced herself to open her eyes and blinked in the pale dawn light. Naomi's concerned face loomed above her.

"You must have been having a nightmare," Naomi said. "You yelled 'No' a few times and woke me up. By the time I reached you, you were whimpering."

Arielle touched her cheeks. They were wet.

"Are you alright?" Naomi asked.

Was she? Arielle wasn't sure. The dream hadn't been like any nightmare she'd experienced before. This one had been so real, it was like being awake rather than a dream. The woman's empty, pleading eyes, and her calls for help, were still present in her thoughts.

"I'll be alright," Arielle mumbled. But she wasn't sure of that at all. Had that been a nightmare or something else entirely?

CHAPTER TWENTY-TWO

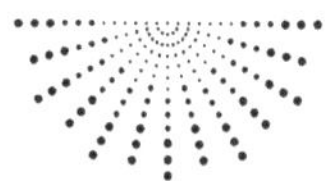

The dream hadn't returned, but Arielle couldn't escape the woman's cry for help. Her pleas intruded even when Arielle was doing something as mundane as watering the tiny cucumber plants. She'd built a tiny earthen wall around each plant, and she used a scoop to put water on each plant. The earthen wall ensured the water stayed near the roots.

"They're looking healthy," Ruth said.

Boaz had refused to allow Ruth to do any of the gardening, but she loved to come out and see the plants and their progress.

"I'm glad Boaz suggested we grow the extra vegetable crops," Naomi said. "None of us are used to doing nothing but light housework."

Arielle had enjoyed the slow times after Ruth's marriage, but it hadn't taken long for her to want something to do. They'd asked Boaz to let them grow cucumbers, onions, garlic, and melons. In the late afternoons, she and Ruth were making the strings for the vines to climb up towards the upper bars of the frame.

"I'm glad Boaz has realized I'm not breakable. I need to be out in the fresh air," Ruth said.

He had been overprotective when he first heard Ruth's news.

"The poor man never expected to be a father," Naomi said. "And now he has to face the fears that every parent feels. Once you're a parent, it is hard work to trust Yahveh and not worry about all the possible dangers. In the end, life and death are in Yahveh's hands."

Had Naomi lost children before Mahlon and Kilion? It was normal for women to lose several children, either before birth or within the first few years of their lives. There were so many diseases that could snatch their little lives away.

"Come inside once you're finished." Naomi headed back to her usual seat on the verandah.

Once she was gone, Arielle emptied the last of the water in her bucket.

"Come on," Ruth said. "I've got someone I want to introduce you to."

Arielle raised an eyebrow. She hadn't noticed anyone but Boaz arrive.

"Boaz found a Moabite girl for sale in the marketplace. He insisted on buying her from the traveling merchant and bringing her here."

Yet another reminder that Boaz was a good man. Who knew what fate he had saved the girl from?

"Where is she now?" Arielle asked.

"Having a thorough wash," Ruth said. "And being fitted with new clothes."

The girl was blessed, although she probably didn't know it yet.

Arielle poured the last of the water onto the final cucumber seedling. "I'll go and find her."

"We can go together," Ruth said, getting up awkwardly off the stone wall she'd been sitting on. Naomi thought the baby would arrive before the hottest months, something which pleased both Ruth and Arielle.

* * *

The girl was sitting in the outside kitchen, wolfing down dried figs as though she hadn't eaten for a month. Maybe she hadn't. Even through the clean tunic, it was obvious she was painfully thin. She scrambled to her feet, bowing, and avoiding eye contact.

"There's no need to bow," Ruth said.

"The master said I must bow." The girl's voice cracked.

"Boaz is master now," the cook said. "And he won't let anyone bow to him. He says we must only bow to Yahveh."

"Who's Yahveh?" The girl's eyes were wide, as though she expected another mighty master to come into the room and demand her allegiance.

"Yahveh is the wonderful Creator of all, and he loves people like you and me," Ruth said gently.

"B-but I'm not like you," the girl said, eyes still downcast.

Ruth smiled. "Arielle and I are from Moab too."

The girl looked up properly for the first time. Almost immediately, her shoulders rose and her head dropped as low as possible as though she was trying to disappear. Would Arielle have ended up cringing like this girl if she'd been sold to the temple as a baby or after she'd been captured?

Ruth continued speaking as though the girl wasn't different from any other person who stayed with them. "I came here as a widow with nothing, but Yahveh has given me everything."

The girl said nothing. Whatever experiences she'd had, silence had probably been demanded of her.

"My name is Ruth," Ruth said. "What's yours?"

The girl blinked as if the question was difficult.

"Your name?" Ruth gently asked again.

"No name," said the girl, her face tight. "They called me child. Or

'Hey you' if they wanted something and cursed me if I was too slow."

And they had hit her, if the partially healed bruises on her face were any indication.

Ruth closed her eyes as though praying, although she might have been merely thinking. "Would you like a name?"

The girl touched her chest, as if doubting Ruth's offer was directed at her.

"What about Zipporah?" said Ruth. "That's a worthy name. She was the wife of our greatest leader."

The girl flushed and swallowed. "Zipporah," she said reflectively, as though she'd been given a treasure.

Thanks to Naomi, Ruth, and Boaz's tutelage, Arielle had known immediately who Zipporah was, but it was obvious this girl knew nothing. Although, if you could ignore her painful skinniness, she probably wasn't much younger than Arielle.

Heavy steps came around the corner of the house. The girl darted behind the cook.

"How are you settling in?" Boaz asked. "Good to see my wife and sister-in-law are looking after you."

Zipporah didn't say a word.

"Boaz, dear," Ruth said. "I think I left my shawl in our room. Could you please bring it to me?"

The moment he left, Ruth spoke to Arielle in an undertone. "Perhaps you could take Zipporah out to see your garden. I'll go and help Boaz understand why he needs to leave her with us."

Arielle nodded. Most men weren't like Boaz, and it was obvious Zipporah's view of men was severely warped by her experiences … experiences that could so easily have been Arielle's own if she had not been adopted by Naomi and Elimelech.

CHAPTER TWENTY-THREE

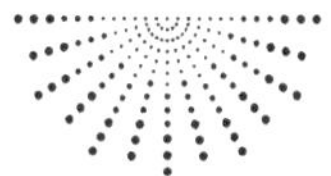

*A*rielle checked that the carpet on the verandah wasn't dusty. It wasn't. Zipporah worked hard to keep the verandah area tidy. Was it out of fear or because she took pride in a job well done?

Naomi came out first and settled herself on the cushions that Arielle had laid ready. Ruth joined them, looking tired and pale.

"Are you unwell?" Naomi asked.

Ruth cracked a smile. "The baby did not want to sleep." She rubbed her belly. "Turning somersaults all night."

"Not too much longer," Naomi said.

"I really hope not," Ruth said.

The whole household was excited. Most of the servants here had been here for most of Boaz's life. They all felt he belonged to them and once they saw how much joy she brought their master, they'd welcomed Ruth.

Zipporah came and placed some dried figs and nuts in front of them, then left as silently as she'd come. Arielle found her silence irritating, but Naomi had urged her to be patient. "Silence is Zipporah's protection. She hasn't learned to trust us yet."

Maybe she never would. They were all praying for her. Zipporah meant bird, but she acted like a bird in a cage who didn't know the door was open and she could have flown free. *Yahveh, free her.*

"Are you going to lay out the clay pictures?" Ruth asked.

"It does make it easier," Arielle said. "But I don't want to bore you by practicing the stories you're already familiar with."

"Daughter, it never hurts us to repeat the history again." Naomi leaned back on the closest cushion.

"And I notice different things each time," Ruth said. "It depends on what I'm going through, as different circumstances make me see things from a different perspective."

Arielle got up to fetch the pictures as Ruth had asked.

"Make sure you bring the ones you made," Ruth said. "They're by far the best."

Since they'd first made the plaques, Arielle had made some new ones as better ideas came to her. She picked up the first pair, brought them over to the carpet, and laid them so Ruth and Naomi could see them. Then she went and brought back another pair. Today she'd tell all the stories up to Avraham. Tomorrow, she'd practice all the Avraham stories.

"Boaz has suggested that we make a special shelf for the plaques," Ruth said. "What do you think?"

Arielle seated herself. "Wouldn't putting them on a shelf make it more likely they'd fall and break?"

"He'll work out some way to make them secure," Ruth said with the confidence of someone who lived with a problem-solver.

Boaz had mentioned that the plaques had become real talking points, and several other farmers had asked about them. Boaz always asked his visitors if they wanted to listen to a story and let them choose which one they wanted to hear.

Arielle left the first plaque on the carpet, the one about the creation of the world and A'dam and Havah. She had tried to tell a story holding the plaque but it hindered her, for she looked at the pictures instead of telling the story. She also liked to gesture as she told a story and she couldn't do that while holding a breakable object.

"In the beginning," Arielle said in the time-honored way of starting this story. She knew this story well enough that she wasn't straining to remember each section. Instead, she concentrated on her gestures and using her voice. Whenever Yahveh spoke, she slowed her voice down and made every word a clear command. "Let there be light." Then she would leave a good pause before she spoke the next line. After every day of creation she let her voice drop and pause after the final line of each day. Those lines became like a drumbeat. "And it was good, and it was good, and it was very good."

Arielle finished with, "By the seventh day, the Lord God had finished all the work he had been doing. So he rested from all his labors. He blessed the seventh day and made it holy."

There was silence, then Naomi clapped, "That was wonderful. Your storytelling has improved so much."

Arielle's face warmed. She had worked hard to polish the stories. It felt good to shine at something. "I practice while I water the plants."

Naomi reached for an almond. "Well, your practice is paying off."

"Don't expect the other stories to be as good," Arielle said.

Ruth rubbed her belly. "Don't stop now. I need to be distracted from the little one's energetic kicks."

Arielle pushed the first of her plaques aside and drew the second one closer. The picture of the tree and snake and A'dam and Havah were easy to recognize. She told the beginning of the story.

"I think you need to slow that line, because it is something you really want us to notice," Naomi said. "Say it more like this. 'You won't die,' the snake said. 'For the Lord knows that when you eat it your eyes will be opened and—'" Naomi slowly drew out the next words. "'And. You. Will. Be. Like. Yahveh, knowing the difference between good and evil.' See, very slow on the phrase you want the listeners to pay attention to."

"Let me try again," Arielle said, repeating the whole story with the slow middle section.

Naomi nodded. "Exactly. It will help people when they want to tell the stories to others."

"It must be wonderful to be a priest and be able to read the actual words of Yahveh that Mosheh wrote," Ruth said.

A single section of a scroll would be worth a fortune.

Arielle continued through the stories, adding Cain and Abel, and Noach and the worldwide flood. She got some details of the flood wrong, but Naomi corrected her. The Tower of Babel wasn't too difficult but her voice was tired by the end. She stood to return the pictures to their safe place against the wall.

"Aren't you going to ask us anything?" Naomi asked.

"I don't know what to ask," Arielle said. She'd been so busy learning the actual stories and making sure they were accurate and told well that she hadn't considered asking questions or anything else.

"Hopefully your listeners will want to ask questions," Naomi said. "It helps them learn and apply the stories to their own lives."

"You could ask us what our favorite story is or which part is our favorite," Ruth said.

Arielle grinned. "And what would be your answer?"

"Let me think." Ruth nibbled her lip. "That Yahveh always goes seeking people even when they'd rebelled against him."

"And where do you see that?" Naomi asked, making a point of showing Arielle how to keep the discussion going.

"In the garden of Eden," Ruth said. "Rather than rejecting or destroying A'dam and Havah, Yahveh went to find them and called them to himself."

"He did the same for Cain," Arielle said. "Giving him an opportunity to tell the truth which sadly he avoided doing."

"Do you think things would have ended differently if A'dam and Havah and Cain had all admitted what they'd done, or even better, had gone to Yahveh as soon as they'd made wrong choices?" Arielle asked.

Naomi leaned back on her cushion. "It's interesting to think about that. Would the consequences have been less if they'd immediately admitted their fault instead of trying to cover it up? Maybe. I certainly was much happier when Mahlon and Kilion did that." She chuckled. "Not that they admitted being at fault very often. They were too busy blaming each other."

"Or me," Arielle said.

"It usually had nothing to do with you," Naomi said.

Arielle had been an outsider to the boys' close relationship. They were more like twins than brothers.

"I sometimes find the stories a little depressing. People turn away from Yahveh so quickly," Arielle said.

"I guess you've only known Yahveh for such a short time," Naomi said.

"And you've had us to encourage you," Ruth said. "It is much harder to follow Yahveh if you're the only one among all your family and friends who follows him. When Orpah went back to Ar, it meant that even if she had some trust in Yahveh, she was going to find it hard. She'd be like a single ember which falls out of the fire. It soon goes cold."

"Do you think there are any followers of Yahveh in Moab?" Arielle asked.

"We only knew of two," Naomi said. "But who knows if they still follow him or if the fire has slowly died."

"How do you prevent the fire from dying?" Arielle asked.

"Yahveh delights in helping us but he also uses other people and ways. He gave you the idea of the drawing," Naomi said. "Even Boaz mentioned how much the drawings are helping him. Every time he sees them leaning against the wall, he remembers the story."

"All this repetition helps too," Ruth said. "And it helps us when we teach another person the stories and—better still—train them to tell others."

Arielle was praying that Zipporah might be willing to listen to stories, but so far Zipporah had remained mostly silent. How did you get someone who'd been hurt to open up? To trust?

"But it isn't just being around encouraging people and going over and over the stories," Naomi said. "It's also making sure nothing becomes a barrier between you and Yahveh."

Arielle raised an eyebrow.

"I see your eyebrow," Naomi said with a chuckle. "You've been asking questions with your eyebrow since you were a child."

Arielle used to drive Naomi crazy with the number of questions she'd wanted answers to. Maybe that was why she'd been closer to Elimelech. He'd never minded her questions. Instead, he'd patiently answered them as best he could.

"I let the loss of Elimelech and the boys become a barrier." Naomi shook her head. "Stupid really, because that was when I most needed Yahveh's help. I needed his help to cope with the losses and his help to know what to do. I struggled on, trying to do things myself. All it gave me was worry lines on my face and an ache in my belly."

The Naomi of today was certainly different than the Naomi who had left Moab.

"How do we prevent that barrier from forming?" Arielle asked.

"It's a daily decision to choose to trust Him no matter what happens. Eventually you will see that Yahveh was worthy of that trust," Naomi said. "We tend to let our feelings rule. We feel Yahveh is not trustworthy because he is not arranging things as we think he ought to, so we declare him untrustworthy."

Ruth nodded. "And when we decide he isn't trustworthy, we stop trusting him and make the whole situation worse."

"So should we instead assume Yahveh is trustworthy and wait to see what he does?" Arielle asked.

"Yes and no. First we should look back," Naomi cast her eyes across the plaques. "Look back and see Yahveh's long history of being trustworthy, caring for his people, and fulfilling his promises. We must choose to trust. Our feelings will eventually catch up. You've heard me singing in the mornings. Having allowed bitterness to grow between myself and Yahveh, I'm determined not to endure that misery again." Naomi smiled. "I'm going to choose to praise him every day."

It was a good example for Arielle to follow. She certainly had no desire to ever live as Naomi had lived in those dark months after the death of all their menfolk. If singing could help Arielle trust God, then she would sing. If telling Yahveh's stories would keep her and her others trusting, then she would keep practicing.

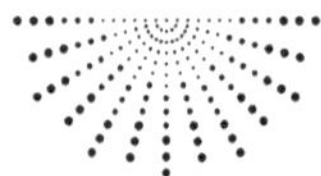

"Fire!"

Arielle jerked upright and whirled around. The goats leapt back with startled bleats as their feed spilled on the ground rather than in the trough.

Behind the main house, a plume of smoke was dark against the blue sky. The kitchen. It had to be the kitchen. Kitchens were separate from houses for this exact reason, but if the wind was in the wrong direction, then the main house could burn too.

"Come on," Zipporah said, face pale. "Close the gate and hurry."

Arielle left the goats and fastened the gate with trembling hands, leaving the feed container where it was. Picking up the skirt of her tunic, she joined Zipporah in a mad run across the fields and up the hill to the house.

They rounded the corner of the house.

Whatever had caught alight had now spread. The smell of burning oil filled Arielle's nostrils and she glanced left and right, trying to sort out what was happening and where they could help.

"There's the master." Zipporah gestured toward the kitchen.

Boaz directed a line of men who were swinging axes at the

supporting posts of the kitchen. Perhaps they hoped to smother the fire and make it easier to beat out the fire on the roof, stopping sparks from leaping the gap to the main house.

Was there even a task for them amongst so many men and so much frantic action?

"Let's get wet sacks," Zipporah said. "They're all so busy that they're not paying attention to where the sparks are going." She pointed to the edge of the verandah and the plants around the edge. How long until something else caught fire?

Zipporah dashed towards the water tank where the cook was submerging sacks in water and handing them out to a line of workers. Arielle joined her. Those waiting in line were already covered in soot and pungent with sweat and the acrid smell of smoke.

It didn't take long before they were each handed a sack. Once she held the heavy, wet sack Arielle followed Zipporah towards the verandah of the main house. Already several sparks were smoldering.

Zipporah made an awkward attempt to throw her sack to smother the sparks but it was obvious it was too heavy.

"Let's work together," Arielle said. "We can hold one corner each."

Their first slap at the sparks was still awkward but by the third attempt they had worked out how to successfully hit and smother the sparks that had taken hold.

Once they'd smothered all they could see, Arielle said, "I'll go and get the sacks wet again. You keep an eye on where the sparks are landing."

Zipporah nodded, her eyes already fixed on the incoming sparks. Arielle gathered their sacks in her arms and got back in line. Over by the kitchen, the men had almost cut through the supporting posts.

Arielle was handed two new sacks and immediately dropped

them. Their weight was nearly too much for her. One of the young men saw her struggle and came over. "Let me help."

They'd just reached the main house when there was a shout and a tremendous crash. The roof above the cooking area had fallen at last.

"Help," Zipporah's voice cried. "We need water here now."

Arielle turned from staring at the destroyed cooking area. The falling roof had sent a cloud of sparks into the air and the breeze wafted them towards the main house.

"Quick, sacks and water to the main house," Boaz shouted.

The young man and Arielle plied the sacks they'd brought, and Zipporah dropped hers over an ember lying among some plants.

Arielle turned to return to the water tank but Boaz was at her side.

"Can you go to your home and check that Ruth is alright? I sent her down there the moment we smelled the first smoke. Please let her know that things are under control. I don't want her getting anxious."

He didn't need to say anything more. Ruth was already big with child and they were all trying to make sure she didn't lift anything or worry.

Arielle handed her sack to someone else.

Boaz indicated the line of people passing water containers to each other. "And bring back any other containers that will hold water."

Zipporah didn't even notice Arielle leave. She was fully involved stamping on sparks or hitting them with the wet sack she'd been given. Arielle was surprised to see her so involved, as though she actually cared what happened to the house.

Arielle ran towards the house, slowing as she approached. Naomi would be upset if she scared Ruth. Naomi was praying hard for the safety of mother and child, unable to let herself believe that a child might come after so much grief.

Naomi met her at the door. "Is everything alright?"

"They had to knock down the cooking area. Now they're making sure the main house is wet enough to protect it," Arielle said.

"So it's not safe yet," Naomi said. "I'll make sure Ruth stays here."

"Boaz has asked me to bring any containers. I can only think of two that I could carry."

Naomi frowned. "Yes, that's right. Please be careful, I don't want anyone getting burned. Burns are difficult to treat."

Arielle fetched the containers and carried them up to the water tank, then took her place towards the end of the line.

Yahveh, keep us safe. Protect Boaz and Ruth's house.

The man next to Arielle in line handed her a full container of water. She turned and passed it on to the next person, then turned back and received a new container in its place. Zipporah ran past with two empty containers to return for filling.

Off to the side, three women were still keeping a sharp lookout on the kitchen, wet sacks in hand, making sure the smoldering embers didn't burst into flame.

Arielle kept passing water containers. Her arms and back ached, but still she handed on the containers to the next in line.

"Enough!" Boaz shouted. "That should be more than enough."

Arielle leaned over, her hands on her knees. She'd be aching tomorrow.

All around her, people were moving to sit along a stone wall. Arielle followed them. The stench of sodden, burned wood filled the air. What a mess. The outside cooking area would have to be totally rebuilt, but at least the house had been saved.

The housekeeper came around with water and a dipper. Arielle took a long drink and then another. The housekeeper moved to the person next to her.

"I need the soot and sweat cleaned out of my hair, as much as a drink."

"Cheeky boy." The housekeeper swatted his ear. "If you lean forward, I'll dump some water over your head."

She did, and he remained leaning forward until the water had mostly dripped onto the ground. Arielle wished she could do the same, but she'd have to let her hair down in private. No woman should let down her hair in front of men.

"In thanks for battling the fire, cakes of raisins all around," Boaz said. "And the rest of the afternoon off."

The workers cheered.

Boaz himself wouldn't be doing any resting. He would be part of the group watching the house in case a wind came up and stirred any sparks to life.

Arielle got to her feet and went past the water supply to get some water for Zipporah. She found her over by the house, handed Zipporah the drink, and dropped down to sit next to her.

"You worked hard."

Zipporah finished the drink and wiped her forehead, smearing soot across her skin. "I didn't want the house to burn."

Arielle didn't say anything. She'd heard more words come from Zipporah's mouth since they'd heard the shouted "Fire" than in the weeks since Zipporah had joined their household. It appeared behind her silence was a sharp and sensible mind.

"I didn't want Boaz and Ruth to lose their home." Zipporah shifted to get comfortable. "I don't want to have to leave here."

"Why's that?" Arielle asked as casually as she could. Somehow, fighting the fire seemed to have unloosed Zipporah's tongue.

"When Boaz bought me in that market, I was terrified. Thought he would be just like all my previous masters."

"But he wasn't?"

Zipporah shook her head. "None of you were. At first I assumed you were all just acting. I've been tricked before." She shuddered. "Thought someone actually cared, but it was all just a show to win my trust." She sniffed. "Now I am very, very slow to trust."

It made sense, but it was sad to see Zipporah so guarded when she could be enjoying all that living here had to offer.

"But I've been watching you together, and I've seldom heard an angry word and if you do get angry you quickly resolve things."

Arielle never did know who was watching. Watching to see if what they claimed matched with how they behaved. So many people in Bethlehem claimed to be Yahveh's people, but so few actually lived according to his law. So few actually treated outsiders or the weak, poor, and vulnerable like they were close family.

Maybe Zipporah would be open to learning about Yahveh at last.

CHAPTER TWENTY-FIVE

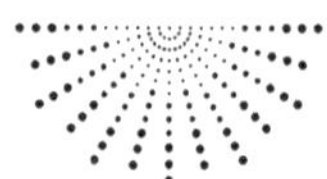

"You've certainly changed since you arrived," Arielle said to Zipporah as they watered the garden. "You were painfully skinny, and even your hair and skin were dull. Now they shine with health."

Zipporah flushed. "None of my previous masters believed in wasting food on me."

"Stupid them. Don't they realize healthy servants work harder?"

"I was treated very differently elsewhere to how I'm treated here," Zipporah said. "Servant isn't the right word to use. I was more a slave than a servant. They didn't really care if I died from overwork. They could always buy another slave."

The idea of buying someone and then treating them badly made Arielle feel sick. If Naomi had refused to adopt her, she might have had a life like Zipporah. Certainly, the priest of Chemosh had not had her best interests in his heart. She felt sick every time she thought of him and the look in his eyes. Eyes that pierced and seemed to assess her usefulness in terms of the temple trades and whether she could be sold and for how much.

Zipporah sighed. "I just wish I had been born beautiful."

Arielle widened her eyes. The fact that Zipporah was plain was something she should have been thankful for.

"There is nothing wrong with your looks," Arielle said. "A beautiful girl would have been in grave danger when you were taken from your family."

"I wasn't taken from my family," Zipporah's voice had become harsh. "I was sold. Sold because I was the least beautiful member of the family, the least likely to marry."

Beauty, health, and wealth were the best guarantees of a good marriage. Families looked for brides who had these qualities and for families they wanted to be aligned with. Poorer families wanted a bride who could work hard and produce healthy heirs.

"But why were they selling you at all?" Sadly, Arielle could think of several possibilities.

Zipporah looked down at her feet. "My father tried to impress some men who were gamblers. Soon he was joining in with their drinking and gambling." She sighed. "He always believed he'd be lucky tomorrow, but tomorrow never came."

The common lie that gamblers believed. There was a gambler in Bethlehem who had lost everything. Now he begged in the market.

"Eventually the men he owed money to suggested they take one of his children to pay off his debts."

"So your parents had to choose? How terrible."

"They preferred to make the choice themselves rather than risk losing their heir or my eldest sister. She was already engaged to be married. Once the decision was made, they closed their hearts to me." She spat. "Of course I had another name before but I don't want to use it. It felt like they took back the name they'd given me just like they took back their love."

Arielle swallowed. There was so much hurt written across Zipporah's face. So many years of suffering for her father's foolishness.

"I'm so sorry for what happened to you. It wasn't your fault or choice, but you've had to pay the cost."

Arielle doled out the water, making sure each plant received enough to keep it healthy. Some people treated their plants better than people. Her shoulders tensed at the thought.

"Naomi told me a little about you. That you are not …" Zipporah flushed and paused.

"Not her real daughter," Arielle finished the watering.

"She didn't use those words," Zipporah said.

"Yes, my life has also been impacted by the choices of others. Someone in my family dumped me on Naomi's doorstep and she took me in."

"It turned out alright then?"

"We haven't always lived like this," Arielle said. "In fact, when we first came back to Bethlehem, we had almost no food or money and had to glean in Boaz's fields."

"I've noticed he allows the poor to glean through the harvest of all his crops."

"It's part of Yahveh's law. He made this provision so that there shouldn't be any poor among the Israelites."

"But there are still plenty of poor people in Bethlehem," Zipporah said.

"That's because few people obey Yahveh. Boaz is one of only a small group of farmers who follow Yahveh's generous ways."

"Perhaps some of the others can't afford to."

"I used to think that, so I asked Boaz about it. He said some of the other farmers think he is mad to give away so much to the poor, yet it is his farm that is blessed. He believes that Yahveh honors obedience."

"Mmm." Zipporah watered a few more plants.

Arielle had been praying for an opportunity to speak to Zipporah about Yahveh. Had the time come?

"Yahveh is the reason Boaz and Ruth and Naomi are like they are. Those who follow a god become like the god they follow."

Zipporah covered her ears with her hands. "Stop. I don't want to hear about Yahveh. The gods are useless."

"I agree that most gods are, but Yahveh—"

Zipporah didn't let Arielle finish but shook her head as if to prevent Arielle's words entering her ears. "When I heard my parents talking about which of us to give away, I prayed to every god I could think of. When they sold me, I prayed again, straining my mind to think of any god I might have missed. There was no answer from any of them." Zipporah's voice was harsh. "Either they didn't care about someone as insignificant as me, or they are not gods at all, merely creations of men. I want nothing to do with any god. It is better to rely on myself."

"Zipporah, I am sad to hear you weren't rescued. Like you, I don't follow the Baals, Asherahs, or Chemosh but Yahveh is different."

"How so? He did not rescue me either, even though I cried out to any unknown gods."

"Didn't he bring you here?"

"That had nothing to do with your Yahveh. It was Boaz who saw me and paid the price demanded."

Boaz had said the price was more than any female slave was worth, but he couldn't bear to leave Zipporah there in the market for she reminded him that Ruth and Arielle might have ended up in a similar situation.

"Boaz seeks to follow Yahveh in all he does. He said it had been a sudden decision to go to the market that day."

"You can believe whatever you want to believe. I think Boaz's going to the market that day could just as easily have been a coincidence."

It broke Arielle's heart to hear Zipporah's words. How could she be so blind? It was so obvious to Arielle and Ruth and Boaz that Yahveh had guided him to the market that day. He hadn't intended to go to the shop where he had seen Zipporah passing by with a heavy bucket. He didn't usually carry as much silver with him as he had that day, but someone had just paid him for their grain. And if Zipporah's boss hadn't yelled at her to get moving and she hadn't answered, Boaz wouldn't have heard her Moabite accent. Once he'd heard that, he said he'd been determined to release her from her slavery.

"You said that normally you weren't allowed out of the house, yet the usual water carrier was sick that day so you had to go out to get water."

"Maybe, but I still want nothing to do with your Yahveh. The last thing I want is more disappointment. Everyone I have ever trusted has let me down."

Arielle sighed inwardly. She wanted Zipporah to know and follow Yahveh, but it was clear that the journey would be a long one. *Yahveh, please help her to discover that you are trustworthy and will never forsake her. Help her to learn that you care.*

CHAPTER TWENTY-SIX

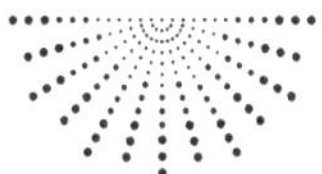

Knock, knock, knock.

Arielle groaned and rubbed her eyes. It was still dark, and someone was pounding on the door. Ruth. It had to be. She'd been dragging herself around for days.

Arielle rolled off her sleeping mat and went to the door.

"Who is it?"

"It's me, Zipporah. Ruth has asked Naomi to come."

Arielle unlocked the door and opened it wide.

"Is it the baby?"

Zipporah nodded as she entered. "She's only just told us, but apparently she's been in labor for hours."

Ruth never wanted to bother anyone, but this was one time they really wanted to be involved.

"I'll get Naomi up. You go back to Ruth. We'll be there as soon as we get some clothes on."

"No, I'll wait. Boaz and the housekeeper are with her. They know enough to heat some water. Boaz wanted me to help you get there."

Arielle went into the back room and knelt down to shake Naomi.

"Wake up, Ima. The baby's coming."

No bleary eyes from Naomi. She sat up straight away.

"I'll slip on my cloak. Everything's ready."

Naomi had packed a bag many days previously, and it sat beside the door. Plenty of cloths, swaddles, and a knife. Arielle wasn't sure if she wanted to help Ruth or not. She didn't want to see Ruth in pain and she knew pain was part of the whole process.

Naomi picked up the bag and they closed the door behind them. Moonlight glistened off the dew on the grass. A goat bleated from the fields and a breeze rustled through the leaves of the closest tree. Arielle shivered and drew her cloak around her shoulders.

It didn't take long to go up the hill. There was a glimmer of light from Ruth's room. Boaz would have lit many oil lamps.

They went into the house and a groan filled the air, growing in volume. Arielle swallowed. If only Havah, their common ancestress, hadn't rejected Yahveh. Arielle had seen animals give birth. It was an effort, but not this level of pain.

Naomi called out, "Can I come in?"

At Boaz's "Come in," she pushed through the curtained doorway.

Ruth was pulling on a rope hung over the ceiling beams and rocking back and forth. Her hair hung limp with sweat.

"Have you got hot water ready?" Naomi asked.

Boaz indicated two clay pots near the wall.

"We might need more. I can take over here for a while." Naomi glanced at the clay lamps. "Zipporah, these will need more oil."

Zipporah scurried to obey as Ruth moaned again. Naomi went and rubbed her shoulders, crooning into her ear. "Well done. That's the way."

"If I'd have known it would hurt like this, I'd never have wanted a baby," Ruth panted, perspiration gleaming on her face.

Naomi chuckled. "That's what they all say. Think about the baby to come."

Naomi had helped many of their neighbors in Moab deliver their children. She said it had been one way she could find acceptance.

Another contraction came.

"That's right, breathe through it." Naomi rubbed Ruth's back in big circles.

Arielle blew out a gusty breath. It was going to be a long night.

Once the contraction had ended, Naomi looked at Arielle. "Why don't you take Boaz out? He looks ready to faint and I've already got my hands full."

Boaz nodded and beat a hasty retreat with Arielle following. She was relieved too. She'd felt awkward standing there, not knowing whether she could help or whether she'd merely get in the way.

"I feel useless," Boaz said.

"Me too," Arielle said.

"And there's nothing I can do to stop the pain."

Arielle matched his strides as they paced outside under the moonlight.

They heard another moan from the house. They were still too close to the house. If she could get Boaz talking, maybe it would both distract him and prevent him hearing the sounds of Ruth's pain.

"Tell me again about this house," Arielle said.

"My parents built it," Boaz said. "I suspect it was Abba's way of trying to make up for the rejection my Ima experienced. They tried living in the village but people weren't willing to talk to Ima. They were more secluded out here." Boaz swept his arm to indicate his land. "It didn't matter if no one came to the house, for there was more than enough to keep them occupied."

And once the farm became successful, people were willing to pretend they'd forgotten Rahab's background.

"What were your parents like?"

Boaz walked a few more steps. "Abba didn't say much but he worked hard. He was always in his fields, struggling as he learned how to make them produce as much food as possible. He got me working alongside him early on and taught me everything he had found out."

A fox barked somewhere out in the darkness.

"Did you like working alongside him?"

Boaz grunted assent. "He was so patient and never thought it a nuisance to explain everything a few times and to guide my hands in a new task. And, he wasn't afraid to give me responsibility and support me doing it. If I made mistakes, he let me make them. Then we talked through what had gone wrong and how things could have been done differently."

Boaz's father, Salmon, sounded like Elimelech—exactly the kind of father any girl would want.

Arielle strained to listen to the sounds from the house. Yes, there was another groan. Talking was working, because the strain had gone out of Boaz's voice.

"What was your mother like?"

"She was a woman of great faith. She didn't let what others thought about her bother her. I guess she was used to people looking down on her. They'd done so in Jericho and it was no different in Yehoshua's camp or here. It was Abba who was bothered. Ima just laughed and said nothing here could be worse than what she'd experienced in Jericho. But she also said Yahveh had blessed her with Abba and me, and that was enough for her."

Maybe that was something that Arielle needed to learn. She already had Naomi and Ruth and Boaz and hopefully a new baby to love. Could that be enough? She'd like to think so, but there was always that place in her heart that felt like it was missing something—knowing who her mother and family were. Did other adopted children think the worst of their birth families? Did they also believe everything would turn out all right if they could only be reunited with their parents? She hated holding these conflicting views simultaneously and hated that she despised her mother for abandoning her at the same time as longing for her. Silly. Better to be like Rahab and be grateful for what she had.

There was a long, drawn-out moan, then immediately a lighter wail.

Boaz clutched Arielle's arm. "What's that?"

Arielle cupped her ear with her hand. "It's a baby's cry."

"Come on then." Boaz broke into a trot towards the house.

Arielle ran after him. "Perhaps let them clean up first."

"Oh, yes," Boaz said, slowing down.

They waited a while and then Boaz squared his shoulders and strode towards the room where Ruth had been laboring. Pausing at the entrance he said, "It is only me, Boaz. Can I come in?"

Naomi parted the curtain. "Congratulations! You have a son.

Boaz's smile nearly split his face and he went into the room. Ruth lay on the bed, looking exhausted but exultant at the same time. "Come and meet your son," she said with a broad smile. "He's amazing."

Boaz moved towards where Ruth was lying. He knelt down and scooped his son into his arms, cuddling him close, and then breaking off to peer at his little face. "Oh, he's beautiful, my love, just beautiful. Thank you, Yahveh, thank you, for my beautiful wife and my beautiful son." His voice cracked. "Thank you for your blessing on this family."

He turned to Naomi and Arielle. "Come and greet our son." His voice was full of pride. "There's not a more handsome babe in all of Bethlehem. No, not Bethlehem, in all of Judah."

"Now, dear," Ruth said. "I agree he is beautiful, but other parents might disagree with you."

He laughed, sounding much younger than his years. "I doubt

they're more excited or more grateful than I am." He handed the baby to Naomi like he was made of delicate pottery.

Naomi kissed the boy's forehead. "Are you going to call him the name we discussed?"

Naomi had been part of the discussions because this child was also hers, a replacement for all she had lost and an inheritor of Elimelech's legacy.

"Obed," Boaz said. "The name suits him, as we all desire him to be both a worshiper and servant of the Most High. The best servants are those who first worship."

Ruth reached out and touched her husband's hand. "Why don't you start Obed's journey by praying."

"Exactly what I was about to suggest," Boaz said. "As we have prayed constantly for him before his birth, we want to continue to pray for him every day."

Arielle had hoped she'd be next to hold Obed, but had to wait because Naomi handed little Obed back to Boaz. He gazed down at the baby's face as if he could not look away.

"Yahveh, you are great and wonderful. Thank you for this wonderful gift that I hold in my arms."

Arielle swallowed at the look of wonder that Boaz gave Obed.

"Yet Ruth and I have not been parents before. We need your wisdom to parent Obed well. Help us to love and nurture him and train him how to make choices that always lead him towards you and not away from you."

That was something Arielle was learning. Following Yahveh wasn't a big one-off declaration of loyalty but a daily series of choices. Each time she chose to go Yahveh's way, it made it easier the next time. If she chose to reject his way and chose her own direction, she became more practiced at turning away.

"Yahveh, you created the mountains and yet you also created Obed's eyelashes." Boaz brushed one finger across Obed's eyes. "This child is a work of your art." Boaz's voice cracked. "He's so beautiful, but he is also small and vulnerable, so please protect him. Protect him from the sicknesses that can come from nowhere. Protect him from danger. Most of all, protect him from evil and from choosing to take part in evil."

A lump filled Arielle's throat. Maybe all followers of Yahveh prayed these kinds of prayers over their children. But what about children in Moab? Their parents were teaching them to follow Chemosh or the Baals. *What of those who don't know you, Yahveh? How will they hear?*

CHAPTER TWENTY-SEVEN

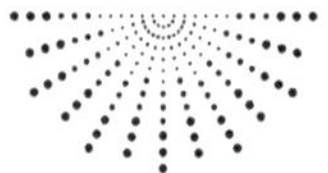

$\mathcal{A}$rielle and Naomi had come to visit Ruth.

"Ima and Arielle, welcome," Ruth said with a smile. "I'm so glad to see you. You can sit over there." Ruth gestured towards the carpet near the far wall.

According to the Law of Yahveh, Ruth had been unclean for seven days already and would be unclean for a further thirty-three days. Then she and Boaz would go to Shiloh to make the offerings required after the birth of a son. Anywhere she slept or sat until that time would also become unclean. If anyone else should touch her then they too became unclean.

"Poor little mite." Ruth brushed Obed's cheek with her finger as he suckled. "He apparently screamed at his circumcision and he's been upset ever since."

Arielle and Naomi had also been absent from the circumcision. It was a men's thing, a time to remember the covenantal promises Yahveh had made to Avraham. A time to mark Obed's body so he would always remember that he belonged to Yahveh's people. It was interesting that the Moabites, Edomites, and Ammonites, all descendants of Avraham and his family, also circumcised their sons.

Yet the practice no longer meant much among the non-Israelites. It was simply what was done.

Not that being absent had prevented them hearing little Obed's cries. He'd refused to stop crying until he'd been returned to Ruth. Now he snuggled at her breast.

"I'd better go and get ready." Naomi looked outside the window. "The guests will start arriving soon."

The circumcision feast would be a big occasion. Boaz was so proud of Obed, he'd invited people from as far away as Shiloh.

"It feels strange not helping," Ruth said.

"This is your chance to rest," Naomi said. "Once you've made the offerings at the end of forty days, you can join us in the garden as you're able but you'll be busy enough feeding and caring for little Obed. And once he starts walking, we'll all be chasing after him all the time. Cherish this time to rest and enjoy your baby. " Naomi laughed as she shook her head. "I was so tired with my sons I barely had time to breathe."

"Mahlon and Kilion were certainly energetic," Arielle said.

Naomi snorted. "They were young ruffians. I was glad when you came along because you slowed them down a little when you were small. They regarded themselves as your protectors."

That was good to know. All Arielle remembered was trying to keep up and usually failing and feeling frustrated at being treated as a pest.

Naomi got to her feet. "Are you coming, Arielle? Boaz has asked me to act as hostess in Ruth's absence."

* * *

*A*rielle exited the cooking area and went back to the guests on mats out in the garden. A lyre and a zither sounded from under the covered area near the house. She'd been to check on the food but there'd been no need. The housekeeper had everything moving smoothly. Zipporah was serving her and Naomi at the mat for family and honored guests.

Boaz leaned towards Arielle. "Do you think you could go and check if the little man could come out for a while? Tell Ruth we won't keep him long."

"Of course." Arielle got to her feet and went back into the house.

She knocked gently on the wall outside Ruth's room, just in case Obed was asleep. At Ruth's "Come in," Arielle peered through the doorway. "It's just me."

"Oh good. I'm feeling left out in here. Tell me who's come and what's happening."

"I'll do my best."

She listed those from Bethlehem, mostly Naomi's relatives or Boaz's contemporaries, then mentioned the visitors from outside their area. Many were people they'd stayed with on their trip to the Tabernacle in Shiloh.

"And as for what's happening, they're just eating and listening to the music."

"I'm glad Boaz put the musicians close by so I can hear them play. I've never heard such beautiful music before." Ruth sighed. "I suppose you're here for the baby. He's probably due to wake up soon. He might be fussy because he's in pain, poor little man."

"I'll be as gentle as I can," Arielle said.

"Please don't let him be passed from person to person," Ruth said. "I know people will want to hold him but he'll start screaming."

"I'll make sure he stays with Ima, or with Boaz, and myself."

"Thank you," Ruth said.

"And you can rest here and listen to the music."

"I might even fall asleep," Ruth said. "Obed is likely to be unsettled tonight."

Having already had a week of practice holding Obed, Arielle managed to pick him up without waking him. She carried him carefully out to Naomi and managed to transfer him, still sleeping, into Naomi's waiting arms.

Almost immediately a stream of ladies approached them.

"He's gorgeous."

"Does he look like Boaz or Ruth?"

The next woman pursed her lips. "Boaz's nose, I think."

"The chin looks like Ruth's," another woman said.

Arielle left them to it and went over to eat some more of the delicious bread and roast lamb. It was much too early to see who Obed resembled.

The wife of Boaz's friend from Shiloh led her partially blind mother over to view the baby in Naomi's arms. The old woman peered at Obed's face and raised her hands to heaven. "Praise be to the Lord, who this day has not left you without a guardian-redeemer. May this child become famous throughout Israel! He will renew your life and sustain you in your old age. For your daughter-in-law, who loves you and who is better to you than seven sons, has given him birth."

Arielle winced. She appreciated the compliment the woman was giving to Ruth, but perhaps now was not the time to remind Naomi of the tremendous losses she and Ruth had suffered along the way. Naomi nodded her head at the blessing but her eyes shimmered with tears. In the midst of all this rejoicing, Mahlon, and Kilion, and Elimelech were not forgotten. They would have loved little Obed, yet he would not have existed without the loss of Mahlon. It raised a maelstrom of conflicting emotions in her.

"What a good baby he is," cooed the old woman.

"All babies are good when they're asleep," Naomi said. "But he certainly cried today. And no wonder, with having to go through such pain."

"They don't remember the pain, thankfully. You will teach him his circumcision is a sign of Yahveh's covenant to his people."

Yes, with parents like Boaz and Ruth, Obed would be well

taught, but what about Arielle's own people? What opportunities did they have to hear about Yahveh and his love and compassion?

"How is Ruth recovering?"

"She seems to be doing well," Naomi said. "Getting as much rest as she can. Once the forty days are complete, she and Boaz will travel to Shiloh to make the required offerings."

"They must stay with us on the way," the woman said. "It is so encouraging to see another family who put Yahveh first."

"Ever since Ruth followed me back to Bethlehem, she has been completely devoted to Yahveh. Through her witness, Arielle now follows Yahveh too. Boaz and Ruth both long for this place to be a testimony to many."

"As we all must seek to be. Lights in a dark night sky."

Was Arielle a light? She didn't seem to be making an impact on anyone. She was praying constantly for Zipporah, but Zipporah seemed closed to any conversation beyond the mundane. *Yahveh, open her eyes and let her see your Light. Let her realize she needs you, that you are what her heart longs to find.*

Boaz came over to Naomi and took Obed into his arms. Obed murmured. Boaz cradled the baby close and he almost disappeared into his father's embrace.

Boaz waited until Obed was quiet. "Yahveh, your gifts are sometimes unexpected but always generous," Boaz prayed before those gathered. "Thank you for your generous gift of young Obed. We give him back to you. May he love you all the days of his life and may he shine your light into many dark places."

Was shining Yahveh's light only for a select few, or was it the responsibility of all Yahveh's children? Even here, Arielle could not escape her dream. The Moabite woman had behaved as if she never saw the water which would help her escape the fire. She'd behaved as if she were blind. Who would take the light to her?

CHAPTER TWENTY-EIGHT

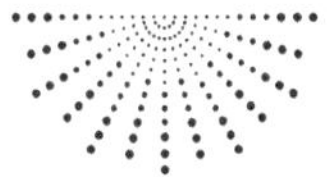

"Welcome, welcome." Yosef and Sarai, their hosts for their first night on the journey towards Shiloh, ushered Boaz and his family into their home.

Arielle couldn't help smiling broadly in response. There was something wonderful about the network of faithful followers of Yahveh. They were a minority among the Israelites but they took the time to encourage each other whenever they met.

"Where's the little man?" asked Sarai. "We have been praying for you, that you'd both be healthy." She touched Ruth's cheek. "You look to be in blooming health."

"I have been feeling well," Ruth said.

Boaz had considered bringing a cart for Ruth and the baby, but the tracks weren't really good enough for carts. In the end, they'd rigged baskets on a donkey and Obed had been secure in his basket-bed. They'd brought several doves in the other basket and Boaz was carrying a lamb. Ruth had started by riding but eventually said she'd find it easier to walk, which she'd done most of the way. As they hadn't brought Naomi this time, they'd made fast progress.

"Thank you for your prayers," Boaz said. "They have carried us as we adjust to someone who doesn't hesitate to cry when he needs something."

Sarai chucked Obed under his chin. "Well, it is not as if little Obed has any other way he can communicate."

Yosef waited until Ruth had scooped up the baby then whistled. A servant came out of the stable, unstrapped the baskets, and took the donkey for a brush down, feed, and rest.

"Come in, I'm sure you're ready for a wash and something to eat," Sarai said.

Arielle and Ruth followed Sarai, and Boaz followed Yosef. Arielle loved traveling but was always happy to wash off the dust and grime from travel.

It didn't take long to freshen up. Then they relaxed while seated on a raised eating platform under a tree.

After they had eaten bread, curds, herbs, and some dried figs, Boaz leaned back against the rail behind him. "How has Yahveh encouraged you since we last met at the circumcision feast?"

"You inspired us with the idea of the pictures representing different stories. That has been hugely encouraging. We came home and tried to use clay but found our clay wasn't as good as yours. We've found it easier to make wooden blocks about this size." Yosef held his fingers apart. "The women sketch the pictures, then my son and I carve the lines into the wood."

"We've been learning the stories to keep up with our progress in making the blocks. Best of all it has led to lots of questions among the servants." Sarai's voice was tinged with excitement. "We're praying they might choose to follow Yahveh."

It wasn't just Sarai who was excited. Arielle could hardly believe that her simple idea to help herself remember the stories was now giving others the opportunity to get to know Yahveh.

"A few days ago, a visitor asked about them and we were able to tell them all the stories," Yosef said. "They've asked if they can come back soon and hear the other stories."

Obed whimpered in his sleep and Ruth swaddled him tighter. "Hadn't they heard the stories before?"

Yosef shook his head. "Seems not. They said they only knew of one genuine follower of Yahveh in their village and no one took much notice of her."

"So sad," Boaz said. "To think that the descendants of Avraham, the Father of Faith, should come to this."

"Why have things become so bad?" Arielle asked.

Boaz sighed. "There's not a single answer to that. The deepest reason is that since A'dam and Havah, our hearts have always wanted to reject Yahveh's ways and go our own ways instead. We want to be in control of our lives. We think freedom means doing what we want rather than living a life of joy and contentment within the boundaries Yahveh has set."

"Many people use their freedom to indulge themselves then find themselves captive to what was supposed to bring freedom," Yosef said.

"And when Yehoshua led the Israelites into the lands promised to Avraham, he was given clear instructions to wipe out every Canaanite within the boundaries of the land. Yahveh knew what would happen if we did not." Boaz shook his head.

Ruth had given Arielle a clear explanation of why such destruction was necessary. It was still hard to think about but every day she saw the results of the Israelites' failure to obey Yahveh in this matter.

"Do you remember the story of Balaam?" Ruth asked.

Arielle nodded.

"He was hired to curse the Israelites, but Yahveh kept turning his words into blessings. When that didn't work, Moabite and Midianite women entered the Israelite camp. They not only enticed the Israelites to worship the Baal of Peor but also to indulge in immorality."

The sour taste of shame filled Arielle's mouth. Why couldn't she come from a more worthy people?

"Boaz, you said Yahveh sent a plague," Ruth said. "I can't remember how many died."

"Twenty-four thousand," Boaz said. "It would have been more, but Phinehas, son of Aaron the high priest, Mosheh's brother, took a spear in his hand and drove it through a man he caught in the very act of taking a foreign woman into his tent. Yahveh not only stopped the plague but made a promise to Phinehas that his descendants would continue to serve as priests."

"When the Israelites entered the land, they were full of zeal to obey Yahveh at first, but somehow they never finished the task," Yosef said. "There remained pockets of Canaanites and they have always been a snare to our people."

"With some notable exceptions," Boaz said.

"Of course," Yosef said. "Your mother was one of the wonderful exceptions, but I don't believe the rest of her family that were rescued from Jericho had her faith."

"No, they did not. It was grievous to her that those who had been rescued from destruction never took the time to understand that Yahveh had shown them mercy and to accept all the other blessings that could have been theirs had they lived his way."

"It wasn't just Rahab's family who was saved, but also the Hivites in Gibeon and the three surrounding towns," Sarai said. "They too demonstrated more faith than most Israelites. They knew Yahveh had told Yehoshua to wipe them out, and they knew the Israelites could not be beaten by conventional methods because they'd heard that Yahveh fought for the Israelites. Victory did not depend on numbers or strength but on whether or not Yahveh was fighting for the Israelites. So they came up with a desperate plan to trick Yehoshua into making a peace treaty with them."

And their plan had worked. Arielle had only heard this story once but it was unforgettable, with its miraculous events and battles, where Yahveh rained down hail large enough to kill the enemies it fell upon, and supernaturally extended daylight hours until victory was complete.

"Along with our inbuilt determination to reject Yahveh and the Israelites' failure to annihilate the Canaanites and their systems of worship, we have also failed to pass on the stories of Yahveh to the next generation. Each generation has drifted further away. All too soon, we have people like our recent visitors who've never even heard the deeds and words of the God they claim to still follow. Yahveh's laws have become outdated traditions taken out of the context of the stories that explain their roots or reasons."

Arielle turned to their hosts. "Then how have you remained faithful to Yahveh?"

Yosef held up a finger. "First, I made a decision that I would not drift away. I kept choosing to follow Yahveh. Second, I made sure I chose a wife who had made the same decision." He smiled across at Sarai. "Boaz made the same decision, which is why he finds himself a father only now, at such a late stage. If he had compromised and married someone who wanted his wealth but not his Yahveh, then he too might have drifted away."

It was a horrible thought. It was Boaz's daily choice to honor Yahveh that made him the man Arielle so respected. Following Yahveh's standard meant she might have to remain single. So few men loved Yahveh as Boaz did, and Arielle was not willing to choose a lesser man.

"Third," Yosef raised another finger. "We make sure to speak with, encourage, and pray with as many faithful Yahveh followers as we can. Over time, our home has become known as a place to stop. As we've encouraged others, they have encouraged us. It keeps the fire hot in our hearts."

"Meeting other faithful Yahveh followers has been wonderful," Ruth said. "Naomi has said one of the reasons her faith faltered in Moab was because there were so few other believers around to encourage her. Now we meet every day to encourage each other, and we're all growing. As we grow, others are drawn in to learn more."

It really was like a fire. The more they encouraged one another, the stronger the light and warmth from the fire, and the more who were attracted.

"Fourth, we go to Shiloh three times a year and sometimes more often. We stay a few days each time and find out when the Levites will be reading Yahveh's word. We go and listen to as much as we can each time."

"Wouldn't it be amazing to be a Levite and have the privilege of reading the very words of Yahveh?" Sarai asked, her face shining.

"Do you think we might be able to hear someone read Yahveh's words at Shiloh?" Arielle asked.

"We can certainly enquire," Boaz said. "I would be willing to stay longer if that was possible."

Yosef cleared his throat. "Back to Arielle's question about how we remain faithful to Yahveh. There is a fifth reason, but it is something you are already doing. Our family gets together often to share what Yahveh is teaching us, to remind each other of our history and what Yahveh has done. And we pray. We pray a lot for each other, for those we meet, and for those who live around us. In fact, we have been praying you would have a son. And here he is."

Obed jerked in his sleep and opened his eyes. He blinked and then opened his mouth and let out a surprisingly loud yell for someone so young.

"There, there, little one," Ruth soothed. "You're safe and we're among friends."

Obed gulped and quieted as she kept soothing him. Then he nuzzled his mother and she slipped him under her tunic to allow him to feed. Once he was settled, she asked, "How have you seen Yahveh answer your prayers?"

"In so many ways. Recently our grandson was sick with a high fever," Sarai said. "We tried everything we could think of but nothing helped. In the end, we just had to pray and entrust him into Yahveh's hands, asking for his mercy. Almost immediately he fell asleep and he was much better by the morning."

"We also pray about our crops and animals. We have seen sick animals healed and even locusts veer away from our farm," Yosef said. "After all, we have no idea what to do in so many situations."

"Have none of your animals ever died?" Arielle asked.

"We have had animals die, but we have learned to trust that maybe Yahveh wants us to learn something through the situation." Yosef grimaced. "It is embarrassing how quickly we start to rely on ourselves. That's almost always the time when we have a loss."

Sarai smiled. "We're slow learners. As we age, although our bodies are slower, we are much faster to turn to Yahveh."

"When we were younger, we were much more self-reliant," Yosef said. "Getting older is not all bad. Our faith is certainly growing all the time, even as we are declining."

Naomi's faith was also growing as she aged. She was more and more willing to share her failures along the way. She also shared what she was learning, even now, from stories she'd heard many times before. Although she hadn't come on this trip to Shiloh, she'd said she wanted to hear all about what they discussed with their hosts along the way. Arielle intended to keep on learning, as Naomi did, all the way into her old age.

Coming here felt like she received a rich meal for her heart, not just her stomach. Yet if a person just sat and ate and never worked, they would become fat and weak. How did that apply to being fed on Yahveh's words? How did one ensure this kind of food was turned into work rather than just becoming flab?

CHAPTER TWENTY-NINE

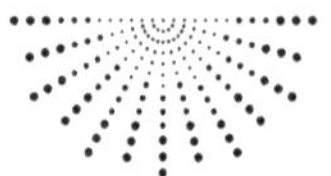

Arielle waved Ruth and Boaz off from the gate of Miryam and Levi's home in Shiloh. Levi was leading the year-old lamb. Boaz carried the basket with the doves—one for the sin offering, another for a burnt offering, and a freewill offering of silver to thank Yahveh for Obed. Ruth carried Obed, who was sound asleep after having been awake for long periods overnight.

"Please feel free to sit and enjoy this beautiful morning," Miryam said.

"I'd prefer to come and help you do the washing," Arielle said. "That will help me calm my excitement that we're actually going to hear some scripture read after they return."

"We're coming too, because it is a scroll I have only heard once before."

They took the clothes, including their travel clothes, to the large rock used for the laundry. Miryam's home had its own well, quite a rare thing in a town, so there was plenty of water. Arielle drew the water for the older woman and they wet the tunics and rubbed any particularly dirty areas.

"Do you know the general story of what will be read?" Arielle asked.

"Job is an unusual scroll," Miryam said. "No one seems to know who wrote it or even how old it is. Various people say he lived in the time of the patriarchs, possibly during Avraham's time."

Arielle scrubbed another tunic. "It must be wonderful to live in Shiloh and to be able to hear the words of Yahveh whenever you want."

"You would think that would happen but some of the Levites don't think the readings are important. Things have improved recently because we have a new priest, Eli. He loves to read Yahveh's word and takes the time to read all of the Law and Job and the few psalms we have."

"What is a psalm?"

"A sort of poem or song." Miryam wrung out the tunic she had washed and laid it over the top of a bush to dry in the sun. "After the reading has finished, we'll teach you one of the songs. We've memorized two, a song of Mosheh and a song of his sister, Miryam. We find singing not only lifts our eyes away from our problems and towards Yahveh, but the more we sing the words the more the truths change our hearts."

Until Arielle had heard the lyres and zithers at Obed's circumcision party, she'd never realized what she'd missed. She'd heard Zipporah humming some of the tunes several times since the celebration. The only time she'd heard music before was the brazen blare of trumpets and the sound of gongs at the temples in Moab. She'd hated those sounds. They'd dug holes in her ears and made her head ache.

"Job was a very wealthy man who lived somewhere near us in the land of Uz." Miryam poured water on the next item of clothing." I won't tell you the whole story, but he was blameless and upright before Yahveh and had many children and flocks and herds.

Yahveh's enemy, Satan, came before Yahveh and said Job only worshiped Yahveh because he had been blessed."

"Let me guess. Satan suggested that if everything was taken away from Job, then he would abandon following Yahveh."

"How did you guess?" Miryam asked. "Have you heard this story before?"

"No," Arielle said. "But I have been thinking about one of our servants. She wants nothing to do with Yahveh because he allowed her parents to sell her as a slave and she had a miserable life."

"Until she came to work for Boaz, I assume."

"Correct." Arielle quickly explained how Zipporah had come to work with them.

"Many of my neighbors are the same. They conclude Yahveh does not love or care for them because they experience difficulties. I was once tempted to think like that when my second child died."

"I'm sorry." Arielle touched Miryam's hand. "That must have been hard. Naomi said she struggled with the same doubts after all her losses."

Miryam scrubbed the tunic in her hands. "It is so important that we don't linger in our doubt. You will hear how Job dealt with his suffering at the public reading after our meal." She glanced at the sun. "A meal we should start preparing the moment we've finished with these clothes."

They wrung out the last of the clothes and spread them on various bushes before going to the cooking area and preparing bread, curds, cucumbers, and herbs.

Arielle used a sharp knife to slice the cucumbers. "Why do you think Yahveh allows people to suffer?"

"I asked lots of why questions when little Simeon died in his sleep. I didn't get many answers. Looking back, I see things differently. I have been able to sit with many mothers who have lost children and they know I understand their pain."

"That might be why I feel close to Zipporah." Arielle picked up another cucumber. "Both of us had parents who abandoned us."

"Tell me about that," Miryam said.

Arielle's eyes prickled with tears. Miryam was the first person apart from her family and Boaz who'd really shown an interest in her background. Arielle told her the scant details she knew of how she came to enter Naomi and Elimelech's household.

"And you're still angry about it?" Miryam asked.

"I guess I am," Arielle said. "Don't get me wrong. I am thankful to Yahveh for my new family but I still want to know why my birth family did what they did."

"You might never know," Miryam said. "Especially as you now live in Bethlehem and don't even know if any members of your original family are still alive."

"That's just it. Does anyone in Ar know about my family? Is there still someone who could answer my questions?"

Miryam swept up some crumbs with her hand. "I wish I could say that the answers are out there but they might not be. Naomi might never know why Yahveh allowed Elimelech and the boys to die. I am glad Naomi didn't get stuck on the endless whys. Getting stuck leads to bitterness and the conclusion that Yahveh doesn't care."

"Zipporah is stuck. She thinks Yahveh didn't rescue her even though she treated him as just one name in a long list of gods."

"Keep praying for her. I've seen Yahveh soften people's hearts. My own father was set against Yahveh but we kept loving him and praying. We didn't speak directly about Yahveh. During his last days, he finally asked questions and we were able to help him to turn his face towards Yahveh at last."

"I like that way of expressing it. We do turn our faces away. He keeps pursuing us until finally we turn to face him and discover he is not what we feared but the one we have wanted more than anyone else." Arielle paused. "I might never find my mother and father, but I have something better."

"Yes, the God of all creation. He has been more than enough for me, and I long for all those I know to come to follow him as I follow him."

There was a creak of the gate and a whistle outside, followed by a baby's cry.

"There's Levi," Miryam said.

Obed's cries grew in volume even as they spoke. Perhaps he sensed he was in a place where his needs could be looked after.

"Let's go and eat," Miryam said leading the way, "Although it sounds like Ruth will have to clean and feed the baby first."

* * *

"How was this morning?" Arielle asked as she and Ruth walked behind the others, up the hill to where Eli the priest was going to read the book of Job.

"Moving," Ruth said. "We offered each of the sacrifices. The priest did not inquire about whether I was an Israelite and I didn't tell him. We were only in the outer court anyway. I stayed well back when the animals were sacrificed."

"You said the experience was moving. Why moving?"

"Several things. It was amazing to finally stand there with Boaz. Then it wasn't just a purification rite. It was also a pledge that we would raise Obed to the best of our abilities to follow Yahveh. I couldn't stop the tears of thankfulness coming." She wiped her eyes. "And then the priest prayed a beautiful prayer of blessing for Obed. It was so unexpected because I assumed all the priests were unfaithful. That is not the case."

"Maybe Yahveh always ensures there is a remnant to shine his light."

"I think that must be true. Although it seems as though there are more faithful believers here in Shiloh."

"They have greater opportunities to hear Yahveh's words and are constantly reminded of him by the rhythm of the ceremonies and festivals."

Now they were approaching the top of the hill, close to the Tabernacle, there were more people moving in the same direction.

"This is a good spot," Levi said. "We should have no problem hearing Eli and—"

"If Obed starts crying, I can move away," Ruth said. "Hopefully Eli has a soothing voice."

They stood in a clump. Levi and Miryam murmured greetings to those they knew.

"Here he comes," Levi said in an undertone.

A man was led through the crowd. In his arms he held an enormous scroll. He climbed onto a raised platform, unrolled a linen cloth, and placed it on a wooden bench. Then he kissed the scroll and opened it at one end. He lifted his head and said, "This is the word of Yahveh to us today from the scroll of Job, the faithful."

Eli waited until all were quiet, then began to read. "In the land of Uz, there lived a man whose name was Job. This man was blameless and upright; he feared God and shunned evil. He had seven sons and three daughters, and he owned seven thousand sheep, three thousand camels, five hundred yoke of oxen and five hundred donkeys, and had a large number of servants. He was the greatest man among all the people of the East."

Arielle stood still, absorbing the story about Satan's taunt and test. Was Yahveh worthy of worship even if he never delivered a single blessing? The breath caught in her throat as all Job's blessings were taken away. All his flocks and herds, then his seven sons and three daughters were crushed when the roof of their house fell in, then his own health as boils caused him agony. When she heard that his wife said, "Are you still maintaining your integrity? Curse God and die!" Arielle was furious. How dare she add to Job's suffering?

Eli continued to read the words of Job's so-called comforters, men who were convinced that suffering implied someone must have done something wrong. They were confident they understood the reason for Job's suffering and therefore urged him to repent to regain Yahveh's blessing. Job kept maintaining his innocence.

The sun beat down on them and an ant nipped her foot. Arielle stood carefully on one leg and rubbed the painful area. Boaz touched her arm and indicated a tree off to the side. He guided Ruth there and Arielle gratefully followed. Ruth was able to sit with her back against the tree trunk.

Eli continued, "Then Job replied."

Arielle leaned forward. What would Job say in response to his comforters who had only added to his suffering?

"How long will you torment me and crush me with words? Ten times now you have reproached me; shamelessly you attack me. If it is true that I have gone astray, my error remains my concern alone. If indeed you would exalt yourselves above me and use my humiliation against me, then know that Yahveh has wronged me and drawn his net around me."

Before Arielle had known Yahveh, she had wondered if the gods were against her. Could she have maintained her trust in Yahveh if she believed he had thrown a net around her and was depriving her of everything that made life worth living?

Eli continued to read Job's reply. "My relatives have gone away; my closest friends have forgotten me. My guests and my female servants count me a foreigner; they look on me as a stranger. I summon my servant, but he does not answer, though I beg him with my own mouth. My breath is offensive to my wife; I am loathsome to my own family."

Poor Job. How terrible to have suffered all this and not know why. How could someone continue to trust Yahveh under these circumstances? Was there ever going to be joy in his life again?

"Oh, that my words were recorded, that they were written on a scroll, that they were inscribed with an iron tool on lead, or engraved in rock forever!"

What would Job think of them, sitting here today and hearing his words? They were not written on lead or rock but they were indeed on a scroll.

Eli paused and raised his head and Arielle couldn't help focusing on him.

"I know that my redeemer lives, and that in the end he will stand on the earth."

Arielle blinked. Here was the hope she had been waiting for. Job had not given up. He still trusted in Yahveh, his redeemer, the one who would make sense of all suffering.

"And after my skin has been destroyed, yet in my flesh I will see Yahveh; I myself will see him with my own eyes—I, and not another. How my heart yearns within me!"

Arielle did not hear anymore for a long time, for she was caught by Job's words echoing across the years. Here was a man at the absolute bottom of a pit, yet he believed he would see his God, his redeemer.

When they'd lost Elimelech, and later, Mahlon and Kilion, Arielle hadn't known what to think. The Moabites rarely talked of life after death. She'd never heard it mentioned among the Israelites either. She'd ask Boaz what he thought. If there was life after death, like Job seemed to say, it changed so many things. It brought hope and meaning instead of grief and loss.

CHAPTER THIRTY

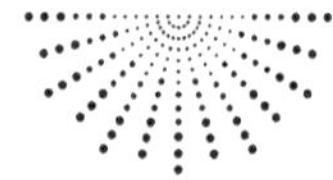

$\mathcal{A}$rielle sat down in their usual outdoor spot. The day was already too hot to be outside. At least here there was a chance of a breeze.

"We had a wonderful trip, Naomi. I think it was even better than going for a festival because there were less people around and we heard Yahveh's words being read."

"Don't forget the two songs," Ruth said excitedly. "They were practicing them for the festivals and sang them several times through."

"And we sang them over and over with Levi and Miryam until we had memorized the words," Arielle said, the memory of the joy they'd experienced making her smile.

"Don't make me wait. Please sing them," Naomi said.

Arielle turned to Ruth, who was feeding the baby. "The song of Miryam and Mosheh first?"

Ruth cleared her throat and hummed a few notes.

"Let's sing the chorus first," Arielle says. "It goes like this."

Together they sang,

"I will sing to the Lord, for he is highly exalted.

Both horse and driver he has hurled into the sea.

The Lord is my strength and defense, he has become my salvation.

He is my God, and I will praise him, my father's God, and I will exalt him.

I will sing to the Lord for he is highly exalted, he reigns for ever and ever."

"Sing it again," Naomi said when they'd finished the chorus. "If I hear it a few times then sing it a few times with you, I should be able to remember it."

Arielle's voice lifted. She'd been singing the song all the way home from Shiloh. This story matched the one about the crossing of the Red Sea and the drowning of Pharaoh's army. Wouldn't it be wonderful if someone could make a song for every story? It would have to be someone else, because she didn't have such abilities. Such songs would be another way for people to remember Yahveh and his great deeds.

By the fourth time through, Naomi was remembering the words. "Once more and then you can teach me another section."

There was no hurry. They only knew two songs. The other was a song of Mosheh which repeated the line, "Teach us to number our days, that we may gain a heart of wisdom."

"I can see the benefit of this already," Naomi said. "Singing Yahveh's words make them go around and around in my head." She smiled. "In the middle of the night, when I wake up for some reason, you might hear me singing them."

"I didn't know you woke up at night," Arielle said.

"You're young," Naomi said. "When you're my age, you'll wake up too. My body gets stiff lying still too long and I have to wriggle about a little. Now, why don't you tell us a story?"

"The Red Sea, to match the song?" Arielle asked.

"No. Start from the beginning and tell us about the creation of all the beautiful things around us."

Arielle would have thought that Naomi knew this story frontwards, backwards, and sideways. She could probably recite it in her sleep, but if Naomi wanted to hear the story of A'dam and Havah again, then Arielle would tell it again.

"In the beginning the earth was dark and formless," Arielle began.

"Arielle, could you speak a little louder?" Naomi asked with a hand cupped around her ear.

Arielle squinted at her. They'd only been away about ten days. How could Naomi's hearing have deteriorated so much in so short a time?

"I'm getting old," Naomi said, but there was a twinkle in her eye as though she was sharing a private joke.

Arielle obligingly raised her voice as she continued telling the story of A'dam and Havah and their rebellion against Yahveh and all the consequences of that foolish choice.

Inside the house there was a scraping of a sandal. Suddenly Arielle understood. There was nothing wrong with Naomi's hearing and she didn't need to hear A'dam and Havah's story again. Zipporah was doing some tidying inside, and Naomi wanted her to overhear the story. If she wouldn't listen directly, then maybe she'd eavesdrop. It was worth a try. Arielle still hadn't succeeded in drawing her into conversation about the things of Yahveh.

Arielle finished the story and went on to the next. She enjoyed rehearsing the stories and was proud of how well she could now tell them. She noticed different things each time she went through a story. It seemed incredible that having heard it and told it so many times, there were still new things to learn.

Yahveh, keep Zipporah there and send your words directly into her heart. She has been so hurt and she needs to know you desperately. Help her to be intrigued so she cannot draw away.

"Your storytelling is much improved," Naomi said. "You're no longer in a rush to get through the story."

"I know them much better now, so I'm not trying to remember what comes next. Instead, I can concentrate on trying to tell them with better pacing and emphasis."

Young Obed let out a big burp. Ruth laid him on his tummy and patted his back. "During the night, when I feed Obed, I've started singing the songs we learned in Shiloh. I'll start telling him the stories soon."

"You can probably start now," Naomi said. "He won't understand them, but he will hear the sound of your voice and be reassured by it."

"Did you tell me stories when I was little?" Arielle asked.

"Elimelech always did a better job than I did. The boys kept me too busy."

There was a question that Arielle had never dared to ask before. "Did you and Abba ever think of not taking me in?"

"Never!" Naomi said with a vehement shake of her head. "I must admit we were daunted about looking after you. A new baby is hard work, but we knew if we had not taken you, then the alternatives were too horrible to consider." Naomi reached out. "And we never regretted it."

"Except that day when I got into the flour bin and spread it all over the floor."

Naomi laughed. "I was pretty angry about that, but you don't reject a child for being a child."

Naomi might not but Zipporah certainly hadn't experienced such kindness. There were no more sounds from the room she'd been cleaning. Had she heard the whole story? *Yahveh, open her heart to you.*

✳ ✳ ✳

he heat was such that all gardening had to be done early in the morning or late afternoon. Arielle and Zipporah were weeding prior to watering. Arielle placed a piece of old cloth under her knees and kneeled down to clear the weeds around the base of her half-grown plants.

"Do you think Yahveh made weeds?" Zipporah asked. "It doesn't seem very considerate of him."

Of all the questions she'd imagined Zipporah might ask, that wasn't one of them. At least she was asking a question. They suspected she had listened to all the stories through, as they'd told them at the same time each day, after singing to alert Zipporah that they were starting. Sometimes she swept nearby and sometimes she found tasks to do in the big room nearest to where Arielle and Naomi sat. Arielle made sure she spoke in a loud clear voice to help Naomi's feigned deafness.

Help me to answer well and please keep Zipporah asking questions.

"Perhaps they weren't weeds when Yahveh created them. Perhaps they only became unwanted after A'dam and Havah had rebelled against Yahveh. The account says the ground was cursed and would now produce thorns and thistles."

"It does seem unfair that we have to weed all the time because of A'dam and Havah."

"It used to bother me that we had to suffer and die because of their choices. But I've come to realize each generation would still have rebelled against Yahveh as they did. Our hearts seem to constantly stray. The other day I snapped at Naomi even though I knew it was wrong and wouldn't please Yahveh."

"Pfft," Zipporah spluttered. "If you'd lived where I've lived, that wouldn't even be called anger."

"But the people who mistreated you weren't followers of Yahveh," Arielle said. "The better I know Yahveh and his ways, the more sensitive I am to how he wants me to behave. I shouldn't have been angry at Naomi. She wasn't trying to annoy me and she has treated me as a daughter all these years."

Zipporah sighed. "You're lucky."

"I didn't always feel lucky. I felt resentful that my mother had dumped me on Naomi's doorstep. I believed she didn't care."

"Your mother was better than mine. She gave you into the care of someone who would look after you."

"Maybe, but that wasn't how I felt. Inside I was angry, sad, and disappointed. I felt like I'd been abandoned and must not be worthy of love. But since I've come here, I've been learning to look at things differently."

"How so?"

"I'm learning to be thankful for what I do have rather than resentful about what I've missed out on."

"You may not have missed out on much." Zipporah wiped her cheek with the back of her hand.

"That's true. In fact, my situation might be better than what I would have had otherwise. Isn't it strange how we long for something else assuming it will be better." Arielle chuckled. "Contentment isn't easy. If I'd grown up in Moab with my own family, it is unlikely I would ever have come to know and follow Yahveh."

"Why do you think he is worth following?" Zipporah asked.

Such a good question and one that Arielle hadn't prepared an answer for. *Yahveh, give me wisdom.*

"In Moab, I was scared all the time. I was frightened of the temples and their priests. I was frightened of ghosts. The funeral processions scared me."

"Aren't all people scared of death?"

"I think we all start that way, but I've been thinking about that exact question since I came back from Shiloh. I heard a story there about a man who suffered terribly but he was confident that he would meet Yahveh. He was longing for that day."

"You all speak about Yahveh as if he can be known."

"I think he can be, but perhaps not in the ways we expect. When I pray, I believe he hears me. My prayers might not be eloquent but he enjoys hearing my prayers much as Boaz loves hearing Obed's noises."

"But you can't see him? He has no images you can point to and say, 'That is Yahveh.'"

You made my mouth Yahveh, please help me speak in a way that helps Zipporah.

"What did you feel or think when you saw images of gods?"

"Angry." Zipporah sat back on her heels. "I felt angry that their faces were impassive and they didn't seem to care and didn't listen to my prayers. Some of them looked beautiful and some were frightening and ugly, but it made no difference. They were equally unresponsive."

"After the Israelites left Egypt and crossed the Red Sea, they went to Sinai. This was the mountain where Yahveh had previously spoken to Mosheh and sent him to Egypt to confront Pharaoh."

Zipporah didn't say she didn't know the story so she must have listened when Arielle told it last time.

"Yahveh called Mosheh up to the top of the mountain and gave him the Law that told the Israelites how Yahveh wanted them to live. While Mosheh was away, the people got restless and Mosheh's brother crafted a golden calf for them to worship. He said, 'These are the gods that brought you out of Egypt.'" Arielle sighed. "And the people worshiped them."

"What did Yahveh do?"

"First he suggested to Mosheh that he was tired of the Israelites, that he was going to wipe them out and start again with Mosheh and his descendants."

"But he didn't?"

"Only because Mosheh begged for mercy on behalf of the people. Yahveh was angry not just because they were worshiping manmade gods but because no image is enough. The golden calf suggested that Yahveh was limited to one place at one time when he is everywhere, at all times. There is no object big enough or wonderful enough to represent him, so he commands that no images may be made."

"So there are no images of him at Shiloh?"

Arielle shook her head. "Not one, not there nor anywhere in the land. Not of Yahveh anyway. Sadly, many Israelites do worship the gods of Canaan and there are many of those images. Too many. You ask why I want to follow Yahveh. Because I believe he made and sustains everything. And he doesn't just sustain it, but he loves and cares for his people. In the desert, where the Israelites wandered for forty years, Yahveh gave them food and drink every day. He forgave them repeatedly during those years and gave them numerous new starts. I believe he gives me guidelines to live a life that is worth living. He gives me joy which gets me up in the morning."

Zipporah held up a hand. "Enough. I get it. You are happy with your choice, but it is not necessarily the choice for me."

Arielle didn't say anything but she would continue praying that Zipporah would choose to follow Yahveh too. Then there would be three Moabites joining Yahveh's family. But what of the thousands of others? What of Orpah and her family and Ruth's family, and their former neighbors? How would they hear? How could they hear if no one went to tell them? And if they never heard, how could they possibly repent and turn towards Yahveh?

CHAPTER THIRTY-ONE

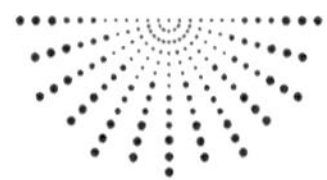

Two mornings later, Arielle followed Boaz into the fields to check the crops. She'd asked if she could accompany him because she had something she wanted to ask. Something she wasn't yet ready to discuss with Naomi or Ruth.

Arielle matched her steps with Boaz's.

"Is everything alright?" Boaz asked. "I'm wondering why you want to talk to me. The only reason I can think of is that you want me to arrange a marriage for you."

Arielle nearly laughed aloud. She hadn't been thinking of such things because she had not met anyone who was anything like Boaz.

She shook her head and took a deep breath. "Do you believe Yahveh communicates via dreams?"

His eyes widened. Her question had obviously caught him off guard.

"He is God. He can do what he wants." He paused and frowned. "There are accounts of angels in all the books of Mosheh. He spoke to Yaacov in dreams and to his son, Yosef. There are many other instances when scripture says, 'And the Lord spoke to so and so.'

We don't know if those were dreams or visions or through some other means."

"I think," Arielle paused and took another deep breath. "I think he has spoken to me."

Boaz blinked. "If that is the case, it is very special indeed. He has never spoken to me or anyone else I know. Let's sit down and you can tell me all about it."

They perched on the edge of a large rock and Arielle tried to collect her thoughts. It felt wrong to even talk about the dream. It was still so vivid in her mind, so personal. She'd chosen Boaz to talk to because he was wise and wouldn't laugh at her. Not that Naomi or Ruth would laugh, but they loved her and would struggle with what the dream seemed to be saying. Boaz would help her discern.

He waited quietly for her to begin.

"I think it is better if I simply tell you the dream and see if you come to the same conclusion about it as I have." Arielle half closed her eyes and thought back to last night. "Last night wasn't the first time I've had this dream. I had a similar dream when I first moved here. I dreamed I was standing on an island in the middle of a lake. It was a large island and I felt completely safe, but all along the shores of the lake the trees were aflame. Huge trees would fall, hissing, into the water."

"Go on."

"I saw a woman standing on the shore, the same woman I saw last time. Her arms were raised and she called, 'Come and save us. Come and save us.' She had a scar across her cheek." Arielle reached up and brushed her hand across her own left cheek. "She bowed down towards the water and called, 'Chemosh, Chemosh, rescue us.' I tried to yell across to her, 'No, don't call to Chemosh. He won't save you. You must trust Yahveh, he alone can save you.' But my voice didn't work."

Arielle's throat tightened for the next part of the dream always devastated her.

"Is there more?" Boaz asked.

Arielle nodded. "The woman spun on her heel and plunged back into the midst of the fire. Every time, I wake up shaking and thinking, 'Who will tell her and the other Moabites about Yahveh?'" She turned towards Boaz. "Do you think it is a message from Yahveh? And if so, what do you think it means?"

"Hm. Is it a message from Yahveh?" He stroked his chin and then looked at her. "What makes you think this dream is different from other dreams or nightmares?"

"I do sometimes get nightmares but they feel completely different. This one felt like I was awake and really there. I could see clearly. I could feel the grittiness of the sand beneath my bare feet. I felt completely safe on the island, because I knew I was in the center of Yahveh's lands and nothing could ever take me away from them." Arielle sighed. "But things were different for the woman. Despite the smoke in the air, I could smell her fear and despair. Her eyes were blank. She couldn't see me or hear me. It was like she was blind. Or dead." Arielle shivered. "Her eyes were like the eyes of the priest who kidnapped me in Moab, except she knew she needed help. It was just that she was turning the wrong way."

"Because she knew no other direction to turn."

"Yes, because no one had told her." Arielle sat with her head bowed under the load of that thought. Ever since she'd first been to Shiloh, she'd felt the burden for her and Ruth's people but she hadn't wanted to think too much about it. Leaving Bethlehem would be like tearing her heart out. Her heart was on this farm with Naomi and Ruth and little Obed and Boaz too. People who followed after Yahveh with all their soul and mind and strength. Besides which, how could she, one woman alone, travel to Moab?

"If Yahveh has sent this dream, which seems to be the case, then we must conclude that he wants someone to go and warn the Moabites. The question is why you have had this dream." Boaz blew out a gusty breath. "I reluctantly come to the conclusion that maybe Yahveh is asking you to go. But—"

"But I don't seem to be the right choice," Arielle said. "It should be someone older and wiser and a man not a woman."

Boaz nodded. "But who are we to question who Yahveh sends? Sometimes courage and strength do not come in the expected containers."

"I don't feel adequate or at all prepared," Arielle said, hating the quaver in her voice.

"Maybe that's a good thing," Boaz said. "Those who feel adequate might trust themselves instead of Yahveh." He got to his feet. "The one thing I am sure of is that we need a day of prayer and fasting. Naomi will want some sort of confirmation from Yahveh herself if she is to let you go. For she will worry and be afraid for you the whole time you're away."

It was going to be a battle against worry for Arielle too. She was afraid. Afraid of what it might cost and whether she would have to face that priest again.

* * *

*A*rielle and the others gathered in Naomi's home the next day. Boaz had told his foreman he was in charge for the day.

Arielle's stomach rumbled. She wasn't used to going without her morning meal. Even Ruth was fasting although Boaz said she didn't need to as she was still breastfeeding. Ruth said she wanted to concentrate on their prayers as much as she was able. She'd feed Obed and let Zipporah care for him while they prayed.

"Well, we have all heard about Arielle's dream," Boaz said. "Now is the time to pray: For clarity, for wisdom for how to go about this task—"

"And for the people Yahveh wants me to talk to," Arielle said. "For open ears and hearts."

"Indeed, but before we start praying for all these things, I am going to suggest that we start with praise," Boaz said.

"Could we perhaps start with confession?" Arielle asked. "I feel like we must approach Yahveh's throne and deal with any sin first."

Boaz nodded. "Let's first pray on our own then return to praise Yahveh together."

Arielle nodded and moved into the inner room. If she was to do this, there must be no sin between her and Yahveh. She must be totally honest. She fell to her knees and bowed her head. "Yahveh, you are great and mighty and I am a mere nothing. I am of the race whose actions meant we are banned from your presence in the Tabernacle for ten generations. My lips may not have kissed Chemosh, but for too long I did not see your beauty, your holiness, your uniqueness. Please forgive me."

She remained quiet for long moments.

"Yahveh, show me my sin, whatever there is in me that offends your holiness."

Again, she remained still.

"Lord, even as I learn your words in songs and stories, there is pride there. I delight in being a good storyteller. Forgive me. If I have any ability, it is a gift from you and to be used for your glory."

She prayed through several smaller things before facing the biggest issue. "I know I still hold bitterness towards my parents. I don't even know who they are but I am angry they abandoned me. It is not something I can understand but I know you want me to forgive them. I ask you to give me a heart that is willing to listen and seek to understand. I ask that if they are still alive, you will allow them to find you."

Arielle prayed Yahveh would wash her clean inside and out. By the time she went back to the others, she felt much lighter, ready to praise Yahveh for his goodness and mercy.

They praised Yahveh until the sun passed its highest point.

"We might be fasting," Naomi said. "But you must not faint because you haven't had enough to drink." She passed around grape juice, its taste sweet with an overlay of tartness in Arielle's mouth.

Naomi prayed the first prayer of the afternoon. "Yahveh, you are master of the world and master of Moab, though they neither know you nor honor you. I would prefer you send someone else to share your words in that land. Can you not send an older man?"

At least she was honest. Arielle had a lump in her throat. How could she possibly leave this, her family? She'd spent years longing for her family of birth and not thanking Yahveh for the precious family he'd given her. *Forgive me. And Yahveh, reassure Naomi and show her your plans. If we have made a mistake, make it clear.*

Once Naomi had finished her prayer, they each prayed asking Yahveh to confirm his will.

"Can we pray by name for all those we know in Moab?" Ruth asked when they had finished.

"Dearest, why don't you start," Boaz said.

Ruth prayed for all the members of her family.

The tears prickled Arielle's eyelashes as Ruth begged for the lives of her family. Family who might not even be alive, for there were few travelers between Bethlehem and Moab these days to share such news.

They prayed for Orpah and her family and for their neighbors, each by name. Naomi particularly prayed for an older woman in their lane who'd been the first to befriend her. Arielle prayed for Kozbi, that somehow they might meet and she would be able to introduce her to the One she so needed.

"We pray for Arielle's journey, if you do indeed intend her to go," Boaz said. "May you protect Arielle and those we send with her. Give them opportunities to shed your light on the way. Help them to meet people who can help them and provide places to stay in Moab. Protect them from evil and keep them in the palm of your hands."

The image of being held in the Creator's hands was comforting. None of them were saying it, but going to Moab was dangerous. The journey was dangerous, because there were always people willing to take advantage of the unwary. And being in Moab would be dangerous, because the people under the dominion of Chemosh would not be happy about one of their own telling them of Israel's god, the Israel who had defeated King Eglon in the time of Ehud. There was no love between these cousins.

Yahveh, give me peace. Your peace to go and face whatever awaits me. Help me not to be afraid. For she was afraid. Afraid to leave these people she loved so much and this place of safety. Here she might hope to one day marry and have a family of her own. If that was not possible, she would be looked after in this beautiful place.

In Moab, there would be no one to protect her except Yahveh alone. He would have to be enough. Had she learned to trust him enough?

CHAPTER THIRTY-TWO

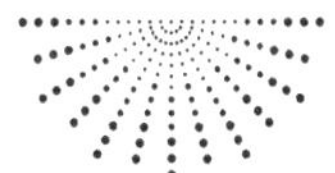

"Naomi, what's wrong?" Arielle asked.

She'd found Naomi weeping on their rooftop as she looked out across the fields.

Naomi turned and enveloped Arielle in a hug. "I'm weeping because Yahveh made it clear to me during the night that you are to go, but when I asked when you would return, he gave me no promise."

"That doesn't mean I won't return," Arielle said. "Just that he didn't answer your question."

Naomi broke out of the hug and wiped her eyes. "You always manage to cheer me up." She sniffed. "Don't ever think you're not precious to me."

Arielle used to think she was just the outsider, but ever since they'd come to Bethlehem, and especially since Ruth had married, Naomi had turned to Arielle more and more.

"I am sorry I didn't tell you how precious you are. When you were younger, I feel I neglected you because the boys kept me on the run."

Arielle had sometimes felt neglected which was why she had turned to Elimelech. He'd always had time for her. Time that she'd so deeply craved to fill the gaping cavern in her heart.

Yahveh had answered their earnest prayers and spoken to Naomi, but Arielle had also had another dream. She just wasn't sure whether she was meant to share it and if so, with whom.

"I'll help you first. Then I'd like to go and spend time with Ruth and the baby."

Naomi stroked her cheek. "You spend as much time with them as possible."

* * *

"Yahveh answered our prayers," Arielle said as Ruth patted a crying Obed on his back. He had not appreciated being with Zipporah for most of yesterday.

"Are you surprised?" Ruth asked.

"Not as much as I would have been in the past," Arielle said. "It is becoming clearer and clearer that his plans for me include returning to Moab. Last night, he gave Naomi a dream that made her willing to let me go."

"She's a mother. It will always be hard to let you go," Ruth said.

"It's hard for me as well. I'd much prefer to stay here, but last night I had another dream. I was surrounded by temptations, all of which urged me to stay."

"Can you remember it?" Ruth asked.

"Too well," Arielle said with a shudder. "I was looking down at you and little Obed, and it was as if I was presented with all the things I would miss if I go. I saw scenes of Obed walking and running and growing up. It wasn't what I saw that was hard. It was the yearning to be part of it."

"Yearning is such a strong emotion. Whenever I see little Obed, I yearn to introduce him to my family." Ruth sighed. "I knew in my head when I left that I probably wouldn't ever see them again but it is much harder to live with that day after day. Obed reminds me of them so often, in the way he chuckles and the tilt of his head. They would have been so thrilled to meet him."

"I will do my utmost to find them," Arielle said.

"If they're still alive. They're not old, but you and I know the precariousness of life. If Orpah cannot have you stay with her, I am sure my parents will open their home to you."

"Even if I follow Yahveh?" Arielle asked.

"They were never opposed to Yahveh," Ruth said. "After all, they allowed me to marry Mahlon. Boaz and I will be praying every day that my family members open their hearts to Yahveh. Please tell them they are most welcome here."

"Of course."

Ever since Arielle had had the first dream, she'd been praying for the people back in Moab, that they would have the opportunity to hear about Yahveh. She'd prayed but always hoped she wouldn't be the person chosen to go to tell them. If she were Yahveh, she'd choose someone like a Mosheh or an Avraham. Not a girl from Bethlehem with few connections back in Moab.

Obed hiccupped in his sleep. Ruth took him off her shoulder and cradled him in her arms. "You said that most of the dream was a nightmare. What else did you see?"

Arielle had seen herself, happily married and with a child of her own. Her eyes stung with unshed tears. Ever since Obed had been born, she'd thought about a family of her own. "It showed me some of the other things I would have to give up. Then it showed me the dangers ahead."

"Real dangers?" Ruth asked.

"Real possibilities." Like being beaten or worse. The fear had almost smothered her. "But then everything changed."

"How?"

"It's hard to describe. The fear was driven back by a light, and a warmth cradled me as you're cradling Obed. I heard a voice. Maybe I didn't actually hear the words. It was more that I felt them like a hug, 'Child, I will never, never, ever leave you nor forsake you' and I felt more secure than I've ever experienced."

"Those words are always true for those who trust in Yahveh but living as though we believe them is another thing altogether." Ruth looked down at the sleeping Obed. "Let me put him in his cradle. Then we can go for a short walk."

They walked back to the house and succeeded in placing Obed in his cradle without waking him.

They walked carefully out of the room. "We'll just be down in the garden." Ruth said to Zipporah. "I might have to help you there when Arielle leaves."

It was only a garden, but it had been another of the temptations in the dream. Seeing and eating the results of all their weeding and watering mattered more than Arielle had expected. Her ties to this place were increasing all the time. She'd better head for Moab before they got any stronger.

Once out in the garden, she and Ruth wandered down the rows.

"Boaz has already started making preparations. Today he is going to ask one of his most trustworthy servants to escort you."

"Do you know who it is?"

Ruth shook her head. "He said the man might refuse. Then he'd have to think again. He's also said you must take a donkey."

"Surely we won't be carrying that many provisions."

Ruth shook her head. "No, but there are other things a donkey could carry."

Arielle scratched her head. Was Boaz intending to send some of his produce?

"We'll send some gifts from the best of our produce for my

family and Orpah. He also wants you to take the second set of clay pictures."

Those would definitely require a donkey.

"He says the pictures do half the work for you, because anyone who looks at them wants to hear what they represent."

It was a clever idea, because one of Arielle's fears was that she wouldn't be able to get a conversation started. The tiles would make things easier.

They picked a few vegetables for their next meal. Arielle swallowed past the lump in her throat. "You know I don't want to leave."

Ruth nodded. "And we don't want you to go. But if Yahveh asks us to do something, we have to do it or miss out on the blessings that come with it." She hugged her arms round her body. "We'll be praying for you constantly. Boaz intends to visit all our friends on the way from here to Shiloh and get them praying for you too."

Maybe one of the reasons Yahveh had given her the dreams was to help some of the Israelites think beyond their borders. Boaz had shared from Mosheh's fifth book last night, about how Yahveh hadn't chosen the Israelites because they were more numerous or intelligent or deserving of salvation.

Instead, Yahveh had rescued them to make them a beacon of hope to the nations around them and to cause the peoples of the world to be envious of their blessings so they'd come and enquire about Israel's God. Tragically the Israelites had done the reverse, chasing the gods of the peoples around them instead of being separate and completely surrendered to Yahveh and his ways. Maybe now, without a faithful people to act as a beacon, some of the faithful remnant of Yahveh followers would have to be people sent to live among the surrounding peoples to tell them of Yahveh's deeds and his desire for all people to worship him.

* * *

*A*rielle and Ruth were spinning wool when Enoch, their steward, entered the room and came over to speak into Boaz's ear.

Boaz nodded and turned to Ruth. "There'll be three extra families here tonight." Guests were common enough but not in such large numbers. Who was coming? What secret was Boaz keeping?

"Shall we let the others know?" Ruth asked.

Boaz nodded. "Better than Arielle and Naomi wasting all day trying to find out."

Arielle was about to protest that she wasn't nosey when she saw Boaz's eyes twinkling. He did like to tease.

"Did you notice Enoch was missing?"

Arielle nodded. She hadn't seen him in three days which had surprised her for Enoch was the man Boaz had chosen to accompany her to Moab. He was an older man, a widower.

"He was worried he wasn't fit enough to travel to Moab, so he volunteered to go to Shiloh as a trial run."

Why Shiloh? It wasn't time for one of the major festivals.

"Stop teasing her," Ruth said. "Tell Arielle why he went."

"He went to meet some of the families we stay with on our travels, Yosef and Sarai, Levi, and Miryam, and ask them to come and send you off properly. You're going to need all their prayers while you're traveling and in Moab."

Arielle nodded, unable to speak. He was so right. Sometimes what she was doing seemed crazy. Knowing people were praying would make all the difference.

"I had the men slaughter a goat. We'll make it a send-off to remember."

And he did. An evening of food and laughter and chatter and admiring young Obed, who had no intention of going to sleep while there were so many interesting people around.

At last Boaz stood up and clapped his hands. "Thank you for

coming all this way to stand with us as we send Arielle off to carry Yahveh's words to places that have not heard them and may not welcome them."

There was a long silence. Just because Arielle had finally welcomed Yahveh's words did not mean that others would. Some wanted nothing to do with Yahveh because they were intent on going their own way. They didn't want Yahveh spoiling their plans. Didn't want light to shine in their darkness, because light illuminated things they'd prefer to keep hidden.

"Our family has committed to praying for Arielle and Enoch every day they are gone, and we would like you to consider joining us."

"We will," Levi said.

Boaz held up his hands. "I don't want you to rush into this. Take your time and consider if you are ready for this commitment. Why don't each of you talk to the rest of your family."

It was a sensible plan for it was easy for the senior man in a household to make decisions and expect the others to follow. Boaz liked to involve everyone in this household and had often scandalized the servants by asking for their opinions on things to do with the farm. As he said, they lived here too and also depended on the farm doing well.

The leader of each family turned to the others. Arielle couldn't hear anything except for a low murmuring of voices. It would ease her mind to have all of them praying for her.

"We will pray," Levi said.

"And us," replied the other families, one by one.

Boaz nodded. "Good. It will be much easier for each of us to remain faithful if we know others are also praying." He turned to Arielle. "Come, sister. Stand in the center and we will gather around and pray for you."

Arielle moved to where Boaz had directed her. The others crowded in close, laying hands on her shoulders and back and head.

She swallowed the lump in her throat. Each hand linked her to the people in the circle, including her in another family she hadn't expected.

The prayers filled the air and fell on her like a rain of blessings. For an abandoned child, she now had far more family than she'd ever dreamed possible.

CHAPTER THIRTY-THREE

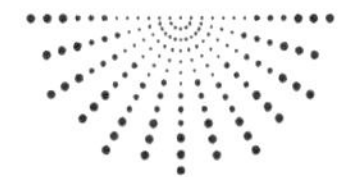

One moon later

"*A*rielle and Enoch, welcome to our home. I am Rahel." Their hostess was a woman with a brown, wrinkled face and a smile from one ear to the other. "This is my husband, Dek."

They had made it to Heshbon, to one of the homes Boaz had confidently said took in travelers who honored Yahveh.

"Any friend of Boaz's is a friend of ours," Dek added. "We lived in Bethlehem many years ago but moved here to offer hospitality to travelers going north or south."

Rahel ushered them into the courtyard. "We hosted Naomi and Elimelech and their two boys on their way to Moab a long time ago. Come in. I'm sure you all need a drink and a rest."

Enoch went to take the load off the donkey while Arielle followed their hosts into the house.

"After we've had a short rest Enoch wants to go and get our cooking pot fixed as its handle is broken."

Which made it difficult to get on and off the fire.

"You're in luck. There just happens to be a family of coppersmiths here at the moment. They're faithful followers of Yahveh and they'll do a good job."

Enoch entered from the stable and heard Dek's comment. "Where can I find them?" he asked.

Dek gave them instructions. "And why don't you ask them back here for the evening meal."

"Just give me a chance to wash my tunic," Arielle said. She always took the chance to change to her second tunic if possible. Washing didn't take long. Soon she and Enoch were weaving through the streets where they found the side gate where the coppersmith had set up his tent.

While they waited in line, Arielle asked people what their favorite story was and told a few to interested listeners: stories about Noach, Yehoshua and the battle of Jericho, and Mosheh and the burning bush. Some were interested and others pretended not to be.

The coppersmith's wife came over and asked them what the problem was. Arielle held up the pot. "Just the handle."

"That will be easy enough for Reuel to fix," the woman said.

It seemed strange to ask someone she'd just met to a meal but Dek had asked them to issue the invitation. "And our hosts, Dek and Rahel, asked if you'd join us for the evening meal."

The woman beamed. "I'm always happy to have an evening off cooking."

When their pot was returned, Enoch examined it closely and gladly handed over the fee.

"We're finished for the day," the coppersmith's wife said. "If you're willing to wait, we'll just wash and close up and come with you."

They watched as the coppersmith, a brawny man with streaks of white in his hair, smothered the fire and then laced up the tents. He disappeared for a while over near a stream.

"Do you think they're Israelites?" Enoch asked.

"I'm not sure," Arielle said. "Maybe they're like me and have entered Yahveh's family by choosing to follow him. I'm sure we can soon find out more."

"This trip has been good for me already," Enoch said. "In Bethlehem, I only saw what I had lost. Here, I'm meeting others and seeing new things."

Reuel returned and introduced himself and his wife, Jael, along with Jael's sister, Zura, her husband, Dedan, and two nearly grown children. Presumably Dek and Rahel knew how many people to expect.

Once back in town, they strolled up the narrow streets back to Dek's place with Dedan tenderly leading his wife, Zura. Much to Arielle's surprise, she was blind. How had she met Dedan?

By the time they arrived back at the house, it was full of mouth-watering scents of roasted meat, probably goat. Rahel must have been cooking all the time they were away. They were all invited up to sit on the roof as the sun was now low in the sky.

Dek broke the bread and handed it to each of his guests. The meal started with Jael's yogurt, cucumbers, dill, chickpeas, and meat.

"We are greatly enjoying staying at believers' homes along the way," Enoch said. "We especially love hearing how people came to follow Yahveh. Reuel, your name is a familiar one in our history, being the name of Mosheh's father-in-law, but from which tribe are you?"

It was the question Arielle had wanted to ask, but she was too young to be asking questions in such a company. By asking about their tribe, Enoch was accepting Reuel's family as Israelites. There was no need to offend anyone by suggesting they were not Israelites.

"Like the first Reuel, we are Midianites," He turned to Arielle. "Do you know who Midian was?"

"A son of Keturah, Avraham's third wife."

Reuel bowed his head to her. "Well done. It is good to find someone who knows the ancient stories in such detail."

"The woman who adopted me has spent a long time teaching me all the stories she knows."

He smiled. "You would get on well with Zura and Jael, for they too are storytellers. They often tell stories to our customers now that we all know Yahveh."

Arielle couldn't stop herself smiling broadly. How wonderful it was to meet other non-Israelites who had found Yahveh. Maybe there were more than she had expected.

"Where do you travel?" Enoch asked.

"We used to travel a circuit among the trans-Jordan tribes to the north," Reuel said. "I have now passed that circuit onto my two sons and their wives. We moved further south with our daughter. I'm not sure where we'll move if Zura and Dedan's son wants a circuit."

"You could always retire," Jael said with a laugh. "I wouldn't mind settling somewhere."

"It wouldn't be long until you got bored," Reuel said. "Maybe we'll have to move west of the Jordan."

She nodded. "You're probably right about me getting bored. I'm used to being on the road, and I enjoy meeting people and telling others about Yahveh. I would never have imagined we Midianites would be telling the Israelites stories of the One they are supposed to know."

"It does seem strange," Zura said. "But what a privilege. Yahveh has shown much grace to us."

"How did you come to follow Yahveh?" Arielle asked.

"Zura knew him first," Jael said. "So she should start."

Zura finished her mouthful. "For me it was fairly easy. My sight was taken away in an accident and I had nothing much to do but think about what my purpose was and if life was worth living. Yahveh sent a woman to tell me the stories of his love for me, and I was ready to accept." She laughed. "My sister was much slower.

In fact, she wasn't willing to listen to anything I had to say for years."

"But you never gave up praying," Jael said.

"I was wrecking my marriage," Reuel said. "And caused my wife and family much heartache."

"But eventually the state of our marriage made me willing to listen to my sister."

"And separately, I met faithful followers of Yahveh who challenged my thinking and introduced me to the One who can change all hearts," Reuel said. "I had no promises that our marriage could be helped but, oh, I prayed."

Jael smiled. "But when we finally met again, we discovered Yahveh had changed both of us."

"Our marriage didn't change overnight, but as we lived according to Yahveh's good law, we learned to see each other with new eyes." Reuel gave his wife a look that made her blush.

"It is interesting how often things have to go wrong before we are willing to listen," Dedan said. "For me, it was the loss of all my family. I tried to drown my sorrows in drink but that didn't work."

"As I also found out," Reuel said.

Maybe it had been the losses of Elimelech, Mahlon, and Kilion that had prepared Arielle's heart, for certainly she had never paid much attention to Yahveh while life was free of trouble.

"What about your story?" Rahel asked.

"Oh, I don't think it's that interesting," Arielle said.

"All stories of finding Yahveh reveal his loving-kindness and bring him praise," Rahel said.

Arielle raised her eyebrows. Perhaps everyone's life was part of the whole testimony to Yahveh's goodness.

As Arielle told her story, the listeners nodded. It seemed that how she met and followed Yahveh could indeed bring encouragement to others.

Dek and Rahel also told their stories. They had been raised in

God-fearing homes. For the rest of them, difficult times had led them to Yahveh.

Yahveh, lead us to people who are disillusioned with Chemosh and hungry to know you, even if they don't know it is you they seek.

"It is encouraging to hear of Midianites coming to follow Yahveh," Arielle said.

"And us of Moabites," Zura said. "But when I think of the stories Yahveh has left with us, I see many others."

"Like who, Ima?" her daughter asked.

"Like Rahab, the mother of Ruth's husband," Zura answered.

"And the Hivites who tricked Yehoshua. They still live in the towns of Gibeon and its surroundings," Dek said.

Enoch was leaning forward, with a shine in his eyes Arielle hadn't seen before. "And in Avraham's time. He lived many years near Kiriath Arba, which was an Amorite town and had close connections with Abimelech of Gerar."

"And two Pharaohs had opportunities to know Yahveh," Jael said. "Although we don't know what they did with those opportunities."

"With Yosef in Egypt all those years, he must have had a widespread impact," Reuel said.

Rahel nodded. "And probably with people of many backgrounds."

"I prayed that the believers we met in Israel would encourage us on our way and you're doing that." Arielle looked around the circle of believers. "I'm grateful."

"Where are you headed?" Jael asked.

"South, to Moab," Arielle said. "To introduce as many as possible to Yahveh."

Jael drew in a sharp breath. "Surely that is dangerous."

"It is," Enoch said. "I have been sent by Boaz to ensure Arielle gets there and to protect her the best I can."

Jael frowned. "How do you know this is what you are supposed to do?"

"It certainly wasn't my idea," Arielle said. "I'd much prefer to stay in Bethlehem with my family, but Yahveh confirmed it several times."

Yahveh, do you want me to tell them about the dreams?

It wasn't something she wanted to talk about, because it felt too personal, as if she was telling them her innermost thoughts. Yet she sensed no objection to her speaking. So she took a deep breath and told them about the series of dreams. All were silent for a long moment when she finished.

"Do you think we should only do such a thing if we have been directly told to do so?" Jael asked.

"I don't know," Arielle said. "But I do know I would have never started on this journey without the dreams. I needed them because I just looked at my weakness. I didn't think I was the right person to go."

Rahel chuckled. "Yet when Mosheh suggested that to Yahveh, Yahveh told him he was the one who made Mosheh's mouth and Yahveh would give him the words."

It was an incident Arielle had thought of several times since leaving Bethlehem.

"I have no reassurances that it won't be dangerous," she said. "But Yahveh did remind me that he will never leave me alone. He will be there and give me all I need. I'm relying on him to do that. Naomi and Boaz and Ruth and several of their friends are praying for me every day."

"We'll add our prayers too," Reuel said.

The others nodded.

Their words warmed her deep inside. "I won't be able to send news, so you'll have to work out what to pray for yourselves."

"Yes, Ima, what should we pray?" Jael's daughter asked.

Jael touched her daughter's cheek. "How about we pray that

Arielle and Enoch are led to people with prepared hearts. To people who are looking for answers beyond their traditions and the things they've relied on."

"And for courage," Zura said. "And wisdom to know when to back away and not persist with certain people."

Even the thought of more people praying bolstered Arielle's courage.

"Why don't we pray right now?" Dek said. He stood to his feet. "Let's stand together in a circle."

They stood and held up their arms to link with the person next to them. Dek led them in prayer, followed by many of the other men and women.

Thank you, Yahveh, for encouraging me with these new brothers and sisters. My family just keeps getting bigger and bigger and more and more interesting. Moabites and Midianites have allied themselves together for evil in the past. Let this be an alliance for your good and honor.

CHAPTER THIRTY-FOUR

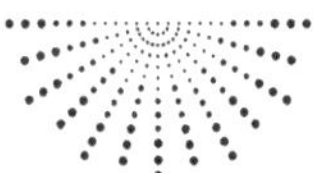

The donkey in front of Arielle disappeared over the lip at the edge of the Arnon Gorge. Now that they were here, it didn't seem that long since she had traveled in the reverse direction with Naomi and Ruth. At that time, she thought she'd never pass this way again. She blinked away tears. She hadn't expected to get emotional. Maybe she would always have ties to her native land.

Yahveh, prepare our way. Save some and bring them to know your compassion and mercy. And please help us to be able to tell one of the accounts of your great deeds around the campfire tonight.

Dek had introduced them to the band of traders they were traveling with. In the past, he'd spoken to one of the traders about the things of Yahveh. Although the man was still a long way from choosing to follow Yahveh, Dek trusted him to deal honestly with Arielle and Enoch and keep them safe. It was much safer traveling with traders than attempting the trip on their own.

Arielle started down the narrow path into the gorge. Their leader wanted them through the gorge and up the other side before nightfall. They would snatch a few mouthfuls to eat and water their animals and themselves in the valley at the bottom.

"Are you managing?" Enoch asked.

He was taking Boaz's instruction to treat Arielle like his daughter very seriously. It had annoyed her a little at first, but now she thought it rather sweet.

There was nothing she or Enoch or anyone could do about it if she hadn't been managing. She simply had to trudge on and look forward to a good rest once they camped on the other side. Praying as she walked helped. She prayed especially for Dek's friend, that his heart would be willing to hear some stories. Maybe others would as well. *Please help them not to reject your message. Give me a way to start the conversation.*

* * *

They'd set up a goat skin awning and would lie on mats under the partial shelter. It wasn't as if it would rain at this time of year and tent walls would be stifling. Arielle asked Enoch to carry some bread, goat cheese, and dried fruit over to the fire. Then she accessed the panniers from which the donkey had been released for its own feed. She drew out three of the picture tiles, hoping they would provoke curiosity.

It didn't take long to eat. Afterwards, Arielle took the tiles and examined them in the light of the fire. One represented the giving of the Law, another the fall of Jericho, and another was the first in the series, creation. She laid them along a log and prayed. *Tonight may Moabites hear your words.*

"Hey, what do you have there?" Dek's friend said.

Arielle silently handed them over to him and kept praying.

He tapped one. "This looks like the destruction of Jericho. Dek told me this story."

Dek hadn't mentioned which stories he'd told this trader. *Give me courage to talk.*

"What other stories did he tell you?" she asked. Enoch's

rock-like presence on the other side of the fire gave her confidence and made it permissible for her to speak to an unknown man.

"Mostly about Yehoshua and how the Israelites came to conquer Canaan."

Another of the traders came and plonked himself down beside the fire. She swallowed. It was much easier to talk to one man on his own. The other man spat into the fire and it sputtered. "Whadya got there, little girly?"

Arielle tensed up then relaxed. Enoch was still here, and Yahveh had told her he would never leave her or forsake her.

She handed the second man the three tiles, praying he wouldn't throw them in the fire or break them as she had no means of creating new tiles.

"Did you draw them, girly?"

She nodded.

"You've got some talent. Are you going to Ar to sell such things?"

She shook her head. "I tell stories that match them."

"Stories. Hey, I like stories." He burped long and hard. "Give us a story then, girly. Let's see if you're any good."

Arielle took a shaky breath. What story would interest him but also be one that wouldn't bore the first man who had heard other stories before?

Yahveh? Which story?

"Why don't I start with the first story ever?" Arielle took the first tile and gripped it, the roughness reassuring in her hands. *Yahveh, give me courage.*

"In the beginning the earth was formless and void, but the spirit of the Creator was hovering over the waters. He said, 'Let there be light!' and there was light. He separated the light from the darkness."

Arielle put down the tile so she could use her hands to tell the story. The firelight glinted on the men's eyes but she couldn't tell if they were interested.

"And the Creator separated the light from the darkness and said, 'It is good.' And there was evening and there was morning on the first day."

"Go on," the rowdier man said gruffly. "This is better than listening to someone snore."

Was that a compliment? She kept going, through day two and three and four. The two men were listening, although the first seemed to be pretending he wasn't.

She reached the concluding lines, "And the Creator blessed the seventh day and set it apart as holy, for on the seventh day he rested from all the work that he had done."

There was a short silence before the big man clapped his huge hands together. "Bravo. You are a storyteller, just like you claimed."

Arielle's shoulders relaxed. *Thank you, Yahveh.* She'd been so frightened before she opened her mouth but once she had started, the fear had left her.

"What are you clapping about?" a voice said as two more traders lumbered into the midst of the group.

"We've got us a storyteller," the second man said. "Told me a story I've never heard before." He scratched his head. "Well, I have heard other versions of where everything came to be, like the stars and trees and things, but not this version."

"Well, come on. Tell us too. It's not as if we have anything else to do."

They sat down on the ground so they could see her. It made Arielle squirm, but she took another breath and retold the story. These men didn't listen as well and didn't stay after the story. The rowdy man asked a few questions then asked, "Have you got more stories?"

She'd thought Dek's friend would be interested, not this man. So far, Dek's friend had kept quiet although she was sure he was listening. She told the account of A'dam and Havah's rebellion against Yahveh and the evil that spread among their own family.

"Stupid fools," the man muttered. "Mucked it up for the rest of us. Now look at us. We have to work every day. No seventh day off for us, and barely any time with our families."

"Don't you ever bring your wife and family with you?" Enoch asked.

"She used to come sometimes, before the children, but we can't dawdle along like she wanted. Eventually she refused to come."

"That must be tough," Enoch said.

"Yeah," he muttered. "You got more of them stories?"

"Lots," Arielle said. But there were only two more nights to tell them. "Do you want to hear what happened after A'dam and Havah?"

He squinted up at the night sky. "One more, then I better get some sleep. I have the third watch."

So she told the story of Noach, the man who walked with God, and the two men who may never have considered walking with Yahveh listened intently. She finished the story and they said nothing. Simply got to their feet and left. Arielle sat there, not sure what to think. Had they enjoyed the story? Or had they been bored?

Enoch leaned forward. "Don't worry about their response or lack of it. Let Yahveh speak through his word. Let's pray they want more stories tomorrow."

It was a good reminder. She was too prone to think that people's response depended on the quality of her storytelling. Yet Yahveh was able to work through the mouths of his servants. The corner of her mouth quirked. After all, the God who had once spoken through the mouth of a donkey could surely use hers.

* * *

The second evening, the fire had barely been lit before the rowdier man said, "So what's our story tonight?"

Arielle assumed it would be just the original two, but one of those who'd walked away the previous night came over. "There's nothing else to do," he said. "A story won't hurt me."

Arielle put a hand up to cover her grin. Little did he know how stories wormed their way into hearts. Stories couldn't easily be forgotten. Stories were dangerous, life-changing things.

She told them the stories of Avraham as a continuous stream of accounts from his start in Ur to his death in Canaan at one hundred and seventy-five. Stories of a man who journeyed with Yahveh, not always making the right choices but learning as he went.

When she finished, the men again said nothing. She wasn't so concerned this time because Enoch had talked with her about it during the day. He'd said the men had to keep traveling together as they traded down the eastern side of the Jordan and further south. They didn't dare show too much interest as they were afraid of being different from the other traders and breaking the harmony. She must be content to simply tell the stories as though dropping seeds in the soil and asking Yahveh to water them and make them sprout.

CHAPTER THIRTY-FIVE

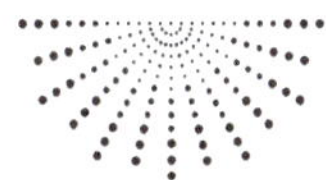

They had finally arrived in Ar, having parted from the traders a little while before. The last night of the journey, Arielle shared all of the Exodus stories she knew, and they'd thanked Arielle in their own ways before they parted. *Yahveh, water the seeds that have been planted.*

Arielle raised her hand and struck the wooden door of Orpah's parents' home with her palm.

A little boy opened the door and peered around it.

"Can we speak to your grandmother?" Arielle asked.

The boy ran back into the house and they heard footsteps coming across the floor.

"Yes?" Orpah's mother asked, suspicion written all over her face.

"Don't you recognize me?" Arielle asked.

Orpah's mother peered at Arielle. "Arielle, is that you?"

"Yes, it is," Arielle said.

Orpah's mother glanced left and right and spoke in a whisper. "Sorry, but you can't come in. My husband spends all his time at the temple. He would never allow you to stay."

Arielle barely had time to get her foot out of the way before the wooden door closed firmly in her face. She looked across at Enoch. "Now what?" she asked quietly.

"Do you know where Ruth's family lives?"

Arielle nodded and led the way. Would she receive the same reception there? If so, where could they stay? *Please Yahveh, let them welcome us.*

They skirted the main streets to avoid crowds. Even so, a man veered their way and spoke to Enoch. "How much for your daughter?"

Arielle drew in a sharp breath

"She's not for sale," Enoch said, and the man moved on.

"Please pull your veil up to cover your face," Enoch asked.

Hands shaking, Arielle obeyed. The veil restricted her view of the path so she took hold of Enoch's arm to keep herself from falling.

As they reached the alley where Ruth's family lived, Enoch checked that no one was nearby. They knocked on the outside gate.

Once again, a young boy answered. Once again, he was sent to get his grandmother. As the gate opened, Arielle pulled back her veil.

Ruth's mother recognized her. "Don't stay out there. Come in quickly."

She swung the gate fully open and they led the donkey into the courtyard. Ruth's mother closed the gate quickly after them and hugged Arielle before releasing her. "Sorry to rush you inside and of course you must stay."

Enoch began to unload the panniers off the donkey.

"We're under suspicion already because of Ruth going with Naomi," Ruth's mother shrugged. "They assume we're in regular contact. How they think we get information I don't know. Pigeon?"

Ruth had always said leaving would be hard on both those who left and those who stayed behind.

"If they knew how we longed for news." She sighed. "Is Ruth well? Does she miss us?"

"She is well," Arielle said. "And happily married with a young son."

"Oh, how wonderful." Ruth's mother's face lit up. "But I must not ask you for more news before you have put down your things and washed."

"I am quite happy to sleep out in the stable," Enoch said.

"We can do better than that," Ruth's mother said. "We have a guest room. If Arielle is willing to share with the younger girls, then we have space."

"That will be more than fine," Arielle said. "They'll smell much nicer than the merchants we traveled with."

Enoch chuckled. "They weren't the kind to wash much."

Arielle went off with Ruth's mother, sighing with relief. She'd begun to think they wouldn't be welcome anywhere.

Washing and settling didn't take long. Arielle was keen to talk with Ruth's family and let them know Ruth was not only happy but richly blessed in every area.

While they'd been settling, Ruth's mother had brought out food. "I apologize that it is yesterday's bread but the fresh bread won't be ready until later."

"We are grateful for what you can give us." Arielle reassured her. "What are we to call you? I can't keep calling you Ruth's father and mother."

Ruth's father stroked his beard. "Why don't you just use our names? I'm Hadad and my wife is Laka. You'll get to know the names of our son and his family soon."

Arielle had already seen various children peering out from behind the different doorways, and the eldest granddaughter had brought her water for washing.

"Tell us about Ruth and her family." Hadad leaned back against the wall.

Thank you, Yahveh, for giving me a natural way to talk about you.

Arielle told them how they had come to be working in the barley fields and how they had first met Boaz. "Yahveh's law makes provision for those who have little."

Hadad leaned forward. "So it was not easy when you went to Bethlehem?"

Arielle shook her head. "Naomi's house had been empty all the years she'd been away, and the garden had run wild. The locals weren't always friendly."

They didn't need to know how unfriendly.

"But Yahveh commanded that all farmers must leave the corners of each field unharvested, so we went gleaning. We didn't know Boaz was a distant relative of Naomi's. He made sure no one bothered us and left generous corners of his fields for gleaners, so we stayed there through the barley and wheat harvests."

Arielle went on to describe Naomi's plan to find Ruth a husband.

"I appreciate that Naomi wanted the best for our Ruth," Hadad said. "But the way it happened terrifies me. It could all have gone so wrong."

"We were worried too but Naomi knew that Boaz is a true follower of Yahveh. She also knew that there was provision in Yahveh's law which meant Boaz was responsible to do something for a widow within his family network. The only potential problem was that he wasn't the closest relative."

Arielle went on to describe Boaz's wisdom in ensuring that the other relative gave up his claim.

"This Boaz sounds like a good man," Hadad said.

"The best," Enoch said. "I have worked for him all my life and would never leave. He is exacting in his standards, which is why the farm is so prosperous, but he works alongside us and is generous once the work is done."

"And the son?" Laka asked.

"His name is Obed and he is a delight," Arielle said. "Boaz never expected to have a son and he spends every moment he can with him. Already Obed goes to the fields, carried on his father's shoulders. They would love for you to visit them."

Just talking about the family made Arielle's chest ache, but oh, Ruth would be thrilled that her family now had news of her.

"Hadad, do you think we could go and visit them?" Laka asked.

"We will talk about it later," Hadad said. "I don't think we could go and then return at this time. We are already under enough suspicion of being Yahveh sympathizers."

Was Ruth's family thinking of leaving, or was Arielle reading too much into Hadad's words? *Yahveh, give us opportunities to tell more of you to these people you created. You want them to know and worship you.*

"How long are you planning to stay in Moab?" Laka asked. "Not that we are wanting you to leave, of course."

"We don't really know," Arielle said. She was beginning to wonder if they'd be able to share any stories in the current situation. "Is it safe to be outside?"

"It is safe enough as long as you don't say anything against Chemosh, the temple, or the priests. You know." Laka laughed nervously. "No proclaiming Yahveh on the street corners."

That had been one of the ways Arielle had planned to introduce Yahveh to people. How was she to get a hearing otherwise? She couldn't stay within these walls all the time. Obviously, she and Enoch were going to have to do some praying. They would start after this meal. They would pray for Ruth's family and for Orpah's, and for opportunities to speak of Yahveh.

"What were you intending to do while you are here?" Hadad asked.

Arielle swallowed. How much should she say? If Ruth's parents cared to keep in favor with the temple, then turning her over to the priests would be an excellent way to do so. Her heart was pounding in her chest and she glanced at Enoch. He bowed his head to indicate that he was praying for her.

Yahveh, give me wisdom.

Arielle rubbed her sweaty palms on her tunic. "You will remember Orpah left with us for Bethlehem but returned after a few days."

Hadad and Laka nodded. "We wondered why."

"We were near the Arnon Gorge when Naomi talked seriously to both Ruth and Orpah. She reminded them that she didn't have any other sons for them to marry. Even if she birthed other sons immediately, they'd be far too young for Ruth or Orpah. Naomi suggested they both return to Moab and find someone else to marry."

"Orpah came back but Ruth didn't," Hadad said.

Arielle didn't know how much Ruth had talked with her parents about the things of Yahveh. *Yahveh, give me wisdom.* "Do you know why Ruth continued on with Naomi?"

Hadad looked across at Laka. "We don't know for certain, but I suspect it is because she wanted to follow Yahveh and she knew that would be almost impossible here."

The tension went out of Arielle's shoulders. "Ruth said to Naomi, 'Your people will become my people. Your god will become mine.'"

"Ruth was interested in Yahveh from the moment she got to know Naomi and her family," Laka said quietly, making sure her voice didn't carry beyond the room they were in.

"Did that interest concern you?"

Laka looked at her husband and he shook his head. "We would not have allowed our daughter to marry Mahlon if we had been concerned." He lowered his voice. "We have not followed him for many years." He gestured towards the temple as though afraid to even mention the name of Chemosh. "We were happy to follow no god, but—"

"But we wish Ruth and Naomi had told us more before they left," Laka finished.

Arielle's joy burst out in a broad smile. *Thank you, thank you, Yahveh. You've led us to people who are seeking you.*

"You asked why we had come," Arielle said. "We have come to find people like you and to tell the stories of Yahveh so you can meet the One both Ruth and I have met."

"When do we start?" Hadad asked.

"As soon as I can unload something from the panniers," Enoch said, getting to his feet. "Arielle has a great way to help you remember the stories."

CHAPTER THIRTY-SIX

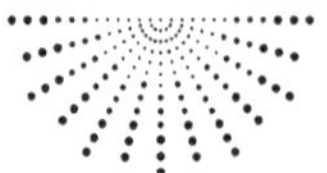

Arielle sorted through her pile of clay plaques and put them in order. Telling the stories in order would help Ruth's family remember them.

"What were you two discussing when Enoch left to bring the clay tiles?" Arielle asked.

"We were discussing if we should ask anyone else to hear the stories," Hadad said. "But we think it is better that we listen first, then tell the others."

"I was going to suggest we do one story each day but go over it multiple times so you are able to tell others," Arielle said. "That's how I learned them."

Whatever happened, Arielle wanted to not only tell the stories but to leave as many people behind in Moab who could pass the stories onto others.

Arielle lifted the first tile and gave it to Hadad and Laka.

"Is this about Yahveh creating our world?" Laka asked. "Ruth told us this story. She was so excited when Elimelech told her Yahveh was the one who made everything."

And now Arielle was telling the same story. One person after another in a long rope of communication. Yahveh was making sure that people of all nations were left with a storyteller, a testimony to his greatness and holiness. It was both a privilege and somewhat sobering to be one of those in the rope of those giving testimony. *Yahveh, help me be faithful.*

Arielle took back the tile and placed it on the edge of the carpet. "In the beginning Yahveh created the heavens and the earth. Now the earth was dark and formless and Yahveh's spirit hovered over the waters ..."

Arielle never got tired of telling the stories. This particular story had a rhythm like good music. It was tempting to tell the story and not think about it, but she refused to let herself disengage from the story for it was a story where Yahveh burst into action. "Let there be ... and it was good."

She finished the account.

Hadad leaned forward. "Can we ask questions?"

"Can you wait until we've gone through the story a few more times?" Arielle asked. "That will help the details sink in and probably mean you have even more questions."

"I'll wait," Hadad said.

Arielle taught them the repeated phrase. "And Yahveh saw that it was good and there was evening and morning on the first day." After hearing the full story for a second time, she got them to practice telling alternate days, then to reverse the next time. By the end of the fourth time, they were already telling the story quite accurately.

Arielle looked at Hadad and Laka. "I won't make you wait any longer. What are your questions?"

Hadad looked at Laka. "You always say I have too many questions."

Laka smiled. "The problem is that so many of your questions are unanswerable."

"I always wanted to know where our lands came from. The

legends we are told are simply foolish. That Yahveh created them makes much more sense than believing they come about because of fighting between monsters of the deep and sky." He turned to Arielle. "The story said the first thing Yahveh created was light. Why do you think that was?"

"I don't know," Arielle said. Naomi had taught her it was much better to admit she didn't know than to make up some answer. "Do you have any ideas?"

Hadad looked thoughtful. "Maybe it is because we all fear the night and what is hidden, so Yahveh not only makes light first but separates it from the darkness." He frowned. "It is as though he controls the darkness and restricts it to its proper place. He is the source of light. By light, we not only see but all living things grow."

"You have always loved the dawn," Laka said. "Now you will keep thinking about its meaning."

"It seems strange that Yahveh first creates light but doesn't create the sun, moon, and stars until much later," Hadad said.

Arielle had considered the same question but had never come up with a good answer.

"I'll think about why that might be," Hadad said. "There must be a reason, for Yahveh is a god of order … unlike the gods in our legends or the Babylonian myths."

It looked like Enoch was enjoying Hadad's questions as much as she was. Arielle was just about to ask a question when Hadad spoke again. "And why does Yahveh rest? He doesn't strike me as a god who needs to rest. Not if he can create plants and animals and the sun and moon just by speaking."

"He might not need rest, but we certainly do." Laka prodded her husband's belly. "You like to have a long sleep on a hot day."

He laughed. "Perhaps that is why Yahveh rested. He knew we needed it, so he set aside one day as special. I remember that Naomi and Elimelech always rested from sunset on the sixth day until the following sunset. They once invited us over for the special meal on that day."

Arielle had forgotten about that. Thinking back, she did remember the excitement of Hadad and Laka visiting. Orpah's parents had been invited too, but they had refused. Perhaps, even then, they'd feared an association with Elimelech's family. If so, why had they consented to Orpah marrying Kilion? How had that come about?

"I have a question," Laka said. "Why did Yahveh mostly create by speaking but then made A'dam out of earth and Havah out of A'dam's rib?"

"That is a very good question indeed." Hadad said. "Why are people made differently from all the plants and animals? I will have to think hard about this question of yours, for I doubt Arielle knows the answer."

Arielle shook her head. "I do not, but I do know Yahveh considers us higher than the animals for he says we are to both name them and rule over them."

"And we alone are made in Yahveh's image, whatever that means," Hadad said.

Enoch leaned forward. "I have thought much about that."

"And what conclusion have you come to?" Hadad asked.

"I turned the question around," Enoch answered. "I asked myself 'How are people different from animals?'"

Hadad stroked his beard. "Yes, I see how that helps. People communicate." He paused. "Animals can communicate pain or danger, but they do not have a conversation such as we are having."

"They cannot learn a new language," Laka said.

"Or plan or make clothing or furniture," Enoch added. "Maybe that is part of Yahveh's image, that we can create even though we do it with our hands and not by simply speaking."

"I am sure I will have more questions," Hadad said. "First, I want to see if I can tell the story. I want to tell it to my son. He can decide if he wants his wife to hear it."

"What about the children," Laka asked.

"No, we will not tell them yet. Children love to chatter and these are not the days for idle chatter."

Arielle swallowed. Within the safe walls of this home she'd forgotten that Yahveh's name might provoke anger in the streets beyond. *Yahveh, protect us.*

CHAPTER THIRTY-SEVEN

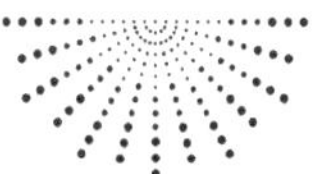

"*A*rielle, are you ready for a walk?" Enoch asked.

She and Enoch had been going for a walk each morning. They avoided walking towards the main temple and usually left the city and went towards the ravine with the pool of water. The place reminded Arielle of Mahlon and Kilion. Her heart still ached at the memory of them, but somehow she felt close to them in the ravine.

Arielle put on her veil and wrapped her cloak around herself to ward off the chilly morning air. "I'm ready."

They slipped out of the gate of Hadad's home and headed for one of the city's side gates. At this time in the morning, they only encountered merchants bringing in their produce from the fields outside the city walls. They paused, pressed against the wall of someone's home to allow a flock of bleating sheep to pass. The guard took no notice of them, as he only asked people's business as they entered.

Outside, the sky was awash with streaks of palest pink. A late bat flew towards wherever it hid from the sun's heat.

Arielle waited until they were out of earshot of any of the

townspeople. "Isn't it exciting to see the family's interest in the stories?"

"Boaz and Ruth have been praying for them ever since they were married." Enoch slowed his pace to match Arielle's.

"I know, but they've also prayed for Orpah and her family and we haven't heard anything from them since we arrived."

"We will simply keep praying," Enoch said.

One of the reasons they came out to the pool was so they could pray. Enoch reminded her every morning that Ruth, Boaz, and Naomi would also start their day with prayer. It was strange to think that over in the direction the sun set, Ruth, Naomi, Boaz, and little Obed were still living and working on the outskirts of Bethlehem. It felt so very far away and yet it wasn't that far for birds that flew.

"It still seems strange to pray and walk," Arielle said. Enoch had insisted it was safer not to stop somewhere and pray because they didn't want to draw attention to themselves. It was better to be viewed as merely walking out to the edge of the ravine and back.

"It's strange to me too," Enoch said. "But it's this way or not at all, and we both need the strength that comes when we pray." He kept walking. "Yahveh, Lord of all. We praise you for the beauty of the sky this morning. For the breeze that allowed us to sleep." He prayed on mentioning the trees and creatures around them.

Then Arielle prayed. "Thank you for the open hearts of Hadad and Laka and their sons and daughters-in-law."

Six adults were now listening and learning the stories. Each was also praying about who else might be interested in the stories.

"Adonai, we know the women are frightened that their husbands might get in trouble for passing on the stories. Please protect each one and guide them to people whose hearts are eager to learn about you."

They took turns praying for all those back in Bethlehem, and for the believers praying between Bethlehem and Shiloh and across in

Hebron and wherever Reuel and his family had traveled. It warmed Arielle to think of those faithful points of light amongst the darkness of those who ignored or rejected Yahveh. *May there always be faithful ones.*

"Do you think we're doing the right thing by only telling stories to Hadad and his family?" Arielle asked.

"I do," Enoch said. "I have not sensed that Yahveh wants us to venture out too far."

"Fear must not be the determining factor," Arielle said. "There are so many others who need to hear."

"Let us ask Yahveh to bring us other opportunities," Enoch said. "And let's also pray for the merchants we traveled with."

Dek's friend had assured them that he would take the other merchant to visit Dek and Rahel the next time they visited Heshbon. The rowdy merchant had seemed scary at first but had turned out to be the most interested in all Arielle said. It seemed she couldn't predict who would be open and who would close themselves off from Yahveh.

By the time they'd prayed for these things, they'd reached the edge of the ravine. The sun wasn't high enough to penetrate the shade below. Did anyone now fish in the waters?

"Will you take a turn and tell the first of the Avraham and Sarai stories?" Arielle asked.

"I knew you'd ask me one day," Enoch said. "I guess now is as good a time as any to start telling them. You'll need to help me with the bits I forget."

"Of course I will," Arielle said. "Naomi helped me a lot when I started."

"Hadad is really making me think."

Arielle chuckled. "You're not the only one. He asks questions I haven't even considered before."

"That is an advantage of telling people who have never heard anything about Yahveh. They make unexpected comments and connections and ask unusual questions. I'm finding it rather stimulating."

He wasn't the only one. It had been wise of Boaz to send Enoch. Not only was he a big help, but his presence allowed her to walk out beyond the city walls in safety. It was also helping him get some distance from his grief after the death of his wife and see that life could still be interesting and full of worthwhile things.

Already heat was radiating off the rocks around them.

"Do you think things are as dangerous as Hadad and Laka tell us?" Arielle asked, wiping the perspiration off her forehead.

"I do. I overheard Hadad discussing it with his sons. He said they must make the choice to hear the stories for their own households because there could be serious consequences." Enoch turned to make sure there was no one else around before continuing. "There is a young firebrand of a priest who is making it his mission to promote Chemosh and eliminate any opposition."

"Is he promoting Chemosh or is it a desire for his own power?" The image of the priest that Arielle had had the misfortune to meet flashed into her mind.

"I think man's ambition is often the root of our problems, and we men often use religion to bolster our own power."

"Let's hope we don't get in the way."

"Yahveh will always be in the way of peoples' ambitions," Enoch said with a sigh. "If we keep proclaiming him, we will offend someone eventually."

That was what Arielle was afraid of. Ever since A'dam and Havah, people had been striving to be in charge and in every generation there were new people who thought they were pharaohs. She was only one woman, and it was hard not to tremble at what could happen. She swallowed and thought back to her second dream. In it, Yahveh had promised to be with her no matter what. That was a promise she could hold on to.

"You don't have to stay with me, you know," Arielle said. "You have safely delivered me here."

"I have no intention of leaving," Enoch said. "I would never forgive myself if I left and you were harmed."

"Thank you for staying. I appreciate having another believer here. Two can work together and encourage one another."

By common agreement, they didn't talk as they approached the city gate. It was now wide open, and a noisy crowd of people and carts and livestock being driven to market would have made talking difficult anyway.

The sun baked the back of Arielle's head as they stood to one side, waiting for the crowd to clear. Finally, a flock of sheep and goats passed through the gate and their way was clear. Treading gingerly around the abundant evidence of the animals passing, they entered and walked back the way they'd come.

Off to one side a heavily veiled woman headed towards them.

"Watch out!" Arielle exclaimed. The woman didn't seem to see them for she continued in a straight line. Seeing the woman wasn't going to deviate from her path, Arielle stepped back. The woman veered closer. Just as it seemed she would collide with Arielle, she spoke.

"Meet me at my parents' place."

Orpah! They hadn't heard anything from her, which had seemed unusual, as she had been a friendly woman.

Orpah had stooped to pretend to pick something up. As she straightened, she murmured. "Go a roundabout route."

Arielle's heart thumped in her chest. Why the secrecy? Was something seriously wrong or did Orpah just want to catch up? Her methods seemed a little clandestine for a mere conversation. Arielle touched Enoch's arm and directed him away from their original route.

CHAPTER THIRTY-EIGHT

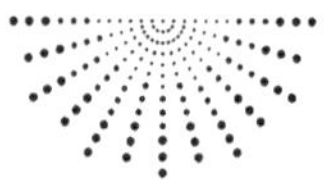

$\mathcal{A}$rielle obeyed Orpah's instructions, which meant it took Arielle and Enoch a considerable time to reach Orpah's parents' place. They'd had to work their way around the outskirts of the town because Arielle also wanted to avoid the central temple area.

They must have been expected, because the door opened before Arielle had even knocked a second time. They were ushered through the darker entrance into the blaze of sunshine in the court-yard. Orpah was just removing her veil. She came over and hugged Arielle.

"You've changed."

Arielle laughed. "It happens."

"I didn't just mean in maturity," Orpah said. "You seem more at peace."

"I am," Arielle said. "I know where I belong."

"And it is no longer here?"

Arielle shook her head. "It is with anyone who truly knows Yahveh."

Orpah glanced over her shoulder and then leaned forward. "It's best not to mention that name here," she said quietly.

A sweat broke out on Arielle's forehead. Mentioning Yahveh's name was why they were here.

Orpah looked around and then indicated the seating area. "I can't stay long, but we have time to sit."

No one came to offer them the usual refreshments.

"My husband isn't keen on me visiting my family," Orpah said. "He tries to forget I was married before. The mere fact that my parents allowed me to marry a foreigner makes him suspicious of them."

"Why have things changed since we left?" Arielle asked, keeping her voice low.

"In the past, most of the priests were fairly casual about such matters as what religion those around them follow." She grimaced. "But that's no longer the case."

"We've heard about the new priest," Enoch said.

"My husband has changed because the priest has been his friend since childhood. The priest singled him out and my husband was flattered. Now I think he is afraid to do anything but be fully committed to Chemosh."

"Do you think he really is fully committed?" Arielle asked.

Orpah sighed. "I do not know, for he no longer shares his heart with me. I distract myself by devoting myself to my children."

"Ima will be thrilled to hear you are now a mother."

"I have two children, a son and a daughter. Sometimes I regret not going with you all, but I cannot regret having them." She took Arielle's hand. "Now tell me all the news."

This might be the only chance Arielle had to talk to Orpah. *Help me to say things that are worthwhile.*

"It took us another week to travel to Ima's hometown after we left you," Arielle said. "We found her house full of pigeons and over-grown with weeds."

She was able to tell of their battle with the birds and weeds in a way that made Orpah laugh, but Arielle made sure to include her personal experience following Yahveh.

"So Ruth helped you understand Yahveh," Orpah asked. "I can't say I am surprised. Ruth was close to her family, but she was still willing to give them up to follow Yahveh."

"Do you ever regret staying here?" Arielle asked.

"What use is regret?" Orpah asked. "I made a decision, and I have to live with it. I just wish … but I can't change my husband back to the man I married."

"We will be praying for you," Arielle said. "We already have."

Orpah said nothing but she reached out and squeezed Arielle's hand. It must be hard being married to someone who was chasing after Chemosh, for those who worshiped Chemosh became like him. Arielle shivered. Becoming like Chemosh meant growing to love his darkness. She did not envy Orpah. Better to never marry than to marry someone who didn't follow Yahveh.

"And Ruth, is she still looking after Ima?" Orpah asked.

"And her husband and young son." Arielle grinned. "Let me tell you how Yahveh blessed her."

Orpah listened with rapt attention as Arielle spoke.

"Send Ruth my love, and Ima too. I often think of you all and wonder whether you found what you sought."

"They found what they sought and I found what I didn't know I was seeking."

"Now you're speaking in riddles," Orpah said. "I don't recall you doing that before."

"I thought I was looking for my birth family, but I was searching for the wrong family," Arielle said. "'When I chose to follow Yahveh, I didn't know I would finally feel loved and accepted. That I'd finally feel like I belonged." Warmth filled her heart. "As a bonus, I found I had many families." She indicated Enoch with her chin.

"Even Enoch now feels like my family, because anyone who follows Yahveh is family and he has more followers than I realized."

"There won't be any here," Orpah said.

Arielle smiled. "I have discovered Yahveh has followers in many places we do not expect."

"If the priest discovers them, they will be expelled from Moab." Orpah shuddered. "Or worse."

"But Yahveh will ultimately win, because no one can live forever or control people's thoughts," Enoch said.

"The priest tries," Orpah said. "He tries, and people are too afraid to resist."

Arielle leaned forward. "Fear will not rule forever."

"I cannot see ahead to a day without it."

"Dear sister, we will be praying."

"Thank you."

Orpah's words were simple but Arielle sensed they held far more meaning. Orpah was surrounded by darkness, which made it all too easy to be afraid. She had not learned to cling to the One who brought light.

Orpah glanced at the sun. "I must go. My husband knows I still visit my family, but they are no longer acceptable to him and he doesn't want me to do things that might affect his reputation."

"Dear sister, do not forget the stories you heard from Kilion and Elimelech. Knowing Yahveh brings hope and peace in dark places."

"I doubt he can bring light into our darkness."

"Yahveh can bring hope into any darkness, for he is light and love and he knows you better than you do yourself."

Orpah got to her feet and kissed Arielle. "I wish I could believe that."

She turned to Enoch. "Wait for a while before leaving, and make sure you take a roundabout route back to where you're staying."

Did Orpah know where they were staying, or was she simply being cautious in case they were overheard?

Orpah slipped out the gate and Arielle sighed. She knew how she'd spend the waiting time. Orpah needed prayer and Arielle bowed her head to concentrate. *Save Orpah and her family. Help her husband flee the dark ways of Chemosh. May the priest be silenced and lose his reputation and powers of persuasion.*

CHAPTER THIRTY-NINE

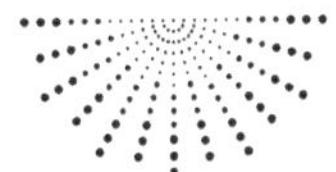

Some time later, Enoch had completed the Avraham stories and Arielle was well into the stories of Iztchak, Yacov, and Yosef. Every day the discussion was more lively as the listeners probed beneath the surface of the words. It was all so different from what Arielle had been expecting. She'd expected to be standing on street corners, telling stories to many, yet here they were, telling the stories to only six listeners.

It seemed so small a start. So inconsequential, but Enoch had reminded her that morning that Yahveh delighted in choosing weak things to achieve his work: a childless couple, a shepherd in the desert far away from his own people, or the people who had adopted him. If Yahveh wanted them to plant seeds, they'd continue to trust him to water them and bring the harvest.

The eldest grandchild put her head into the room. "Excuse me. There is a woman asking for Miss Arielle. At least, I assume that is who she is asking for as she doesn't seem to know her name."

Arielle's gut tightened. Who knew she was here? She couldn't think of anyone.

"I doubt a woman poses any danger," Enoch said in an undertone.

"I'm sure you're right, but I can't think of who it might be," Arielle said.

Enoch clambered up stiffly from the carpet. "I'll come with you, just in case."

Arielle nodded and got to her feet.

"We'll discuss things while you're gone," Hadad said.

He had been the first to lead the discussion, but already they were all taking turns. The women had been a little slower, but once they discovered how easy it was to lead, they'd been willing.

Arielle followed Enoch and Hadad's granddaughter out of the room. She put on some slippers and they walked into the courtyard. A veiled woman was standing with her back to them but she turned at their approach. Was it Orpah? Surely Orpah would have sent in her name or been recognized.

The woman lowered the veil although still only her eyes were showing. She took no notice of Enoch but stared at Arielle as though searching for something. Arielle was sure she didn't know the woman, but there was something familiar about her eyes.

Taking a deep breath, Arielle said. "I am Arielle. How can I help you?"

"Are you the adopted daughter of Naomi the Israelite?" the woman asked.

"I am," Arielle said, more confused than ever. "Why do you want to know?"

The woman ignored Arielle's question. "And were you adopted by her as a new baby?"

"I was. Naomi found me crying on her doorstep." Tension gripped Arielle's shoulders. No child should be abandoned in such a way.

The woman reached out a hand and then withdrew it. "I knew she could be trusted to take care of you."

Arielle's eyes widened and her heart pounded in her ears. Surely this was not … Surely this was not her mother?

She swallowed. "Are you saying you know me?"

"Know you?" The woman's voice rose. "I bore you. You are flesh of my flesh."

"Then why did you abandon me?" Arielle's voice grated in her own ears. "Why would you leave me on a stranger's doorstep?"

"Do you think I wanted to put you there?" the woman claiming to be her mother asked. "I put you there because it was the safest place I could think of."

"Safe? It wasn't safe to leave me on the doorstep."

"Why do you think I made you cry and waited until Naomi found you and took you inside? I was trying to do the best for you."

"Surely the best for a child is to be with its mother," Arielle said, an ache in her belly.

The woman hung her head. "That is usually the case, but our family was not a safe place. Not for me and not for my children. I did the best I could, but I could not protect the children from beatings."

Sourness burned up Arielle's throat.

"When my husband knew that I had borne another girl, he told me to get rid of you."

Arielle wrapped her arms around her waist.

"He meant me to take you to the temple, but—" the woman's voice quavered. "I could never do that."

Maybe Arielle had been too quick to judge. At least this woman could not stomach sacrificing her to Chemosh.

"I had seen Elimelech with Naomi and knew he loved her and his children. I knew they followed Yahveh and Yahveh hates child sacrifice and temple prostitution. I believed they would raise you as their own, for their god protects the weak."

"How did you hear about Yahveh?" Arielle asked.

"I heard the stories of what he did in Egypt and about Mosheh and Yehoshua when I was a child. My grandfather loved those stories."

Joy flooded through Arielle. "So did your grandfather know Yahveh?"

The woman put her head to one side. "Can anyone truly know so great a god? Grandfather certainly loved the Yahveh of the stories."

"And you? What do you think of Yahveh?"

"I have not been allowed to think for many long years. Your father did not want a thinking wife."

"Yet you did think," Enoch said. "And you saved your daughter."

"I did, didn't I? And it looks like I made the right choice. You have had a better life than your sisters."

"How many sisters do I have?" And did she have any brothers?

Arielle's mother counted them off on her fingers. One, two, three, four, five. "They're all married with children of their own."

This morning Arielle hadn't known of any of this family and suddenly it was expanding moment by moment.

"And does my f—" She couldn't quite bring herself to use the word "Father." "Does your husband know where you are now?"

She shook her head. "I don't need to worry about him anymore. He got into a drunken rage a moon ago and reached out to strike me, but he was struck down. He died in moments."

So she had come too late to meet her father. She must not miss the chance to get to know her mother.

"Can you stay?" Arielle asked.

Behind her mother's back Enoch held his hand up as though to halt her invitation and pointed to a side room. Did he want to talk with her?

"Excuse me for a moment," Arielle said. "My friend wants to talk to me."

She followed Enoch to where he had indicated. He waited until she was next to him before asking, "Are you sure it is wise to ask her to join the others?"

"I don't believe she would do anything to harm me."

"Not intentionally maybe but having extra people come to this house is a risk Hadad and Laka might not be willing to take. It is their home. They must make the decision."

He was right—it was not her decision to make. "We will discuss it with them and let them decide if she can join us or not. Can I ask her to return tomorrow?"

"That should be alright. If it isn't, I will wait outside and arrange for us to meet her somewhere else. Is that agreeable to you?"

Arielle nodded. "I will ask her to come again tomorrow."

Enoch returned to their hosts, and Arielle went back into the courtyard. She walked over to where her mother was waiting under a gnarled olive tree. Her mother! She'd never really expected to see her in the flesh.

"Thank you for coming. Would you be able to come back again tomorrow? That will give us time to absorb all you have revealed."

Her mother nodded. "I understand much of what I have said will be a shock, but I am thankful to be able to see you again. I saw you sometimes as a child, but it was always just a glimpse from a distance."

And Arielle had never known that the mother she longed to know had been there, watching and hoping that she was happy and well looked after.

Arielle escorted her mother towards the outer gate. Her mother gave a sudden yelp and leaned down to slap at an ant that had fastened itself on her foot. The veil that had covered her face swung aside and Arielle gasped.

"I am sorry that my scars shock you," her mother said.

"It is not your face that shocks me, but that I have seen you before."

"What do you mean? You have never seen my scars. They were

inflicted when your father found out what I'd done in giving you to Naomi."

She'd been angry at her mother, but here was evidence that her mother had protected her at great cost.

"I have not seen you in the flesh before," Arielle said, her hands clammy. "I have seen your face in a dream. A woman with your face called for me to return to Moab."

"This is a strange thing," Arielle's mother said.

"Strange and wonderful," Arielle said. "We have much to think about, and I look forward to seeing you tomorrow."

Her mother had her hand on the gate but she swung round and cupped Arielle's chin in her hand. "I too will look forward to tomorrow. I have dreamed of this day for far too long."

She opened the gate and quickly went through it. Arielle closed the gate and leaned against it.

She had never expected the woman in the dream to be a real woman, let alone her own mother. A mother scarred by the man she had called husband. A man completely unworthy of the name. A man who was now beyond any response Arielle could make. She wasn't sure if that was a relief or a frustration.

Arielle pushed herself back from the gate. She must talk to Hadad and Laka and let them know of the dream that had brought her to them. A dream that might lead to transformed lives.

CHAPTER FORTY

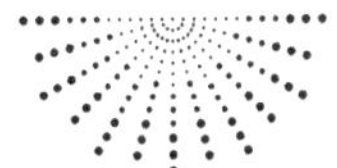

"Stick close," Arielle said to Enoch.

It wasn't because she needed Enoch nearby, more that he had the kind of face that disappeared in a crowd. The other problem was that her veil severely limited her view. She didn't want to lose him, although it might not matter as they both had instructions on how to reach her mother's house.

Arielle had barely slept all night. Today she was going to meet more of her family. Her mother had joined the story times and discussions at Hadad and Laka's home. However, when she said she'd love some of Arielle's siblings to hear them too, Hadad and Laka had looked uncomfortable. After they'd talked about the situation, Arielle had suggested it might be better to have two separate groups. Fewer people coming in and out of Hadad's house would attract less attention.

Two Israelite merchants had been beaten and expelled from the town a few days ago, and that morning Laka had been spat on in the market and called an "Israelite lover." Arielle had overheard Laka and Hadad discussing whether now might be the best time to go to Bethlehem to visit Ruth.

"Not that way," Enoch murmured close by.

Arielle had to turn her head all the way to the right to see which way he was indicating.

"Down here," Enoch said as he ducked into a lane opposite the ancient tree with its well-used shrine at the base they'd been told to watch for.

They knocked on the fifth gate down the lane, as instructed. Arielle's mother must have been waiting right inside, because the gate opened immediately and she stood back to let Arielle and Enoch enter. Once the gate was closed, Arielle removed the veil and attempted to lift the hair now plastered to her head with sweat. She wanted to look her best to meet her sisters. Her mother had said they were looking forward to meeting her but she wasn't depending on that. It was just as likely that at least one of them would resent the arrival of another sibling, not realizing she had no desire to take anything that was theirs.

Not that there looked like much to take, for the house was unusually bare.

"Sorry there is so little to make you feel welcome." Arielle's mother flushed, as though she'd guessed Arielle's thoughts. "My husband took anything that wasn't tied down."

To pay for his drinking habit, or for some other reason? Arielle wasn't going to humiliate her mother by asking further questions. One thing that had changed since the first time they'd met was that her mother no longer bothered to hide her scars. Scars that were from the burning hot soup Arielle's father had flung at his wife when he heard she'd disobeyed him and taken Arielle to Naomi and not the temple. Scars that spoke of love and sacrifice.

Arielle's father might not be someone to be proud of, but Arielle had already moved her mother to tears by telling her how proud she was to be her daughter.

Enoch had stayed outside in the courtyard to wait until after she'd met her siblings, although only the eldest and third sisters had come.

"The others weren't able to come at short notice," her mother said.

Or they were waiting to hear what the other two reported. Arielle's hands were clammy but she followed her mother inside to a room that at least had a carpet on the floor. Her sisters rose from their seats on the floor.

"Arielle, this is your eldest sister, Avith, and your third sister, Shuma," Arielle's mother said.

"I don't recall the name Arielle," Avith said.

"I wasn't allowed to name her. Arielle must be the name Naomi chose."

"And I'm sorry but I don't remember you at all," Shuma said.

"I remember your birth but father said you had died. Like a fool, I believed him," Avith said. "I hadn't yet learned he only spoke the truth if he benefitted from it."

The light in the room was enough for Arielle to see the strain lines on her sisters' faces. According to her mother, all of her daughters had married early to get away from this household.

Arielle studied their faces. "Looks like you and I have similar eyes," she said to Avith.

"And you and Shuma have the same chin," her eldest sister said. "Both stubborn, by the looks of it."

"Determined would be a nicer way to say it," said their mother. "I wish I'd had more of your determination."

Avith snorted. "Then you might not have put up with Father for so long."

Arielle's mother touched her arm. "I'll fetch some refreshments. Why don't you tell each other about your families?"

Once they were alone, Arielle found herself a place on the carpet and then looked at the other two. "Who is going to go first?"

"I'm the eldest, so I will." Avith placed a cushion behind her back and leaned against the wall. "I married soon after you were born. We have seven children. Three sons and four daughters. The eldest two are already married."

There were so many more family members than Arielle had ever imagined. Would she even be able to meet them all?

"I only have five children and they're younger," Shuma said.

"I'm not married as yet and so I don't have any children," Arielle said.

"Will Naomi arrange a marriage for you?" the eldest sister asked.

Arielle nodded. "If we can find a suitable husband."

"Are husbands scarce in Israel then?" Avith asked.

How could Arielle explain? Was it safe to talk with these sisters about Yahveh? *Yahveh, give me the wisdom to not say too much but also the courage to say what is needed.*

"We Moabites tend to think of all Israelites as followers of Yahveh ..." Arielle's voice trailed off as she saw the puzzled looks on her sisters' faces. She wasn't explaining herself very well. "I mean, many Israelites aren't really followers of Yahveh."

"Isn't that the same with many followers of Chemosh here?" the third sister asked.

Yahveh, give me courage.

"Many people in Israel claim to be followers of Yahveh, but their hearts are far from him."

Avith crooked her eyebrow in just the way that Arielle always did. *Get to the point, Arielle!* She took a deep breath.

"Shortly after I moved to Bethlehem, I decided to follow Yahveh."

Her sisters looked both unsurprised by her news and also indifferent. That hurt, because she wanted them to be curious and to ask questions which would allow her to say more.

"Ruth, who was married to one of Naomi's sons who died, later married a faithful follower of Yahveh. If I'm to marry, I want the same."

Avith looked thoughtful. "Just make sure he is not too fanatical. Fanatical men are putting a lot of pressure on people here."

Loving Yahveh with all her heart, soul, and mind was totally different from being fanatical about Chemosh, but they probably wouldn't see any difference. They thought of Chemosh as real and powerful and didn't know his worship allowed evil men control over people. *Yahveh, save them.*

Avith stood up. "I must get to market before there's nothing left."

"And me," Shuma said, standing too. "Tell Ima we'll organize for the others to meet you."

Arielle walked them to the gate, then she and Enoch sat with her mother and drank some warmed goat milk.

"I'd hoped they'd be willing to hear stories too," Arielle said.

Her mother chuckled.

"What are you laughing about?" Arielle asked.

"You don't need to worry about them. I'm passing on the stories to both of them." She grinned. "But neither wants the other to know."

Enoch finished his drink and wiped his beard clean. "I've been thinking about the way we're doing things. Originally you hoped to be able to speak to larger groups at a time but the current situation makes that impossible." He looked at her. "How long do you think it will take to talk to everyone in this city?"

She stared at him. She hadn't thought that far ahead. She'd been happy that anyone was willing to listen. "A lifetime, I guess."

"It will take far more than that," Enoch said. "And this is just one city in Moab. There are hundreds more towns and villages."

Arielle's mother stared at the ground in front of them. "One person could never do the task, or even two or three."

Arielle sighed sadly. It had always seemed like a crazy idea.

"The only way," Enoch said. "Is to have many storytellers each telling the people they know."

He picked up a stick and sketched a figure. "This is you. You're telling your mother." He drew another figure below. "And she's telling your eldest and third sisters."

"And I'll try and tell the others," her mother said. "I worry that I don't know the stories well enough and might make mistakes."

"That's why we suggest people learn one story then tell others immediately." Enoch drew on the ground again. "This is Ruth's parents. They've enabled more of their family to hear. I heard Hadad say he told a story out in his fields to the man who helps him plow."

Yes, and Laka had told some to a woman she knew. It was exciting to think about this net of storytellers. So different from what Arielle had envisioned, where she'd take out a clay picture and people would gather to see what it was and she'd tell the story. She was barely using the clay tiles.

"I think it's working better without the clay tiles," Arielle said. "They worked well in Bethlehem because they led to questions and conversations. But if I insisted on using them here it would slow things down because I only have one set. They can't easily be shared."

"And they're much more obvious," Enoch said. "Here we're wanting no one to notice what is happening."

"Now we've reached the account of Mount Sinai with Ruth's parents, do you think you could start at the beginning with me?" her mother asked.

"Of course," Arielle said. "I'd be delighted."

Yahveh, help them to want to hear all the stories. Help them to recognize who you are and to choose to follow you for the rest of their lives.

CHAPTER FORTY-ONE

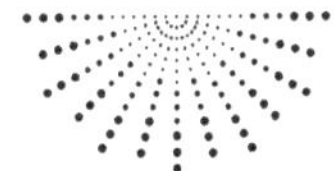

*T*wo moons later

Arielle and Enoch were on the way back from their usual morning walk and prayer time. "Why don't we go via my old home?" she asked.

She'd been thinking about visiting for days but wasn't sure if it was a good idea or not. She had many happy memories of the house. It was where she'd learned to cook and help around the house, and where she'd felt so secure. Secure until Elimelech, the source of her warm security, had died.

However, memories of the end of her time in the house were marked by the loss of all three of their menfolk and by how their neighbor had taken advantage of Naomi by not giving her a fair price. Yahveh would tell her to forgive. Maybe that was why she felt the urge to visit.

"You'll have to lead the way," Enoch said.

It took a while to get there as they wound through a series of back streets, but here it was, looking just as it always had.

"Do you think I could knock on the gate and ask to see into the courtyard?" Arielle asked.

"As long as the people who bought it are the kind to be helpful," Enoch said.

She thought it would be alright.

Naomi's best friend was sitting on a stool just outside her gate. Arielle went to greet her.

"Arielle, I'd know your voice anywhere, even if your face is mostly covered up. Let me see you," the older woman said.

Arielle uncovered her face. She'd put her veil back on when she left the lane.

"How are Naomi and the lovely Ruth?" the woman asked.

Arielle updated her on the family news.

"And you like it there?"

"I didn't at first," Arielle said. "But it is much easier now that we've got friends."

The old lady nodded. "It's always hard in a new place. I found it hard when I came here from Nebo after my marriage. I remember Naomi also found it hard here. We were all a bit wary of foreigners. When I saw she wasn't too much different from us, I became her friend."

"I remember your many gifts of food to our family. Ima appreciated your friendship. You were one of the reasons she found it hard to leave. She'll be delighted to hear you're still so well." Arielle glanced around to check there was no one nearby. "Do you remember the stories Ima told you?"

The old woman leaned closer. "They comfort me every day." She put her finger up to lips. "But shush, don't tell anyone."

"I follow him too," Arielle said in an undertone. "He makes all the difference in my life."

"Yes, please pray for me."

Arielle prayed right there, praising Yahveh that even in this little lane there was a point of light. If she could, she'd return and encourage this dear woman again.

After they'd finished praying, she went over and knocked on the gate of their old home. Her stomach felt like it was full of grasshoppers.

Footsteps crossed the courtyard and a little window in the gate was opened. The woman's eyes widened and she threw open the gate.

"Welcome!" she said.

Arielle took a step back. She hadn't expected such enthusiasm.

"Come in, come in," the woman said. "And sit a while."

Arielle couldn't back out now. She stepped into the courtyard which was achingly familiar. The tree that she'd fallen out of trying to follow the boys was taller now and promised a good harvest to come.

The woman insisted on giving them something to drink.

"How long are you here for?" the woman asked. "And where are you staying?"

"We're staying here and there. We're not sure how long for." This woman made her uncomfortable, there was no way Arielle would tell her where they were staying. As soon as possible, she stood and said they must be on their way.

"That was odd," Enoch said once they were outside. "She treated you like a long-lost relative."

Arielle agreed. The question was why. Why, in a city where everyone seemed wary, had she been given such a welcome?

* * *

They had not been back at Hadad and Laka's home long before someone knocked. Arielle was closest to the front gate. She covered her face again and opened the gate just enough to see who was outside.

"Figs," the veiled woman said as she held one up for Arielle to see.

"We don't need—"

The woman didn't give her a chance to finish but shoved the gate further open and slipped through the gap, closing it immediately behind her.

Arielle's heart pounded. What was going on?

"Are you Arielle?" the woman asked urgently.

"Who wants to know?" Arielle asked, still not sure whether she dared to reveal herself.

"It's me, Kozbi," the woman said, showing her face.

"Kozbi! What are you doing here and how did you find me?"

"Saving your life," Kozbi said, putting down her basket. "The priest isn't the only one looking for you."

Arielle was more and more confused. "What are you talking about?"

"I don't know what you did to that man, but once he discovered you and others had left for Bethlehem, he promised the new owner of your home a reward if any of you ever returned."

Arielle gasped. "But I went there—"

"Which was very, very foolish. Now he knows you're back, and it won't take long to find you. I'd asked the widow in the alley to let me know if you ever visited and I've come as fast as I could."

Yahveh, give me wisdom. What do you want us to do?

You've prayed for Kozbi, here she is. Speak to her. The thought was as clear as if Yahveh had spoken aloud.

"Kozbi, we will consider what you've said about the danger, but I must talk to the others."

"Don't delay. If I could guess where you'd stay, the priest will be able to do the same."

There was going to be no time to dance around, worrying how to open up the topic for which they'd come. *Yahveh, give me wisdom.*

Arielle took a deep breath. "I have been praying that I would find you."

"And I have been praying that somehow I could find out more about Yahveh," Kozbi said.

A wild joy coursed through Arielle. "More?"

"I vowed to never worship Chemosh again after Tozbi was killed, and I have kept my vow." Kozbi lowered her voice. "I remember you said Yahveh created our lands. Every day, I thank him for all the beauty."

If Kozbi was right, they had little time. *Help me, Yahveh.*

"I ask him for wisdom and I share my struggles. But I want more." Kozbi clutched Arielle's arm. "How do I find out more?"

"Can I come to your place?" Arielle asked.

"No. My husband would report you at once," Kozbi said. "And you shouldn't stay in Moab." She cocked her head to listen as though expecting heavy footsteps already. "It might already be too late."

Could Arielle risk telling her where to hear more stories? *Yahveh, I need wisdom. Protect those I love.* She had prayed for eager listeners every day since she'd known she would travel to Moab. She'd prayed for Kozbi, not sure how she could find her. How could Arielle now deny her an opportunity?

"I will tell you where I go to tell stories every day, but you must be careful. If I can't be there, the woman there knows enough to tell you more."

Yahveh, protect my mother and sisters.

"I will be careful. It's my life too."

Arielle told Kozbi how to find her mother's house and prayed that she'd be able to meet her there soon.

"I must go," Kozbi said. "My husband thinks I've gone out to buy these ripe figs and he knows I shouldn't take long."

She turned to envelop Arielle in a huge hug. "I am so glad to see you again." Kozbi murmured in her ear. "Yahveh has heard my prayers, and I no longer feel so alone."

"He sees you and he loves you," Arielle replied.

Kozbi picked up her basket and handed Arielle some figs. "So the neighbors think you bought some."

Then she refastened her veil and left.

Arielle needed to talk to Enoch. Was it time to leave?

* * *

Bang, bang, bang.

Someone else was now seeking entrance, and they were far more demanding than Kozbi had been only a short while ago. Fear clutched at Arielle's throat and she strove to control it. Loud knocking didn't mean someone was coming for her. It could so easily just be that someone was in trouble. Perhaps someone was in labor and needed Laka's help.

Bang, bang, bang, again.

"Alright, I'm coming," Hadad said.

Arielle could hear the slaps of Hadad's still unfastened sandals as he crossed the courtyard towards the gate. Then she heard the creak of the gate opening and the growling of men's voices. So it wasn't a woman in labor.

Arielle moved close to a window and strained her ears to listen.

"No, don't come in," Hadad said. "We don't need your feet tramping through the house and scaring the children. I'm sure our guest has done nothing wrong. She'll be happy to come and explain."

The fear returned with a surge. *Yahveh, help me.* With shaking hands, Arielle smoothed her hair and put on her veil.

"Arielle, are you there?" Hadad called.

"Just coming." She hated the wobble in her voice. *Yahveh, keep me calm.* It could be something simple. But she doubted it. She'd been introducing people to Yahveh in the center of Chemosh's kingdom. Chemosh was not a rival for her god, but there were people or powers behind the facade and they definitely wouldn't be happy at what she'd been doing.

As she came out into the light outside, blinking, Enoch joined her. Together, the three of them walked over to the gate. It was hard not to tremble at the sight of the men outside. They were a muscular, rough-looking trio. One held a spear and two held swords, as though they were expecting trouble. Arielle nearly laughed. It was ridiculous. She wasn't to be feared, and even Hadad's grandchildren had quickly spotted that Enoch was a gentle soul.

"Are you Arielle? The woman who used to live in the house once owned by Naomi and Elimelech of Bethlehem." The man's voice was menacing. Maybe she only imagined that because she was so afraid.

"I am," Arielle said.

"What need do you have to speak with Arielle?" Enoch asked.

"That is our boss's business," the man replied. "We don't question him so he doesn't ever need to question us."

Yahveh, give me courage.

The words of her dream came to mind immediately.

I will never leave you nor forsake you.

Arielle straightened her spine. Now was the time to remember the feeling that promise had given her. No matter what happened, those words were true.

"You must come with us," the man said.

"I'll come too," Enoch said.

The man with the spear took a step forward and used the spear to block Enoch's way. "No. The woman is the only one required."

"Her brother-in-law is an important man in Bethlehem, and he requested I stay by her side."

"Hear that, men," the leader sneered. "This man thinks we care about someone in far-off Bethlehem."

"It's alright," Arielle said out of the corner of her mouth, careful not to say Enoch's name. These people didn't need to know anything more about them. "I am not alone."

"No, she is not alone," the leader said. "We'll escort her to our boss with extra special care."

It wasn't what she had meant but Enoch would understand. They had talked several times about what to do if something like this happened. He was not to attempt to rescue her. Rescue belonged to Yahveh.

The leader took her arm and drew her forward. Two of the men moved behind and she followed the two in front. The route they took her kept away from all the main roads. Even with her sight restricted by her veil, she sensed where they were heading. Always moving towards the center like a spider in a web. Her stomach was paining and she clenched her hand in a fist. In the several moons since she'd arrived back in Moab, she'd always avoided going anywhere near the main temple.

No one had ever named the fanatic priest who ruled this city with a grip of fear nor had they shared details of his background. *Don't let him be the one.* Arielle shivered, remembering the intense malevolence of the priest she'd encountered here before.

The men continued marching forward, deeper and deeper into the rotten heart of Ar. Arielle bit back her gasp as the building she had dreaded appeared before her, the main temple of Chemosh, still squatting like an obese toad and still belching out the smoke from its sacrifices.

The men turned into a dark alley. Before she could sneak a last look at Yahveh's sky, they were swallowed by a dark doorway. The men halted and she ran into the back of the leader.

"Pay more attention, woman," he growled.

Someone struck a spark and lit the torch waiting in a bracket on the wall. The torch spluttered and caught, and Arielle sneezed as the smell of burning oil permeated the darkness. Once the torch was burning brightly, they set off down a series of passages. Passages she had probably already traveled when slung over her kidnapper's shoulder. It was stifling under her veil and her vision was restricted to what was directly in front of her.

Oh Yahveh, be my light, for I am afraid.

Even as she prayed, she remembered the dream and being cradled in Yahveh's hands. He was here, even here.

She stumbled down some stairs and along a passage to a closed door. The leader passed the torch back to one of the men behind her then knocked twice, once, then twice again. A code?

A muffled, "Come in," came from the room.

The leader pushed open the door, grasped her arm, and pulled her into the room. Fear gripped her by the throat.

It was him.

The poisonous spider himself.

He'd aged more than she'd expected, but his eyes still looked as flat and dead as they had when she'd last seen him. He smiled and the torchlight glittered on the few teeth he had left. She clamped her jaw tight to stop her teeth chattering. She would not show fear before this man. He'd enjoy it too much.

"You may leave us," the priest said.

The leader backed out of the room and closed the door behind him with a clang. The priest went over to it and shut the bolts. "There will be no interruptions this time," he said grimly.

It was difficult to breathe in this enclosed space full of menace. The sweat trickled between her shoulder blades.

Yahveh, you are with me. You will never forsake me. I cling to you.

"Now what is this silliness?" he asked. "There must be nothing between you and me."

Before she could guess his intention and step back, he reached up and yanked her veil off.

"Beautiful, just as I remembered."

She'd never considered herself beautiful, but for some reason this man did. It was no compliment.

"How did you know I was here?" she asked.

"Women are so sentimental, I was sure that you'd go back to your old home. I simply told the woman at your old home that I'd pay them well if they reported when one of your family returned." The rings on his hands glinted in the light of the oil lamps.

As Kozbi had said.

He rubbed his hands together. "Now, where were we last time before we were so rudely interrupted?"

Arielle stood straight and tall, trying to look neither defiant nor cowed. It was hard to know which response would be safest. She was in deadly danger. Here was a man who was used to power, one who wielded menace and manipulation as weapons.

Yahveh, thank you that are with me and will never forsake me. Help me to honor you.

"I believe I was offering you a chance to have all your wishes granted at once."

Arielle said nothing.

He leaned forward. "I can offer you the world: wealth, position, servants galore. You'll be the best dressed woman in the city."

He had a low opinion of her to think she'd be interested in such things. Yahveh, give me wisdom to answer. "I am content with what I have."

"You are naive. You have nothing. No family, no home of your own."

Arielle shook her head. "I used to think that, but it's not true. I have the family I was born into." She wasn't going to tell him she now knew who they were. She must protect them. Too many of them were now listening to stories. "I have Naomi's family, who accepted me as their own, and I have the best family of them all." Did she dare to say it? She took a deep breath. "I am a member of Yahveh's family. That has given me brothers and sisters and mothers and fathers too many to count."

His eyes flamed. "I told you never to mention that name in front of me."

"One day Yahveh will judge us all."

The priest's eyes were wide and staring.

If this priest hated Yahveh, then she was going to mention him with every breath, for his so-called god was an abomination. "Nothing can be hidden from Yahveh. He sees what you are doing today."

His hand shot out and he struck her across her cheek, connecting with her nose. Her eyes swam with tears, but she blinked them away rather than give him the satisfaction of seeing her wipe them.

"How dare you say his name again." A globule of spit hit her chin. "You're an insolent woman. I don't know why I bother with you."

He leaned towards her, the smell of his recent meal still upon his breath. "Even now, I will relent if you are willing to denounce the Israelite god." He paused. "Remember you are a Moabite. To be a Moabite is to follow the great, the marvelous Chemosh."

Yahveh, thank you for being with me.

Arielle looked him straight in the eyes. "I will never, ever denounce Yahveh, for he loves and saves his people. He is worthy of all my praise and devotion."

The priest's cheeks were a mottled red and foam was at the corner of his mouth. "You foolish wretch. There is only one place for you."

He punched her. The force of the punch threw her against the wall. Her shoulder connected with the wall and her arm tingled down its length. Blood trickled down into her ear.

Yahveh, thank you I did not deny you.

Arielle closed her eyes to lessen the dizziness. She heard him go to the door and slide the bolts back. "Guards!"

They came at a run. "Yes, sir!"

"Bind her," the priest said. "We will let Chemosh deal with her."

CHAPTER FORTY-TWO

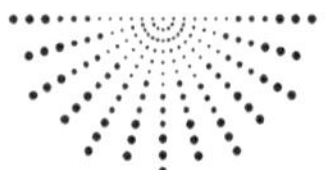

The lead guard hauled Arielle to her feet. The room whirled and she slumped against the man's shoulder.

"Hey, you," the leader said to one of the other guards. "She can't stand. She'll have to walk between the two of us."

"Are you suggesting this woman didn't deserve all she received?" the priest asked, a dangerous sharpness to his voice.

"No, sir!" the guard said.

"Good," the priest said. "I'm sure you don't want to share her fate."

Yahveh, you are with me. Keep me faithful.

The men tied her arms behind her back but not as tightly as Arielle had expected. A second guard took her other arm.

"To the dais," the priest commanded. "We will see what Chemosh's will is."

Arielle did not doubt that Chemosh would agree with whatever the priest commanded. The priest would play his games as though he was the servant of Chemosh and not the master.

The guards hustled her along the dark passages lit by flickering torchlight. This time they were moving upwards.

Yahveh, thank you. You are with me, no matter what happens.

Arielle stumbled.

"We can slow down a little," the leader said.

Thank you, Yahveh. Her head didn't feel quite right. The priest had hit her with all his anger and resentment behind his fist.

Ahead, a rectangle of light filled her sight. They continued up some stairs and a sloping tunnel towards the light. When they reached the doorway, the bright sunshine outside dazzled her. Arielle closed her eyes tight before slowly opening them. Now she could see that she'd been led up onto a high place. The open mouth of the furnace belched forth smoke and she shivered. How many children had ended up here, fed into its gaping mouth because of her people's desire for blessing?

She turned her gaze away from the furnace. The dais was surrounded with horn-like structures, and the priest was already waiting for them. Somehow, he'd managed to change into full priestly attire. Perhaps to make himself appear more impressive than he actually was.

They marched her over to a cage-like structure that rose higher than her head and pushed her inside. What did they think she would do? Fight the lot of them?

Below a crowd had gathered, expecting a spectacle.

Arielle's gaze scanned the crowd, looking for Enoch, who she was certain would be there. If things went as she expected, he must carry the news back to Naomi and Ruth and Boaz and all those who prayed for her.

There! He was right at the back of the crowd, partially hidden by a tree. Her mother was nearby. The breath caught in Arielle's throat. Oh, how terrible that her mother should be here to watch the priest get his thrill from holding power over her. *Yahveh, thank you for reuniting us. Bring her and the rest of the family through to trust in you. May she also teach Kozbi.*

"See this woman," the priest's voice rang out. "Here is a woman who has come into our midst to take followers away from our great Chemosh."

There was a howl from the crowd below.

"She is a Moabite, yet she works against our people."

The boos from the crowd got louder, but there were plenty of people in the crowd just watching. Arielle peered down at the faces looking up at her. She suspected the priest had put his own people in the crowd to influence it.

She gripped the bars in front of her. They were probably designed to make her look guilty and helpless, but they were also solid and held her upright. She had no intention of fainting or collapsing. It would please the priest too much.

Yahveh, give me courage.

"What should be done with such a woman?" the priest yelled.

"Sacrifice her!" screamed one voice then another.

Arielle's shoulders slumped and her head spun. She had been expecting this ever since she saw the furnace. *Yahveh, give me courage. You promised to be with me. I need you now.*

The priest cupped his hand around his ear. "I can't hear you."

Peace flowed into her. She straightened and looked at the crowd. This fate was better than being sold into the temple. She was afraid of the pain to come, but at least she would not be forced into dishonoring Yahveh.

Below someone started thumping out a rhythm. Boom, boom. Boom, boom. Once they'd established the rhythm, they added a word into the space.

Boom, boom. "Sacrifice!" Boom, boom. "Sacrifice."

Arielle looked towards her mother and Enoch. Her mother had drawn her veil across her face. Enoch was standing rigid.

Don't object, Enoch. It would only get him killed with her. Then who would carry the news home? Home to where faithful people prayed. Little did they know how essential their prayers were.

The crowd were getting noisier as the drum beats swept them

up to the fervor the priest had intended. He wanted to appear as if he had only bowed to their demands. Fool! He could not hide from Yahveh, the judge of all men's thoughts. *Yahveh, have mercy even on him.*

Arielle strove to block out the beat and shouts against her. *Thank you that you are here with me as you promised. With you by my side, I cannot be shaken. You are my rock and my foundation. May I honor you.*

The dais below her feet throbbed with the beat. The priest stepped forward. "Enough! The people have spoken."

There was absolute silence.

Now! My daughter, speak!

The command was as clear as a trumpet blast. Arielle drew herself up tall and opened her mouth.

"I know that my redeemer lives, and that in the end he will stand on the earth."

She'd never heard her voice so loud and clear.

"And after my skin has been destroyed, yet in my flesh I will see Yahveh; I myself will see him with my own eyes—I, and not another. How my heart yearns within me!"

The words seemed to come out of nowhere but she recognized them. They were the words that had so stood out to her as she had listened to Yahveh's priest in Shiloh reading from the scroll of Job.

In the crowd, Enoch was standing straight and tall. Her mother had thrown back her veil. Arielle's fear had gone and she did indeed yearn to see Yahveh. Yahveh, who had given her more family than she'd ever dreamed possible.

Footsteps raced towards her as the priest rushed to silence her. Now he was fumbling to open the door of the cage he'd placed her in.

She drew in another deep breath.

"May all my beloved people in Moab come to know the ruler and judge of all. May you know his never-ending compassion—"

Hands reached for her and grabbed her by her throat.

"You worm," the priest hissed in her ear. "How dare you!"

Already things were going dark but she dared, oh yes she dared, because Yahveh had given her courage.

He dragged her, half fainting, from the cage.

"Get over here, you idiots," he screamed to the guards.

They dragged her towards the mouth of the furnace, but it no longer mattered. *Thank you, Yahveh.*

"Throw her in," the priest said. "Be quick, you fools, before she says anything else."

They dragged her over until the heat smote her in the face. There was no time to fear. No time to say anything else. Only time to murmur, "Thank you, Yahveh," before she was falling into scorching heat.

But his arms were around her. She heard his voice, a voice greater than the flames, greater than the whole world.

"Well done, daughter. Welcome home."

EPILOGUE

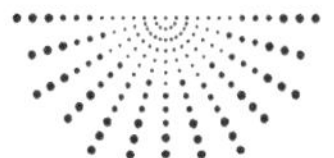

nd then …

ENJOYED LOSS AND LOYALTY?

A book can never have too many reviews. My first novel has now passed 1600 ratings and I appreciate every one.

This book is independently published which means the only way it will be discovered is if readers tell others. Online reviews are an easy way of doing this.

How to write a review — easy as 1—2—3

1. A few sentences about why you liked the book or what kind of readers might enjoy this book. Even one word turns a mere star rating into a review.
2. Upload your review — the same review can be copied and pasted to each site. This post, https://www. storytellerchristine.com/blog/reviews-the-how-and-where/, shows the priority sites.
3. If you loved the book please also share your review on social media or by word of mouth. Anywhere you can spread the word is helpful.

Don't forget libraries! If you've enjoyed my books, then you could request them in ebook or print. You can also check if my books exist in audio or large print versions.

HISTORICAL NOTES

Anyone crazy enough to write a book set in the time of the Judges is going to struggle with their timeline.

The book of Judges is written as though each judge followed the one before. They judged Israel for periods of as little as three years (Abimelech) or as long as eighty years (Ehud). The question is how long did the whole period of the Judges last? Might some of the judges have been concurrent in different parts of Israel? If so, then the length of this period of Israel's history might have been much shorter.

We do have a few Biblical references to help us. 1 Kings 6:1 states,

In the four hundred and eightieth year after the Israelites came out of Egypt, in the fourth year of Solomon's reign over Israel, in the month of Ziv, the second month, he began to build the temple of the Lord.

This article (https://www.thebiblicaltimeline.org/articles-videos/the-judges/) does a full analysis and I find his reasoning plausible.

Ruth 1:1 tells us that the events of Ruth took place "in the time of the judges." I have chosen a time after Ehud because the story links with Moab. I've placed it in the time of the latter judges and thus post-Gideon as well. That allowed me to link back with the characters from an earlier book.

Rahab as the mother of Boaz?

Ruth 4:21-22 gives this as the direct ancestor and descendants of Boaz.

> Salmon the father of Boaz, Boaz the father of Obed, Obed the father of Jesse, and Jesse the father of David.

We know that Boaz was indeed the father of Obed and Jesse the father of David. However, scholars believe that the term "father" can also refer to ancestor and thus may mean grandfather or great-grandfather. I have chosen to assume Rahab and Salmon were the parents of Boaz (Matthew 1:5) even though there are some challenges with the timing.

Arielle is of course a made-up character. However, Naomi, Ruth, Boaz, Orpah, Elimelech, Mahlon, and Kilion are all found in the book of Ruth. I have done my best to make them feel real.

DISCUSSION QUESTIONS

- Who were your favorite characters? Why?
- What were significant steps in their spiritual journeys?
- What were significant barriers?
- Did you learn any new things about the ancient cultures?
- Did you learn any new things about the biblical stories?
- What were the religious beliefs of the Moabites?
- Without written scriptures, it would have been easy to forget the Lord. How did believers remain in the Lord?
- Choose a character and trace their faith journey.
- Which faith journey do you most relate to? Why?
- How did this story encourage or inspire you?
- How did Arielle adapt the stories of Yahveh to suit different audiences?
- What did you learn about the proclamation of truth when in an anti-truth environment?
- What did you learn from this story that you can apply to your life today?
- Talk about the final chapters.

- It's an unusual epilogue. Why might the author have only written "And then ..." ?

Please feel free to write your own discussion questions. I would love to see them and am happy to include them for others if you give permission.

STORYTELLER FRIENDS

Becoming a **storyteller friend** (https://subscribe.storyteller-christine.com/) will ensure you don't miss out on new books, deals, and behind the scenes book news. Once you're signed up, check your junk mail or the promotions folder (for gmail addresses) for the confirmation email. This two-stage process ensures only true friends can join.

Facebook: As well as a public author page, I also have a VIP group (https://www.facebook.com/groups/242910632748639) which you need to ask permission to join. Those in this group pray for this book ministry. They also vote on covers, comment on book blurbs…and are free to ask questions.

BookBub - allows you to see my top book recommendations and be alerted to any new releases and special deals. It is free to join.

ACKNOWLEDGMENTS

What a team I have! Laura Tharion is always the first to read the manuscript and she is brilliant at pointing out its flaws. Thank you.

Continued thanks to Iola Goulton for her editing around her busy job and own writing. I love it that you take the time to tell me which sentences you especially like. I work much better with a little encouragement.

Joy Lankshear you've done it again with the gorgeous cover.

Welcome to Chun, our new proofreader. It's great to have a male perspective on the book. Thank you too to the other proofreaders: Stephanie M, Elizabeth W. (to check all the U.S. spellings and word usage), Anne M., Lizzie R., and Suzanne R. Thank you for your quick and accurate work.

And thank you too to all who pray throughout the whole process of each book. Many others participate and give suggestions in my VIP group on Facebook.

And lastly, a special mention of those that review. I read every one. Reviews are gold for books.

ABOUT THE AUTHOR

Christine worked in Taiwan from 1999 to 2021 and still works with OMF International, but now based out of Australia.

It's best not to ask Christine, "Where are you from?" She's a missionary kid who isn't sure if she should say her passport country (Australia) or her Dad's country (New Zealand) or where she's spent most of her life (Taiwan, Malaysia, and the Philippines).

Christine used to be a physiotherapist, but now writes storyteller on airport forms. She spends as much time as possible telling Bible stories or training others to do so.

Christine loves hiking, cycling, swimming, birdwatching, reading, and genealogical research.

facebook.com/storytellerchristine

bookbub.com/authors/christine-dillon

FICTION BY CHRISTINE DILLON

Prior to writing Biblical-era fiction, I wrote a six-book contemporary Australian set of novels.

I prefer you to buy the ebooks/audio directly from my online store (https://payhip.com/ChristineDillon). It uses PayPal or Stripe (Visa/Mastercard).

Book 1 is also available in Dutch (*Verborgen Genade*).

Of course the books are available from a wide range of other stores.

The *Light of Nations* series may be fifteen books. The best way to hear about upcoming books is to subscribe and become a storyteller friend.

NON-FICTION BY CHRISTINE DILLON

*1-2-1 Discipleship: Helping One Another Grow Spiritually
(Christian Focus, Ross-shire, Scotland, 2009).*

*Telling the Gospel Through Story: Evangelism That Keeps Hearers
Wanting More (IVP, Downer's Grove, Illinois, 2012).*